MW00533716

Her chin rose, and slowly, so did her gaze, until she made visual contact.

She cleared her throat, the sound delicate yet deliberate, then spoke. "Like you said, we're attracted to each other. I thought my reaction to you was a fluke. But this..."

"But this was real," he finished for her. "No aberration. No fluke." He knew not to press her, but rather to let her draw out her own conclusions.

She shook her head, sending her hair flowing in the gentle evening breeze. "I want you and you want me."

He wove his fingers under her hair and stroked the soft skin covering the back of her neck with the pads of his thumb. "That's a truth I would never deny. But my job. Your brother. Our feelings complicate things, Rachel."

"I know." She took a step back, breaking their contact, and blew out a sharp breath. "So while this was fun..." She waved her hands in the air, as if gesturing to their momentary lapse of judgment.

"So while this was fun, it's over now," he said firmly.

"Exactly."

Yeah, they could both wish that were the case. But he knew in his bones it simply wasn't true.

Dear Reader,

The last few books I've written for the Harlequin Romantic Suspense line have involved heroes in law enforcement, and this one is no different. Dylan Rooney is a U.S. marshal who is tracking down a fugitive in Texas—a place very different from where he grew up in California. That's just one of the reasons Dylan feels thrown off balance throughout the book.

The other big reason is Rachel Kincaid, the heroine, who just happens to be the sister of the man Dylan is hunting. Rachel is a strong, independent single mother who believes deeply in her brother's goodness, so when Dylan shows up accusing him of murder, it's natural for Rachel to view him as the enemy. Then the real enemies show up.

As Rachel is forced to rely on Dylan for protection, the more she begins to like and respect him, and this includes his dedication to upholding the U.S. Marshals motto: Justice, Integrity, Service. Throughout the story, Rachel and Dylan face a similar dilemma: how to reconcile one's duty with feelings of desire and love that seem to conflict with that duty.

I hope you enjoy their story as much as I enjoyed writing it!

Wishing you much love and happiness always,

Virna DePaul

TEXAS STAKEOUT

—

Virna DePaul

HARLEQUIN® ROMANTIC SUSPENSE

If you purchased this book without a cover you should be aware
that this book is stolen property. It was reported as "unsold and
destroyed" to the publisher, and neither the author nor the
publisher has received any payment for this "stripped book."

Recycling programs
for this product may
not exist in your area.

ISBN-13: 978-0-373-27895-4

Texas Stakeout

Copyright © 2014 by Virna dePaul

All rights reserved. Except for use in any review, the reproduction or
utilization of this work in whole or in part in any form by any electronic,
mechanical or other means, now known or hereinafter invented, including
xerography, photocopying and recording, or in any information storage
or retrieval system, is forbidden without the written permission of the
publisher, Harlequin Enterprises Limited, 225 Duncan Mill Road,
Don Mills, Ontario, Canada M3B 3K9.

This is a work of fiction. Names, characters, places and incidents are
either the product of the author's imagination or are used fictitiously,
and any resemblance to actual persons, living or dead, business
establishments, events or locales is entirely coincidental.

This edition published by arrangement with Harlequin Books S.A.

For questions and comments about the quality of this book,
please contact us at CustomerService@Harlequin.com.

® and TM are trademarks of Harlequin Enterprises Limited or its
corporate affiliates. Trademarks indicated with ® are registered in the
United States Patent and Trademark Office, the Canadian Intellectual
Property Office and in other countries.

Printed in U.S.A.

Books by Virna Depaul

Harlequin Romantic Suspense

Dangerous to Her #1674
It Started That Night #1706
Deadly Charade #1754
Texas Stakeout #1825

Harlequin HQN

Shades of Desire
Shades of Temptation
Shades of Passion

Love Bites anthology
  "Molly Wants a Hero"

_____

VIRNA DEPAUL

was an English major in college and, despite a passion for Shakespeare, Broadway musicals and romance novels, somehow ended up with a law degree. For ten years, she was a criminal prosecutor for the state of California. Now she's thrilled to be writing stories about complex individuals (fully human or not) who are willing to overcome incredible odds for love. She can be found on Twitter at @virnadepaul or at virnadepaul.com.

For James. I miss you!

Chapter 1

U.S. Marshal Dylan Rooney was on a stakeout. Only in the hill country of Texas a stakeout didn't mean sitting in an unmarked sedan, drinking coffee and eating donuts. Nope. A Texas stakeout meant sitting on the back of a horse. And Dylan, who was a mediocre rider at best, had drawn the short straw in more ways than one. As a marshal, it wasn't uncommon for him to work away from his home base in California. It was, however, uncommon for him to be this bored. And this sore.

He much preferred traveling by plane, train or automobile—the faster and sleeker the mode of transportation, the better—than relying on a four-legged best from hell.

While two other marshals from Dylan's five-member team, and several other marshals from vari-

ous states, scoured the country for Jackson Kincaid,
a prisoner who'd recently escaped transport in California, Dylan was on his third day in Nowhere, Texas,
binoculars trained on the ranch owned by Jackson
Kincaid's sister, Rachel. Besides the sheer boredom
of it all, it wouldn't have been a bad assignment, but
he hadn't counted on his damn horse having anxiety
issues. Ginger, the horse he'd rented from an adjacent
farm, wouldn't stop dancing in the red Texas dirt,
kicking up a cloud of dust in Dylan's face.

It would be the height of stupidity for Kincaid to
run here, especially given that it was where he was
first taken into custody, but it still had to be covered.
Dylan and his team would do whatever it took to apprehend Kincaid, even if it meant endless hours of
watching Kincaid's ten-year-old nephew popping soda
cans off fence posts with a BB gun.

The kid wasn't a half-bad shot, Dylan thought just
as his mother came into view. Dylan sat up higher
on the horse and pressed the binoculars tighter to
his face, watching as she made the long hike up the
western fence line and across the field to where her
kid stood, BB gun at his side. Just as it had when he'd
first seen her picture—hell, every time he'd caught
a glimpse of her in the past few days—Dylan's pulse
accelerated. Rachel Kincaid was nothing like the sophisticated women Dylan normally dated, but she was
hands-down gorgeous. Willowy and tall, she had a
dark Texas tan and dark eyes that clashed with the vi-
brant near white of her blond hair. She worked hard—
too hard—and there was no doubt she loved her son,
Peter, to distraction.

Too bad she had lousy taste in men, her brother

and deceased husband included. Her husband's alcohol problem and subsequent drunk driving accident had left Rachel a widow.

And her brother?

He'd taken everything his sister had sacrificed for him and flushed it down the toilet the minute he'd agreed to transport drugs across state lines.

Now Rachel was basically running the ranch by herself. She had some help, but not much.

Earlier, the woman had been conferring with her only ranch hand—records listed him as Josiah Pemberly, age sixty-three—down at the natural spring. Though Dylan hadn't been able to hear their conversation, it had appeared pleasant, with both parties smiling a lot. Now that Rachel had reached her son, the conversation going on between them seemed far from pleasant. As Rachel spoke, the child stood motionless, his back to her. Frowning, Rachel lifted a hand as if to reach out to the boy, then stopped. Shaking her head, she wheeled around and strode quickly back to the ranch house, her entire posture stiff with frustration.

The woman was sexy as hell, Dylan thought, but it was obvious she had no control over her kid. And she'd obviously lost control of her brother, whom she'd essentially raised, a long time ago. Dylan just hoped her kid didn't end up taking the same path in life that his uncle had.

Dylan dropped the binoculars so they hung on their leather strap around his neck. Day three in the stakeout for Jackson Kincaid, and all Dylan had seen at the Kincaid ranch was one gorgeous yet overworked woman, her sullen brat, one elderly ranch hand and a bunch of weird-looking llamas. At least, he figured they were llamas. Texas was getting too froufrou. Whatever had happened to sheep and cattle ranching?

The next fifteen minutes passed in a drone of boredom. The ranch hand kept mending the fence. The kid continued popping soda cans off fence posts. Dylan gulped down water until the wind picked up, snapping more dust into his eyes and sending a tumbleweed straight at his horse.

"Whoa," he murmured, tightening his grip on the reins with one hand and wrapping his other hand in Ginger's mane. The mare shied, as expected, but Dylan managed to hang on and focused on maintaining his seat and keeping his feet in the stirrups. He fought for control, working to recall the instructions his camp counselor had taught him the year the state had sent him to summer camp in the boonies.

"Keep your seat. Don't yank on the reins. Dig your heels down."

And then he heard a shriek wend its way upward from the valley below.

The kid? The mother? Dylan wrapped the reins around his fist to control the horse and brought the binoculars back to his eyes. The kid had dropped his BB gun and was running toward the house. Dylan panned the lenses over to the house but didn't see the porch door swing open. In the few days that he'd been spying on the Kincaid Ranch, Rachel had always come running whenever the kid wanted her. Now? Nothing. Had something happened to her?

"Mom!"

The single word caught on the edge of the wind and whipped up the ridge to Dylan. Desperation filled the boy's single word.

Dylan loosened his grip on the reins and squeezed with his knees, yelling, "Yiya!"

Ginger responded by leaping forward. Immediately she settled into a gallop and headed down the ridge to the valley. The ranch house was only about a quarter mile away as the crow flies, but the trail down the ridge zigzagged like a pinball machine. Still, even with all the switchbacks, he'd probably be able to reach the kid in time to help.

Assuming he didn't get thrown and break his neck first, of course.

Rachel Kincaid let her long hair drip water down her back. The cold shower had felt good and had taken the biting edge off her nerves. With their higher elevation, the Texas heat usually stayed away from the ranch, but not this summer. This summer the heat got to her. Or maybe it was that Peter kept getting to her.

God, she loved her son, but he'd never been an easy kid. Often affectionate and sweet and funny but also hyperactive. Defiant. Impulsive.

Six months ago he'd been diagnosed with attention-deficit hyperactivity disorder. At the time, she'd been relieved to have an explanation for his moodiness that didn't come with being labeled a failure of a parent. But she'd also been overwhelmed and uncertain of her ability to do right by her son. After doing tons of research on the subject, she'd reluctantly agreed to get him on medicine, something that had seemed to help right away. Putting Peter on a schedule that still provided him lots of downtime had helped even more. By the time the school year had ended, he'd been doing so much better and their relationship had become downright rosy.

Now, however, the prolonged time they'd been spending together over summer vacation was beginning to take its toll. So was the fact that Peter missed his uncle Jax; even if he didn't know the real reason Jax had left last year, he was confused by Jax's failure to visit or call. Peter missed him, and he was bored with just her and Josiah for company. And Rachel? She missed her brother, too. Missed him terribly. She was also tired from working the ranch. From working Jax's appeal. From her frequent battles with Peter. It made her feel guilty, but she wanted summer to be over. Wanted the heat gone. Wanted Peter back in school where he could sass his teachers for part of the day instead of her.

She stepped into a worn but clean pair of Levi's jeans and pulled a tank over her still-dripping hair, knowing it wasn't fair to compare Peter to what her brother, Jax, had been like at ten but doing it, anyway. Jax had been…easy. Then again, Jax hadn't had ADHD. And, when Jax had just turned ten, their parents were still alive and she was in her first year in college; she probably wouldn't have noticed if Jax had given her parents attitude, anyway. Afterward, with their parents gone before he turned eleven, Jax had been so grief-stricken it had taken months before he'd smiled again, let alone thrown attitude.

Peter, on the other hand, had been offering up enough sass to fill a silo. The way he'd turned his back on her earlier when she asked him to stop shooting the pellet gun and fill up the alpacas' water trough had just about driven her out of her skin. She'd had to walk away before she lost it and started yelling at him.

She grabbed her boots but stopped when she heard something.

Peter calling her. The tenor of his high-pitched voice came through the open bedroom window, urgent and scared.

Her heart leaped into her throat. Her baby needed her.

She didn't bother with the boots, and instead rushed down the stairs and burst out onto the porch, looking for her son.

There, racing from the western fence line where she'd left him only fifteen minutes ago, came Peter. And coming toward him from the opposite direction, in a cloud of red dust, rode a stranger on a galloping chestnut quarter horse.

"Peter!" she screamed, and ran to him. She stumbled as the rocks on the drive bit into her feet but kept on going.

"Mom, you've gotta help!" Peter cried out when she reached him. He wrapped his arms around her and sobbed into her shoulder.

Heart pounding, Rachel held her son tight and faced the rider who brought his horse to an ungainly stop next to them. He seemed about her age, or maybe just a few years older—maybe early thirties. Wide shoulders, legs long against the barrel of the horse. Blue jeans, a plaid snap-front long-sleeved shirt rolled to the elbows and his Stetson said *cowboy,* yet his unscuffed boots and the clean felt of his hat screamed of falsehood.

Wait. She knew his horse: Ginger. A horse from her

neighbor Aaron Jacobson's herd. The same neighbor harassing her about the fence line. Hell. Today of all days she didn't need to deal with a stupid land dispute. And she didn't need some city slicker to give her a hard time about the spring.

"I don't know who you are or why Aaron sent you to hassle my kid," she snapped out at the stranger, "but I swear to God, if you don't get off my property, I'll call the sheriff on you. You and Aaron leave my kid alone," she nearly growled, holding a sobbing Peter even tighter. "Whatever issues that man has with the property line can be handled in court—not by intimidating a child."

The man slid off Ginger in an awkward motion and stepped forward, palms held upward in a universal gesture of peace. He came closer and she stood shaking, watching his every step, until he stopped a few feet in front of her. His deep blue eyes were steady and without malice. Didn't matter. He was tall—at least six foot two—and he towered over her and Peter; his wide shoulders and military posture screamed *intimidation.*

But she was a mother. She wouldn't let him intimidate her. Not when her kid was crying against her shoulder.

"My name's Dylan, ma'am," the man said. "Dylan Rooney. And I'm not here about your neighbor. I was riding the ridge, uh, bird-watching, and I saw the kid playing with his BB gun. Next thing I knew I heard him screaming and running to the house. I figured something had happened and came down the hill to help. Kid—" he directed his statement to Peter, who'd raised his tear-streaked face away from her shoulder "—are you hurt?"

Peter pulled away from Rachel and swiped futilely at the tears that kept streaming down his face. "No, it's not me. It's…it's…" Anguish froze his expression, his mouth gaping and open, shutting off whatever he'd been about to say.

Rachel reached for him, but Peter took another step away from her. The distance, a mere two inches, ripped yet another hole in Rachel's heart. He'd needed her—and then he hadn't. She couldn't help thinking of all the family she'd lost—her parents and even her brother in a way. She swallowed the lump of emotional pain down and said, "I heard you ask for my help, Peter. What's wrong?"

The man—Dylan—came forward and placed a solid hand on Peter's shoulder. Somehow the masculine grip held Peter together in a way Rachel's soft hold hadn't, because Peter took a shaky breath and the tears stopped flowing.

"It's Josiah…"

Josiah. Her ranch hand. And friend. A sensation like a cold hand slid up her back. Twenty minutes ago she'd checked in on him as he repaired the fence on the property line she shared with Aaron Jacobson. Had Aaron gone too far this time? Was Aaron causing Josiah trouble?

Her neighbor had been a real pain in the neck ever since he discovered a natural spring right on her side of the fence line a couple of years ago. He'd been digging around the courthouse records, trying to prove the spring was actually on his own land. She'd been too preoccupied with running the ranch, keeping Peter in line and working on the appeal process for her brother to deal with Aaron's constant haranguing, but she'd finally referred him to Julia Rickel, her friend and lawyer, who'd threatened lawsuits and police action and whatnot if Aaron didn't back off. Aaron had made it clear he hadn't liked what he considered to be Julia's threats.

She opened her mouth to speak, but the stranger beat her to the question she was about to ask.

"Kid," Dylan said, "what happened? Where's Josiah?"

Peter hitched a breath and pointed back to the fence line. "He's over there. B-b-but it's too late. We're too late."

The cold hand on Rachel's back now gripped her throat. *No.*

"Too late for what, Peter?" she whispered.

"Too late to help. Josiah's dead."

Chapter 2

Rachel's face had turned so white that Dylan expected her to faint at any moment. He reached out a hand, offering to steady her, but she waved him away. Of course she did. He was a stranger. She had no reason to trust him.

He turned to Peter, whose expression was still alight with panic. Had Jackson Kincaid snuck on the property without Dylan noticing? Seemed unlikely, but...

He followed the kid's pointing finger with his line of sight.

The boy's voice shook as he said, "Way up the fence line, next to the spring."

"Did you see anyone up there with him?" Dylan asked.

The boy shook his head.

"Are you certain he's…dead?" Rachel's voice came out on a whisper of a breath.

Peter swallowed and nodded, his eyes filling back up with tears. "He has a big hole in his head and there's a lot of blood and his eyes are open and not moving and he doesn't have a pulse," he said breathlessly. "I checked. Then I ran to get you."

Oh, hell. This wasn't some kid making a desperate bid for attention. This was real. "You and the kid get into the house and lock yourselves in," he ordered even as he mentally cursed. As if that would do a lot of good if Jackson Kincaid was on the ranch. He was her brother, for God's sake. It wasn't as if she'd view him as a threat to her or her son. And truth be told, Dylan had no reason to think Jackson would hurt them. Still, the man had proven himself to be violent and if he'd killed Josiah…

Rachel started, staring at him with wide brown eyes, pupils dilating. "What— Why?"

"Just to be safe. Call 911. Use the landline. Tell them to get an ambulance here immediately."

Rachel looked from Dylan to her son, then raised her chin. "Peter, do as he says. Lock all the doors and wait for the ambulance, okay? I'm going to check on Josiah."

"I can do that—" Dylan began, but Peter was already running into the house.

"Not without me," she said. She watched the house until Peter had slammed the door behind him, then strode toward Ginger. She put a bare foot into the stirrup and easily swung herself up onto Dylan's horse, then kicked her feet out of the stirrups. "You coming?" she asked. "Because I'm not leaving you here alone with my kid."

Dylan struggled with indecision. He wanted to insist he check on the ranch hand by himself, but this was her private property and what reason could he possibly give for thinking there might be something or someone dangerous out there? Not the truth, certainly. Not yet. Not when the most likely explanation was that her ranch hand had had some kind of accident.

When Rachel raised her eyebrows impatiently and leaned forward, he slid his booted foot in the stirrup and pulled himself up behind her. Ginger danced for a few seconds, then settled as he used his knees to nudge her forward. He wrapped an arm around Rachel's waist and pulled her in tight to his chest. She was stiff but didn't resist. The quarter horse, her hooves steady despite the added weight, settled into an easy lope.

"So, are you a friend of Aaron's?" Rachel asked over her shoulder. "Did he send you out to spy on us? Did he tell you about the crazy widow and her bratty kid?" Bitterness edged her words, which came out jumpy and breathless as Ginger continued to cover the uneven terrain.

Not exactly, Dylan thought. The Department of Corrections had told him about her brother and his brazen escape, and research had informed his team about Rachel, the sister whom Jackson Kincaid thought of as his mother, and Rachel's son. Of course, Dylan didn't tell Rachel that. Lying to her wasn't his first choice, but he also didn't want her clamming up and getting irrational when there was a potential crisis to deal with.

"He just loaned me a horse. We're not friends. Does Josiah have a history of any sort of heart condition? Stroke?"

"No health issues. He's older, but healthy. He's repaired the fence line time after time. I don't know what could have harmed him."

Dylan immediately thought of her brother again. "Maybe your son is wrong about him being dead." In his arms her body loosened fractionally, and she twisted her torso to face forward again. Whether she completely believed him or not didn't matter—she trusted him enough to help her ranch hand.

"I'm not holding out hope. Peter's been raised on a ranch. We raise alpacas for wool, so we don't do a lot of butchering, but he's seen dead animals. He knows what lifeless eyes look like."

So did Dylan. Personally and professionally.

Professionally? The duty of a marshal was to bring in fugitives whether they claimed to be innocent or not. It wasn't his job to investigate their crimes, nor to believe them or not believe them—that was for the cops, the courts and the jury system to decide. Fugitives didn't see it that way. They wanted their freedom. Sometimes they fought to keep it

Sometimes they died.

Personally...

He fought to erase the dead eyes staring dully at him in his mind's eye, but he couldn't.

Dead eyes all looked the same: unblinking and missing life's sheen. But the first set of dead eyes he'd ever seen—his mother's—haunted him every day of his life, reminding him of what could happen to a person who refused to accept the bad in others before it was too late.

"So your son's name is Peter. And you are?"

"Rachel. We're almost there," she said. "Down the gulley to the right. Then the spring's a few hundred yards south."

He knew how to get to the spring already but kept silent, and instead neck-reined Ginger in the direction Rachel had given. The horse headed downhill and Rachel leaned back to compensate for her weight on the horse's shoulders. Her still-wet hair brushed his face and he breathed in the scent. Soft and floral, with a hint of freshness. Ginger stumbled and Dylan tightened his grip on Rachel, appreciating the soft weight of her breasts on his forearm. *Get a grip,* he mentally chided himself. Yeah, Rachel was one hot woman, but she was also the sister of the fugitive he was hunting, and they were on the way to find out if her ranch hand still lived. Appreciating her sweet smell or the luscious weight of her breasts was the last thing he should be doing.

He reminded himself it had been three long months since he'd bedded a woman. Before that, he'd been in a long-term relationship with Ashley, a deputy D.A. back in San Francisco. They'd dated for several years and she'd been pressuring him for more. She'd wanted to move in together. Wanted to move toward marriage. He hadn't been able to commit. He'd cared about her. Appreciated her in bed and out. But he'd known she wasn't the one, just as the handful of women he'd dated before her hadn't been the one. The ones he'd dated after her?

They'd been beautiful. Smart. Urban chic. But

they'd bored him. Body, mind and soul. It had been far easier to immerse himself in work. Now there was Rachel Kincaid. Stimulating him in so many different ways and distracting him from his duty. It not only surprised him. It was beginning to piss him off.

Dylan grabbed his binoculars and scanned the surrounding area. It looked clear, but he was still conscious of the presence of his firearm inside his boot. Knew it would take mere seconds to draw his weapon if he needed it.

"There!" Rachel exclaimed, pointing to a spot of blue, deep down among the green rushes that surrounded a bubbling spring. She grabbed the reins herself and pulled Ginger to a halt.

Dylan swung himself off the horse, then helped Rachel to her feet. She stumbled and he caught her—their faces inches from each other. Her eyebrows swung together in a V before she pulled away.

"Josiah?" she called out, pushing through the rushes, gray mud sucking at her bare feet.

She came to a halt next to the bright spot of blue they'd seen, and Dylan came up behind her. When she sank to her knees in front of the crumpled figure, Dylan knew Peter had been right.

The man was dead.

On her knees, Rachel swallowed against the heave in her stomach. Josiah lay at an odd angle, a few yards from where the spring water bubbled to the surface. Coagulated blood stained his face, no doubt from the severe wound on the side of his forehead. Next to his head, a large jagged rock protruded from the ground. He must have slipped. Hit his head.

She hated that Peter had seen Josiah's open eyes, so devoid of life. Was that what Jax saw when the school bus had dropped him off and he'd come home to find their parents, dead from carbon monoxide poisoning? She reached a hand out to close his eyes but was stopped by a firm grip on her elbow.

"Don't touch him," Dylan growled.

For a second, the timbre of his voice and the weight of his touch made fear shoot through her. This was a stranger, a stranger who'd appeared as suddenly as Josiah had been hurt. Killed. Dylan Rooney claimed he'd been riding after Peter because he'd only wanted to help, but what if that wasn't the case?

But just as panic and fear started to choke off her breath, she reminded herself that he'd told both her and Peter to stay at the house to call 911. Someone bent on trouble would hardly want more witnesses to deal with, and he would most likely have tried to separate them.

After taking a deep breath, she slowly pulled her arm away from his grip. "I only want to close his eyes. Give him some dignity," she argued.

"We can't disturb the scene any more than we already have. This man is dead. We need to back up and wait for the authorities."

Dylan's words buzzed inside her head. Two phrases hung in the air, as if a spotlight was on them. *Disturb the scene. Wait for the authorities.* Then she remembered the way he'd initially ordered her and Peter to go inside the house and lock the doors after them. As if he'd wanted to make sure whatever had hurt Josiah couldn't hurt them.

Aaron had been beastly over the past month, demanding rights to the water he'd found on her land. Even before that, he'd always been a bit of a jerk, which was why she'd initially wondered if Aaron had been causing Josiah trouble.

But she hadn't been thinking murder. Now, based on the position of Josiah's body next to the rock, the most logical assumption would be Josiah had fallen and hit his head.

Clearly this man suspected foul play.

Why?

Dylan held out a hand and after a slight hesitation, she took it. He tugged her upward and she came to standing, facing him.

"Why can't I touch him?" she asked hoarsely. "What do you mean, 'disturb the scene'?"

"I'm sorry. I didn't mean to frighten you," he soothed. "It looks like he fell, but it's always possible something else happened to him."

"Like what?"

His fingers tightened around hers right before he ran his hands up and down her arms in a comforting motion. Her first instinct was to push him away and tell him she needed answers, not sympathy. But that would be a lie.

She suddenly felt on the verge of collapse. Wanted nothing more than to rest her cheek against his chest and beg him to hold her. Comfort her.

He sighed and lifted one hand to run his knuckles against her cheek. "There are always those who want to hurt others, Rachel. There's always a possibility that there's danger where we think we're the safest. But I'm here. And I'll help you. You just need to let me."

Chapter 3

"I don't understand," Rachel said even as she pulled away from him. Fear had made her large eyes grow rounder, and Dylan barely suppressed a curse. Scaring her was the last thing he wanted, but he couldn't dismiss the possibility that her brother had killed this man. For all he knew, Kincaid was still on the property somewhere, a threat to them all.

And yet for all Rachel knew, Dylan was the threat. He needed to extinguish the fear in Rachel's eyes. Sometimes only the truth could do that.

"I told you my name is Dylan Rooney, ma'am. What I didn't tell you is I'm a U.S. Marshal and I'm here on important business."

Rachel backed farther away from him, her bare feet sinking even deeper in the mud that his boots protected him from. She winced, and once again he held out a hand to provide stability. This time she ignored it, staring at him warily.

"Business that has something to do with what's happened to Josiah?"

"Could be. I'm not certain."

"But you think he's been murdered."

"That remains to be seen," Dylan said. She shifted, then winced again, reminding Dylan she'd run out of the house barefoot. She had to be in pain. "Here, let's get you back up on the horse while we wait for help. No sense in you continuing to beat up your feet if you don't have to."

He moved toward her, but she held out her hand. "Stop. You think I'm going to just take your word you're a cop? That you have any legitimate business being here?"

"I can show you my credentials. Will that help?"

She frowned, then nodded. Slowly, he reached into his back pocket for his wallet. He held it out and she took it. As soon as she flipped it open, she saw his badge and official ID. Her shoulders seemed to relax somewhat and she held the wallet back out to him. When he'd pocketed it, she turned and started walking toward Ginger, limping the whole time.

He placed a hand on her shoulder. "Let me help you, ma'am. Please."

She looked up at him, silent and looking a little lost, obviously numb from the shock of finding her ranch hand dead. She didn't protest when he scooped her up in his arms and walked her the few yards back to Ginger, who was calmly grazing on green grass. Tall as Rachel was, she didn't weigh much, but she did remain stiff in his arms while he raised her up onto Ginger's back. Apparently dead bodies had no spook value the way tumbleweeds, bees and the occasional butterfly did, because the horse stood still.

When he settled Rachel onto Ginger's back, she slumped in the saddle, as if all the strength had seeped out of her bones. "You were spying on us. Josiah? Or me?" she asked, her voice hollow, as if she'd forced the words out using what little energy she had left.

That was an answer he didn't want to give just yet. Not until after Josiah was dealt with and he knew he'd have some uninterrupted alone time to explain everything to Rachel.

The sounds of sirens in the distance gave him an out. "Will Peter be able to lead the EMTs here?" he asked.

Rachel nodded, then sat up straight, agitation showing in her blanched face. "But I don't want him to see—"

"I won't let him near the spring. I'll make sure he stays back, okay?"

A faint smile of gratitude curved the corners of her lips upward. Dylan realized that was the first time he'd seen even the hint of a smile on the woman's face.

Rachel Kincaid was beautiful, but when she smiled it made him long for the rest of the world to disappear so he could spend hours simply staring at her.

"Thanks for that," she murmured. "He's just a kid. Seeing death at a young age can be so harmful. So destructive."

Yeah, he knew.

In less than a minute, they heard the voices of the EMTs and he left Rachel to clamber up the gulley,

intent on holding Peter back from going to his mom.
From seeing Josiah's body again.

But Peter wasn't with the EMTs, who said they'd
instructed the kid to go back to the house after he'd
brought them close enough so they could find their
own way to the spring. Silently, Dylan cursed. Now
that he'd confirmed Josiah was dead, he was regret-
ting letting the boy go off on his own. He wanted him
near. To ensure his safety, yes, but also to settle Rachel's worry about him.

Dylan showed the EMTs his badge. They confirmed Josiah Pemberly was deceased and made the
appropriate calls to the police. Within a few minutes,
a deputy from the sheriff's department showed up.
Dylan and the other man, whom Dylan had met days
earlier, exchanged tense looks.

Deputy Mark Todd was one of the three sheriff's
deputies Dylan and his team had contacted when they
first arrived in town. He knew who Dylan was and
why he was here. Thank God he also knew better than
to say anything in front of Rachel.

By the time a half hour had crept up and passed
them, the deputy had agreed to make sure the body
made its way to the medical examiner. He'd also
agreed to call in another deputy so they could do a
thorough search of the property together.

Dylan walked Ginger back to the house, an emotionally drained Rachel still perched on her back. He'd
get her into the shower, bandage up her feet if need
be and check in on the kid. Then he planned to see if
Rachel had any whiskey in the house, pour her two
fingers and tell her why he was in Texas, scoping out

her house with high-powered binoculars on the back of a borrowed horse.

The odd thing was, part of him didn't want to tell her. Instead, he wanted her to smile again. And he wanted to do whatever it took to keep that smile going, not extinguish it.

Rachel wasn't sure what to make of Dylan Rooney. Correction: U.S. Marshal Dylan Rooney. By the way the sheriff's deputies had deferred to his authority, he appeared to be law enforcement, just as his credentials indicated, but was there truly any reason for him to think Josiah's death had been the result of foul play? Some reason to think that she needed his help?

Maybe he was simply being paranoid because of the work he did. At least that was what she told herself as the marshal led Ginger, with Rachel in the saddle, back to the ranch. When they got there, he gently lifted her off the horse and put her on the front porch, then told her he'd take off Ginger's tack and set the mare up in one of the empty corrals.

Rachel immediately went in search of her son. She found Peter sitting on the floor in a corner of his room, his arms wrapped around his knees. "I was right. He's dead, isn't he?"

"Oh, baby," she whispered, knowing there was no easy way to break the news. Peter had loved Josiah. She fell to her knees beside her son and reached out to place a hand on his shoulder. "I'm sorry, Peter, but yes, Josiah's dead."

"I knew it," he choked out. Shooting to his feet, he pushed her arm aside and bolted away.

"Peter," she called, jumping to her feet to follow

him. But her feet hurt and she was blinded by tears
and her son was so much faster than she was. By the
time she reached the top of the stairs, he'd barreled
down them and had slammed out the back door. She
had covered her eyes with one hand, choking back
sobs, when the front door opened and Dylan Rooney
stuck his head in.

"You want me to bring him back?"

She shook her head. Peter often hid out in the huge
cottonwood by the creek—he'd always liked to process difficulties alone, and she'd always respected his
needs even before she came to understand that because of his ADHD, giving him extra space was important. Now, however, she wanted him by her side.
Safe. She'd shower, get some clothes and shoes on,
deal with Dylan, then find Peter and keep him with
her so they could grieve Josiah's passing together.
"He'll be fine," she said. "I—I just need to clean
up and then we can talk. You can wait in the living
room."

Before he could reply, she headed into the master
bedroom and quickly shut the door behind her. Then
she rushed to the bathroom and shut that door behind
her, as well. Only then did she lean back against the
door and allow herself to break down, trying her best
to stifle the sounds of her sorrow. She cried for Josiah, taken too soon. For Peter, who'd seen the stare of
death. And she cried for her parents and for Jax. Jax,
too, had seen empty, lifeless eyes when he returned
home from school and found their parents. She hadn't
been able to protect him from that pain any more than
she'd been able to protect her son.

Some mother she was turning out to be.

For the second time in as many hours, she stepped inside the shower and let the cool water wash her clean. Her feet were a mess, cut by the sharp stones she'd run across on her way to comfort her crying son, then sliced again by the knife-sharp reeds at the spring. Jackson Pollock-ish designs were painted in gray clay from her feet to her calves.

Numbly, Rachel stared at the water sluicing down the drain and, even though part of her hated herself for it, her thoughts drifted to the practicalities of Josiah's death. After her husband Phillip's death so long ago, the only way she'd been able to afford a ranch hand was that Josiah had been happy to do extra chores for a place to sleep and three meals a day. He'd been with her for years, and was the only alpaca shearer her flock tolerated. Between her and Josiah, they'd been able to shear the entire flock in a couple of days. With spring upon them and shearing season right around the corner, she'd have to find some way to come up with the money to hire a professional outfit.

Money she didn't know where she'd find. Money had always been scarce; Phillip's parents were still alive, adored Peter and would help if they could, but they barely got by on a minimal fixed income as it was. Rachel had used what little money she'd had in her bank account for Jax's appeal. Her friend Julia had insisted on taking on Jax's second appeal pro bono, but even with Julia offering her services for free, money was tight. And Josiah had no one in his life besides her and Peter—she'd need to pay for a funeral. It was the least she could do to pay homage to a man who'd been a loyal employee for years. A man

who'd tried to steer her son right when Peter acted
out. A man who hadn't deserved to die.

A man who, according to a U.S. marshal, could
have been murdered.

Broken and choked sobs wrenched their way out
from her body, the harsh sounds clashing with the
soft raindrop lullaby of the shower spray. Her legs
turned to jelly and she dropped to the tiled floor of
the shower with a crash.

Strength seemed to have left her, so she sat, knees
tucked in tight under her chin and arms wrapped
around her shins, and sobbed. She closed her eyes,
only to see Josiah's vacant stare as he lay in the green
reeds, his blue-checkered shirt covered in wet mud.
"No, no, no," she choked out, repeating the word until
it became a mantra. Something that took her away
from this place. Something that let her drift away
from conscious thought, into the ether of nothing-
ness where she could feel no stress, no pain. No fear.

"Rachel."

Dimly, through the fog of pain and anguish, she
became aware of someone calling her name.

"Rachel."

There it was again. Her name. Spoken in a soft,
male voice. A voice full of compassion and sorrow.
A voice close by.

She forced her eyes open to see the shadow of a tall
form standing outside the steamed-up glass shower
walls.

U.S. Marshal Dylan Rooney. In her private bathroom. Invading her space. How dare the man? "Get
out," she managed to say. Instinctively, she cringed,
then realized she was curled into herself, all the im-

portant stuff covered up, even if he could see anything more than her shadow through the foggy glass.

"I heard a thump and you crying out. Are you all right?"

"My son just saw his first dead body, and you told me my ranch hand and friend has possibly been murdered. No, I'm not okay."

Silence followed her statement. Finally Dylan spoke again. "I meant, are you okay physically? I want to make sure you didn't hurt yourself."

"I'm fine," she sniffed.

"Yeah, right, and I'm Santa Claus," he muttered. A deep exhale of breath followed his words, and then he said, "I guess you sound okay. When you're done crying—I mean, when you're done taking a shower—I'll be in your kitchen. We need to talk," he said, his voice grim. "You need to know why I'm here. And why I think Josiah may have been murdered."

With dread, Rachel listened as he walked out of the bathroom.

Her mother had always told her to be careful what she wished for. Learning the truth about why U.S. Marshal Dylan Rooney was here was what she'd wanted.

But now she wasn't so sure. Now she'd give almost anything to believe he really had been bird-watching…and she desperately wished he'd turn around and leave—not just her house, but her ranch—just as abruptly as he'd appeared.

Chapter 4

Rachel stared at the man who'd claimed to want to help her only to then deliver the killing blow that might finally defeat her. "No," she said. "I don't believe you. Jax would never have escaped prison."

Rachel's heartbeat thudded so heavily her chest ached. She glared at Dylan, who sat across her kitchen table, flicking a thumbnail against the rough-hewn wood. Her father had made the table when she and Jax were young. Jax had insisted on using the hand planer and ended up slicing off the tip of his finger, right on the spot Dylan was toying with.

Innocent, sweet Jax, who'd followed their father around as though their dad was his own personal hero. Rachel knew that sweet boy was still inside her brother even though he'd refused to show him in the past year. Even though he'd confessed to police that he'd knowingly transported drugs across state lines, a crime that had landed him a prison sentence.

According to police, Jax had been contacted by someone who'd heard he was looking to make a quick buck. All Jax had to do was drive a package from Texas to east L.A., give the package to the man at the drop site, receive a package in return and drive back to Texas. All for two thousand bucks and the cost of gas. He'd been told the package contained vital documents needed for signatures to sell some high-level computer tech company to a big conglomeration. But he'd known better than that. He'd known the package contained drugs.

When he'd arrived at the drop site, men with guns came storming into the warehouse. Jax had managed to escape and had hopped a freighter back to Texas.

Rachel hadn't known any of this was happening. Jax had told her he was going out of town to look for work. She'd been so proud of him she'd been willing to let him go off for a few days, even though the ranch desperately needed his help.

Then DEA agents and the local sheriff, Howard Ryan, had arrived at the ranch a few days after Jax had taken off, scaring the hell out of her and Peter with their guns and yelling and stomping about. The sheriff had found Jax near the barn and handed him off to the DEA. With her crying and begging them for information, the agents had handcuffed her brother and hauled him away, leaving her with unanswered questions. Jax had refused to look at her. He'd refused to say one word to her. After he'd confessed, he'd refused to say another word to the police.

The last time she'd seen her brother was the day

of his sentencing, before they took him away. The two times she'd tried to visit him in prison, he refused to see her.

She didn't know why—whether he was ashamed of what had happened to him or whether he blamed her for his troubles. One thing was for sure in her mind—Jax's confession had to have been coerced.

No matter how bad things looked, she had faith in her brother. He was a good man. And he had to know Rachel was doing everything in her power to get him out of prison—legally. He'd never put everything she'd done for him on the line by escaping his prison sentence.

Numbly, she stared at the bottle of whiskey and two tumblers Dylan had placed on the table. He'd obviously thought she'd need something to soften the news he was about to give her. The mistaken news, she told herself again. He was wrong about Jax. He had to be.

"There must have been a mix-up in the head count or something," she insisted. "The wrong name answered during roll call. Jax didn't run off."

"Rachel," Dylan said, setting an elbow on the table and leaning closer to her. "Your brother's a fugitive. Has been for a few days now even though we've managed to keep his name out of the press. The U.S. marshals—including my team back in California— got the notification he was being transported from High Desert State Prison to San Quentin for overcrowding when he escaped custody. I'm the one who ended up stuck out here on top of Ginger with binoculars glued to my face and no bathroom for miles, on the off chance Jackson turned up."

"And what were you planning on doing if he did?" she asked, anger revving her words to a fast tempo.

"The same thing I'm still planning to do. Watch and wait until capturing him doesn't present a danger to you or your son, then nab him and bring him back into custody."

"What do you mean wait until capturing him doesn't present a danger to me or Peter? Were you planning to come in with guns blazin'? Have the big shoot-out at the O.K. Corral on my property?"

Instead of answering, Dylan stared at her, holding her gaze with his. She'd noticed before how startlingly blue his eyes were, but the expression he held now, one mixed with pity, compassion and a hint of fury, made the blue seem all that brighter. He shifted, and his plaid snap-front strained against the breadth of his shoulders. Under different circumstances, she'd label him a hunk. If she'd met him at the grocery store or the post office, she'd probably check for a wedding ring. And if she was being completely honest, she'd admit she'd already done the labeling and checking several times.

She mentally chided herself when her gaze once again dipped to his left hand. His ringless left hand. Damn it! This was not some friendly guy seated next to her at a Back to School Night. This man was the enemy.

She pushed her glass forward and waited as Dylan unstoppered the alcohol and poured her a drink, then used a finger to push it back across the wooden table to her. Despite wanting to down the entire glass in one gulp, she forced herself to sip elegantly, letting the firewater drift down the back of her throat, wishing she could be sharing the drink with Josiah. Tears filled her eyes and she tipped her head upward. She cried easily, always had, but she didn't want He-Man to see her tears. Not after he'd watched her sob, naked, on the floor of her shower. Granted, the glass of the shower surround had been so fogged Dylan hadn't actually seen her naked. But still...

Dylan cleared his throat. "I don't understand why you think it's so unbelievable your brother would run from the law. He's a convict."

"A convict who was falsely accused. A convict whose case is under appeal. A convict who will win that appeal and be fully acquitted."

Dylan shook his head slowly, his gaze piercing hers. "You can't possibly be that naive, Rachel."

"And you can't possibly claim to know me. Just because you did the whole gallant-knight thing today, riding in on a charger, coming to the rescue, doesn't make you the good guy. It doesn't make you right."

The corner of his mouth tipped upward in a crooked smile. "So I was a gallant knight, then?"

Funny how that curl relieved some of the tension of the day. The man probably made women melt and teenage girls swoon. But Rachel was far from a teenager, and she wasn't in a melting or swooning mood. She wasn't sure if she wanted to rip Dylan's head off for being against her brother or spend the night crying into her pillow over Josiah's death.

She let out a deep sigh, allowing the alcohol to blur her emotions, smooth the jagged edges. But then a thought suddenly occurred to her, and the jagged emotions were back with a vengeance.

"Josiah," she breathed. "You implied he might have been murdered. You can't possibly think…"

But he did. She could see it in his eyes.

"Josiah fell," she said baldly.

"Maybe," Dylan said. "Maybe not."

She stood abruptly. "I think you've said all you needed to say. My brother's escaped, and he might be on his way here. The U.S. marshals have my place staked out. Now I need to find my son and go about our evening chores. Tomorrow's a big day—I have a funeral to start planning, and I need to figure out how to hire a ranch hand I can't afford. So I think it's time I thank you for your help with our crisis today." She gestured to the front door.

The man remained seated.

"Seriously, did you not get what I said? I'd like you to leave now."

He nodded. "I heard you. And yes, I understood the subtext without the need for added direction. But I'm not leaving. Not until you understand what kind of threat your brother truly represents. Not until you understand that you and your son may be in mortal danger from Jackson Kincaid."

Dylan figured no one wanted to hear someone they loved could hurt them, but he'd seen too many instances of domestic violence not to know that sometimes the ones you loved the deepest were the ones who could cause the most harm. He also figured Rachel Kincaid had heard and experienced all she should have to in one day. Unfortunately he couldn't give her the reprieve he wanted to.

He had a duty to the citizens of the United States to keep them safe.

Justice. Integrity. Service.

The motto of the U.S. marshals wasn't simply words on letterhead. Those words meant something to him. If he did his job, fugitives were brought to justice. He did his job with integrity, respecting the rights of all concerned, be it family, victim or the fugitive himself. And he did it all for personal satisfaction, yes, but mostly to be of service—to his country and to its inhabitants.

Right now being of service meant convincing Rachel Kincaid her brother could harm her.

He wished he didn't have to. The woman had gotten under his skin in just a few hours. If he were a lesser man, he'd say his connection to her was simply physical. The woman was a looker, no doubt. And although those glass walls in her shower had been steamed up pretty well, he'd seen the swell of her breasts, the roundness of her naked hip, when he went to check on her.

But he knew there was more to his feelings for Rachel than physical attraction. He admired her. She certainly put up with a lot from her son. Before that... According to the files he'd read, she'd taken over running the ranch when her parents died, and had raised her younger brother, Jackson. He'd been ten and she'd just turned eighteen. She'd quit college and moved back to the ranch. Six months later she'd married a local boy—Phillip Wright—who'd killed himself a few years later in a drunk driving incident, leaving Rachel a widow with a three-year-old son to raise even as her teenage brother got himself into more and more trouble. She'd been struggling to do the right thing for all of them ever since.

"I know you raised him, Rachel. That you were little more than a child yourself when your parents died. You had your hands full with him, didn't you?" he asked.

She shot him a hard look. "Jax was like any other teenager. He got screwed by life and screwed things up in response."

"Detention throughout high school. He didn't even graduate—had to take his GED. Then two DUIs and a few minor drug busts followed. All that I could see blaming on losing his parents so young. Typical messed-up kid stuff."

"So?" Rachel snapped at him.

He paused before going on. "Then a B-and-E that he got a light sentence on because he was a juvie. Then another B-and-E. Again, maybe you could blame the loss of your parents on him acting out. Being stupid. But then there was the bust for possession of marijuana for sale. His first potential felony. He got off on that one on a technicality. Still sounding like a screwed-up kid to you?"

Rachel sagged back down in her chair and let her hands fall into her lap. She stared at the floor. He followed her gaze to the cracked checkerboard floor tile that had her transfixed. At least she was listening. Not running. Not fighting.

He sucked in a deep breath. Time to wake up Rachel Kincaid. "But what convinces me he isn't some stupid screwed-up kid anymore was the drug deal gone south. Your brother took a job delivering heroin to a drug dealer in Los Angeles. When the DEA showed up to raid the place— Well, you know what happened." He let his words hang in the air.

"Jax never had a chance to fix the tile," Rachel said, dully, still staring at the floor. "That week Peter had the flu. We needed money desperately—I couldn't even afford to take Peter to the doctor. I was exhausted, trying to tend to Peter and the livestock. Jax was trying to help. He was making me a sandwich when he dropped the mayo jar and shattered that tile there." She nodded to the broken tile. "Three days later he was arrested. Poor Jax. He hadn't even turned twenty before he was taken from me and now he's barely twenty-one. He's spent the past year in prison. He's been without his friends. His family…"

"Rachel," he said softly, "Jax isn't a victim. He admitted he knew what he was doing. He confessed. His first appeal was rejected for that very reason."

She raised her gaze to meet his, her eyes nearly as dull as Josiah's earlier in the day. "He was harassed into giving that confession. Scared."

They stared at each other until Dylan sighed. The day had settled into evening. His teammate Eric Haynes had the night shift and would probably already be in position to spy on the ranch. No sense in staying any later. He didn't want to ride Ginger back to Aaron's ranch in the dark.

Besides, if Rachel was naive enough to believe her brother wasn't the drug-dealing scumbag he knew the kid to be, he knew nothing he could say right now would change her mind. Hell, his own mother had been handed irrefutable proof that his brother was bad to the core, time and time again, and she'd never accepted it, even up to the day she died.

"I can see you've got your mind made up about Jax. But sooner or later, Rachel, you're going to have to face the truth." Dylan stood and headed toward the door.

"Where are you going?" she asked, her voice catching in her throat.

Hand on the door handle, he stopped. "The Sleep-E-Z Motorcoach Lodge."

"So the U.S. Marshals will be leaving me alone now?"

"Nope. The sheriff's deputies swept your property—it's clear. They're gone, but my teammate Eric is already in place. He'll keep watch until I show back up in the morning."

"Jax is a good kid," she stated. "He's innocent. And if he did escape, and I'm not saying he did, he must have had a good reason, if only that he was scared."

At that, he turned and caught her gaze with his. "A good reason? He—" He bit off his words. He was pretty certain that Rachel would collapse under the weight of any more bad news. He'd be back to tell her the rest of the story. Until then, maybe some rest would enable her to see reason come morning. So Dylan contented himself with saying, "Good night, Ms. Kincaid." He stepped outside into the humid Texas evening air, frustration crawling around inside his skin. As he slammed the door behind him, he heard a crash and the breaking of glass.

Then he heard her crying.

Again.

He stood there a long time before he found the will to walk away.

Chapter 5

After Dylan Rooney left, Rachel threw herself a very brief pity party and then went looking for her son. Just in case he'd snuck back inside without her knowing it, she combed the inside of the house first. When that proved fruitless, she headed outside and to his favorite tree. Down at the creek, even with dusk not yet set and cool light still diffusing the air, Rachel could tell the cottonwood's branches hung empty. No Peter.

She called Peter's name, but only the trickle of the creek and the rise and swell of the cricket and frog chorus rose around her. A nearby bullfrog stopped its low bellow, but no boy's voice responded. She doubted Peter was in the barn—the grass hay gave him allergies—but she'd try there.

She'd crumbled when she saw Josiah's dead body. Peter had to be freaking out. He liked to be alone when he got upset, but still, this was going on too long.

Fifteen minutes later, with all the light from the fading dusk gone, she headed back to the house. Peter hadn't been in the barn, either. Nor in the toolshed, or in the woodshed or in any of the corrals.

Upstairs, she paused in front of his closed bedroom door. She'd deliberately left it open before she headed outside to look for him. Relief swamped through her even as she braced herself and knocked on the door. "Peter?" No answer. She knocked again. "Peter, honey, I know you're upset, but we need to talk. Peter?" When there was still no answer, she opened the door.

She let out a cry of dismay upon seeing it was still empty. Immediately she saw the piece of paper propped on Peter's pillow. There, in Peter's dismal scrawl, was a note addressed to her.

Mom. I wasn't paying attention to where I was shooting the BB gun. I think I killed Josiah. I don't deserve to live here and decided to be a railroad bum. I have a hat and extra socks and I took five dollars from the cookie jar. I'll pay you back some day. Your son, Peter Kincaid.

An empty ache filled her heart as she realized what Peter must have felt, thinking he'd shot Josiah. She'd seen the wound on Josiah's head. No BB could have done that kind of damage. It had never dawned on her that Peter could have assumed he'd killed a man.

"Oh, God, Peter," she murmured, staring at the note she now held in her hand. She'd thought she was doing the right thing by leaving her son alone to work through his pain, when she really should have been seeking him out, making sure he was okay. Instead, she'd spent time wallowing in her own grief and arguing with a U.S. Marshal over her brother.

What kind of mother was she?

And where the hell was the rulebook on how to be a parent? Why didn't kids come with a user's guide?

Within minutes she called the sheriff's department and reported Peter missing. The call didn't go well. Sheriff Ryan expressed frustration over how many times Peter had run off in the past few years and how many times he'd been caught trespassing. Disturbed by the edge of warning in the lawman's voice, Rachel listened with growing trepidation and worry for her son, then called her best friend, Julia. Her brother—and now maybe even her son—needed a lawyer.

Rachel needed more than that.

She needed a friend. A break. A hint of hope that her life was finally going to take an upward swing.

But given everything that had happened today, given everything that U.S. Marshal Dylan Rooney had told her, she couldn't imagine her life going anywhere but completely downhill.

Hours later, morning brought bright Texas sunlight streaming through Rachel's kitchen window, but there was still no sign of Peter. She'd searched the surrounding area of the ranch until it got dark, and then she'd paced and worried and paced some more, praying for her son to come home. He'd run off before, but never for this long. The sheriff had called just over an hour ago, indicating his men had searched her property and the adjacent land—no signs of Peter.

Peter knew how to take care of himself, but Rachel's mom Spidey senses had the creepy crawlies making their way up her spine. Even if Josiah hadn't been murdered, Texas hosted a number of bad things that went bump in the night. Rattlesnakes, cougars, scorpions and brown recluse spiders. And the occasional bad guy. Scary stuff she didn't want to think about. Not with her son out there, alone and thinking he'd killed a man.

Rachel busied herself making two foaming lattes. One for her, and one for Julia. Thank God for Julia, who'd shown up fifteen minutes after Rachel called her, then taken over with lawyerly efficiency, querying Rachel about U.S. Marshal Dylan Rooney's presence and why Peter had run off. Then she'd shoved Rachel in the direction of her bedroom and promised to bed the alpacas down. Of course, Rachel hadn't slept a wink, but she didn't tell Julia that.

"Thanks again for spending the night," Rachel said, handing over Julia's latte. There wasn't anything she could do to find Peter, and until she heard otherwise, she had to assume he was okay. She needed, however, to distract her mind from her worry, and working on Jax's case would help. "Did you find anything out?" She nodded to the open laptop on the kitchen table.

"Some," her friend said, blowing on the foam of her drink. "According to the internet, this guy Dylan Rooney is who he says he is. U.S. Marshal. Part of a special ops team."

"What makes him so special?" Rachel asked. Besides his wide shoulders, long legs and tendency to rescue kids and widows in need. She gave herself a mental smack. This marshal might be sexy as sin, but he was still after her brother. That meant he might have rescued them, but not because he'd wanted to keep them safe. He'd done it because he wanted something else. He wanted her brother, and she and Peter were just means to an end.

"His team usually goes after the really bad guys. International drug cartel kind of people. I'm surprised they're interested in Jax. Yeah, the bust was big and two people were injured, but it's not like Jax held the smoking gun or anything."

"Have you found out anything about an escape?"

Julia grimaced. "I'm sorry, Rachel. I wish I had different news. But according to prison officials, Jax managed to escape during transport and the only reason they told me that is that I'm on record as his lawyer. He really got himself into a world of trouble with this escapade. Legally, he's screwed himself, big-time."

Rachel groaned and slumped against the refrigerator, letting the metal cool her skin. How was it she'd failed her brother so badly after their parents died? "How bad is it for his appeal that Jax took off?"

"Bad. Completely, totally, I-really–hope-there's-been-some-kind–of-mistake bad."

"There's no mistake," a male voice boomed out. "Jackson Kincaid is bad news. And if you want to keep yourselves and Peter safe, you need to accept that right now."

Dylan knew he shouldn't be staring, but wow— Rachel Kincaid had excellent legs. Dressed in purple cotton sleep shorts and a white ribbed tank, barefoot yet again, and even with her hair in a wild and disheveled ponytail, she looked delicious. His gaze traveled up her legs to meet hers.

She looked delicious and pissed.

And she wasn't moving from where she leaned against her refrigerator, giving him the glare of death. Only her body had tensed, tightened. As if she were expecting a fight.

"Planning on letting me in, or doesn't Southern hospitality extend this far west?" he asked, grabbing the handle of the latched screen door and giving it a rattle.

"Southern hospitality is reserved for gentlemen. And since you're staring like a largemouth bass at a lady in her pj's, you're obviously no gentleman," Rachel snapped out.

She'd shown some backbone yesterday, too, although the ordeal with the dead ranch hand had about done her in. Tough exterior, soft heart, he thought, remembering how devastated she'd been, crying for her friend in the shower. And how heart-wrenching her sobs had sounded as he'd stood outside her door, wanting nothing more than to stride back inside, gather her in his arms, and comfort her.

"Seriously, though, we need to talk about your brother. I'm happy to wait outside while you dress." *There. Gentlemanly behavior, right?*

Ignoring him, Rachel headed up the stairs. The woman Dylan hadn't been able to see popped around the corner and unlatched the screen door and held it open.

"I'm Julia Rickel," she said. "I know why you're here. I'm Rachel and Jax's attorney. And Rachel's best friend."

"U.S. Marshal Dylan Rooney. Rachel's...well..." Rachel's what? Yesterday, she'd sarcastically referred to his knight-in–shining-armor routine. And that was before he'd told her that her brother was out to get her. Before she'd flipped on him and thrown a bottle of booze at what most likely was his head. "Rachel's nemesis."

Julia flashed him a quick grin, then stuck her hand out. He shook it, noting the lawyer's strong grip. She looked to be about ten years older than Rachel. Nice looking, with short brown hair and a trim figure, and with very much a lawyer-type attitude, he realized as she checked him out just as thoroughly.

"Mind if I grill you while you wait for Rachel?" she asked, pulling her hand away and then motioning for him to sit at the rough-hewn kitchen table.

No polite chitchat for this woman. But if she was truly Jackson's lawyer, he probably couldn't say much in front of her. "Grill away," he said, anyway.

"What on God's green earth made you stake out the Kincaid place on horseback? And on Ginger, of all horses?" she asked.

He shrugged. "We didn't want to call attention to ourselves. Aaron Jacobson had a notice in the paper that he rented out horses, so the team's operations officer rented one for me, saying I was a bird-watcher."

"Lame," Julia said, then focused her attention on her laptop.

"Completely lame," Rachel agreed, walking back into the room, this time wearing shorts that covered just an inch or two more than the other ones had, and a bra under her tank.

"Agreed," he said, bringing his gaze from her rounded breasts up to her face. "I would have gone for a hiker so I could have stayed on foot. But at least Ginger got me down the ridge and to your place when Peter started hollering. My partner, Eric, told me some sheriff's deputies came back to search for Peter. They told him he has a habit of running off. He's not back yet?"

Rachel's eyes welled up with tears and her muscles seemed to lose their strength, contradicting her earlier rigidity. "No."

She turned and crossed the kitchen, then opened the refrigerator door, as if looking for ingredients. But he could see her swipe at her eyes. Once again, the woman was crying.

"Look, if he runs off a lot, then—"

"He doesn't run off 'a lot,'" she snapped out, slamming the refrigerator door shut and glaring at him, but tears still glistened in her eyes. "But in addition to being a kid and needing some space sometimes, he's got ADHD. We've been working on different coping skills and it helps being able to run. To move. He knows this land. He always finds his way back safely, but…"

"But he's grieving," he said quietly.

"More than that. He came back when I didn't know it, but only to grab some things and write me a note. He thinks he killed Josiah with his BB gun."

Holy hell. Dylan shifted on the bench seat. The kid thought he'd killed someone with a BB gun? Those things could maybe take out an eye, but not a human. "The M.E. called late last night. Cause of death was a cerebral hemorrhage. Although we don't yet know if he fell or was hit in the head, I can assure you, your kid and his BB gun had nothing to do with Josiah's death."

"I never thought Peter shot Josiah," she snapped out. "He fell. He hit his head. End of story."

"It's just the beginning actually. He could have been murdered. The coroner's running more tests. If Jackson is here, there should be—"

"Jax," Rachel ground out, her face going red. "His name is Jax. No one calls him Jackson. And you're not going to find any evidence that he's here or that he killed Josiah. How many times do I need to tell you he's innocent?" Her words revved up, adrenaline ramping up the speed. "Get it through your thick head—even if my brother escaped, he did it because he was scared. Jax is not a killer."

He waited, allowing her time to calm down, to get her emotions back in check. Quickly, he shot a glance at Julia. Jackson—Jax's—lawyer. Like him, she sat on the bench seat, only she'd pulled her knees up to her chin. Her fingers had stopped their dancing across the keyboard and instead she stared at the screen as though riveted. Interesting. Had the lawyer found out the real reason Dylan was there? Did she now know what he knew?

What Rachel obviously didn't know?

If she did, that meant the information had finally leaked to the press.

"I raised him," Rachel said, breaking the silence, pulling his attention back to her. "Whatever decisions Jax made, I led him there. I know he's not perfect. But if he's made mistakes, it's partially my fault."

Dylan snorted. Barely stopped himself from cursing and snapping at her. She was acting just like his mother. Making excuses for someone else's bad behavior. Blaming herself. "Listen to me—"

On the other side of the table from him, Julia snapped her laptop shut and rose to her feet. "Rachel," she said, sliding the laptop under her arm and coming around to face her friend. "How long will you keep taking the blame for what Jax did? And are you really going to take the blame for what he's done now?"

"So he ran away from jail. I know that's bad, but it's not like he's killed anyone."

"You have to tell her," Julia said.

Dylan caught the woman's full-on glare. Worry and not a small amount of anger shone in her eyes.

Justice. Integrity. Service. Those words meant something to him.

Neither Rachel nor Julia could see that. Rachel was worried about her son and brother. Julia was worried about her friend—with good reason. He wasn't here to hold the hand of a widow who refused to accept her brother was dangerous.

Even so, what he had to say was going to devastate Rachel. He had to tell her, if only to get her to take this situation seriously. To take him seriously.

He had no other choice.

Chapter 6

"Tell me." The deepness of Rachel's own tone sent a vibrato through her throat. What did the marshal know that he hadn't told her? What was her best friend keeping from her?

In front of her, Julia shifted from foot to foot, her laptop slung under one arm, the other arm crossed in front of her chest. As if she was on guard. From Rachel? Or from what they were about to tell her?

Dylan had risen to his feet, as well. Unlike with Julia, his arms were wide—hands fisted and placed on his hips. With his feet apart, he reminded her of some top-notch official in the military. Or a bully.

Neither spoke.

Rachel fought back a swearword. "I said tell me. Tell me what's happened to Jax."

Julia took a tentative step forward. "You know

what? Maybe I was wrong. You're dealing with too much, Rachel. Maybe you should focus on Peter right now. Let your concerns about Jax go for a bit. You've had a shock, with Josiah passing away and Peter running off. I'll handle Jax's situation."

Rachel turned on her. "I handle Jax. Me. You're his lawyer, not his mom."

"And you're not his mom, either," Julia pointed out. She'd used a soft tone, but the words pinpricked Rachel's heart. "Your son needs you. Be there for Peter. Let me and the marshal handle Jax."

Rachel fought for control. "How did you get my best friend to suddenly be on Team U.S. Marshals?" she snapped out at Dylan. "I know my son needs me. And I know my brother needs me. He's alone out there, scared."

"Who are you talking about, Rachel?" Dylan asked, his voice low. "Peter or Jax?"

She slumped. Both, she thought. How was she supposed to be a mother to two boys who needed her—one who was her biological son and still a kid, and the other whom she'd parented for the past eleven years and who could barely be considered an adult?

Tightening her spine, she stood straight, then stalked out of the kitchen and onto the wooden porch, letting the screen door slam behind her. The wind, light and gentle but stronger than a breeze, ruffled the tops of the grass in front of her. Peter needed to run the mower over the lawn. The alpacas needed feeding, the babies needed worming, the chickens and pheasants needed to be fed and watered and to have their cages cleaned. The horses needed to be turned out into the pasture. And it was just her. No ranch hand. No son. No brother.

Tears pricked her eyes. She ached to hold her son in her arms. To rock him and tell him Josiah's death was not his fault. But the days when she could rock her son were long over. He'd be home soon. He always came home—either willingly or yanked by the ear by one of the deputies. But he wouldn't want a hug. Would deny comfort, both for himself and for her.

And what of her brother? How could Rachel fix things for him this time?

The squeak of the screen door and the heavy thud of boots on the porch let her know Dylan had joined her. She remained standing, staring into the distance at the faraway creek, at the brush that rose on either side, and at Peter's favorite cottonwood.

"Julia's headed back to her office. She said she has some paperwork to file on your brother's behalf." Dylan stepped closer, his heat emanating off his chest and meeting her back. It made her feel as if a warm blanket of comfort and care had been placed on her.

Although he didn't touch her, her hair was up in a high ponytail and the hairs on her neck quivered. She shivered involuntarily as she imagined him touching her—massaging the back of her neck with his strong fingers, his warm palm pressed against her skin.

And her body responded.

Aching in long-forgotten places that emphasized how different they were. How strong and masculine he was. How perfect he was made to press against and inside her softer more feminine parts.

God, how she wanted to lean back and rest her weight on this man. The man who'd come riding to her son's rescue. The man who'd stood by her when she dealt with the death of her ranch hand and friend. The man who smelled of mint and melon.

The man who thought her brother was a scumbag drug dealer who'd kill an old man and endanger his family.

His very presence was a threat to her and those she loved.

She turned and shifted away from him, making him frown. The rough wood of the porch railing dug into her back. "Tell me," she said quietly. "Please."

His jaw clenched before he abruptly nodded. "I'm sorry, Rachel, but there's not much a lawyer can do for Jax now. I'm afraid it's bad. Jax didn't just run off, though believe me, that would be no small matter to deal with. During the escape, two U.S. marshals who'd been transferring him to another prison were shot."

"Oh, God…are they…" She couldn't bear to say the word.

"One's dead. The other's been in a coma and is in critical care."

She dropped her gaze to the faded wooden planks of the porch floor. The bones in her legs threatened to break into a thousand pieces and the shaking started. Surely he wasn't telling her that Jax—

He slid a finger under her chin and tipped her head up.

"Rachel, I need you to look at me. I need you to understand."

Unwilling, she met his deep, dark gaze.

Dylan continued, saying, "The reason we have

such an intense operation targeting your brother is that he's dangerous. He's a killer. And we need your help to trap him."

Rachel jerked her head away from Dylan's touch and barreled into the kitchen, the loud crack of the screen door swinging shut behind her sounding like thunder. Dylan's entry through the door was notable but much softer.

"Rachel—"

She shook her head as she paced alongside the kitchen table, the floor cold against her bare feet. The sensation was in complete opposition to the heat running through her veins: the heat of anger, of fear and of…denial?

She'd raised Jax since he was ten. Held him in her arms when he'd woken up with nightmares about their parents' dead and empty eyes. Admonished him and yet felt a sense of pride when he stayed up all night with his favorite alpaca when she was about to give birth. Got annoyed with him over the countless frogs and baby birds he brought into the house to rescue.

And she'd been there when the troubles in school had started. Then the troubles with the law. It hadn't mattered.

Jax saved baby jackrabbits from coyotes. He didn't kill people. No way would she ever believe otherwise.

And no way in hell would she help the U.S. Marshals trap her brother.

A whinny came from the barn—a subtle reminder it was well past time to feed the livestock yet one strong enough to act as a lifeline. She grabbed on to it for all she was worth.

Trying to convince Dylan of her brother's innocence was a waste of time. She knew her brother; he didn't. She turned, strode outside once more, then headed down the patio steps and toward the barn.

Once again, she heard Dylan following her. Heard him say, "Damn it, Rachel, stop."

When she didn't obey him, he gently took hold of her arm, halting her progress and turning her toward him.

With a vicious tug, she ripped her arm away. "Don't touch me," she shrilled.

He immediately put his hands up in a placating gesture. "Rachel, you have to listen to me—"

"No! I don't. Because you refuse to listen to me. No way is Jax a killer. And no way will I help you trap him. Please leave. I have animals to feed. After that, if he hasn't come back on his own already, I'll go looking for Peter."

He put his hands on his hips, his expression radiating impatience. "Have you considered that maybe if you help me, I can help you?"

"I don't want your help!"

"You sure about that? Because the U.S. Marshals have resources, Rachel. One call and I can get a chopper in the sky, looking for your son."

An incredulous bitter laugh tore out of her. "You're telling me you have the resources to find a kid, lost and alone somewhere out in the wilderness of Texas, and you're refusing to put those resources to use unless I help trap my brother? Isn't that called blackmail?" When the man refused to answer, she showed him her back and continued marching down the trail to the barn, aware of Dylan on her tail.

"That's not what I meant. Look—I was going to get the chopper in the sky whether you agreed to help us trap your brother or not. I'd already asked my team administrator to look into it before I got here, just in case Peter hadn't returned. She's likely got a pilot at the ready."

"Ready to move if I do what you want," she said with a sneer.

"No," he snapped. "I won't put your kid's life in jeopardy by playing games. I'm just pointing out that our relationship doesn't have to be contentious. You don't have to fight me because you think I want to hurt your brother. I don't. I just want him safely returned to custody."

She stopped and whirled, facing him with arms crossed over her chest. "So you...what? Think we can be friends and do each other some favors? You'll help me find Peter and you expect me to believe you won't expect something in return? Something like me handing over my brother?"

He stood only a few feet in front of her so that she could almost feel the fire burning in his eyes. She forced herself not to retreat.

"I know you'll never hand over your brother," he said. "All I want is your cooperation, Rachel. No, strike that. That's all I can ask for. Because anything else I want from you has nothing to do with your brother."

She sucked in a breath. Looked away. Refused to acknowledge the heat in his eyes that seemed to flare a thousand times brighter as he'd finished speaking. He wasn't admitting he was attracted to her. And even if he was, so what? Sexual attraction meant nothing;

family did. "How, exactly, do you want me to coop-erate?"

"Don't treat me like the enemy. Don't do anything to warn Jax away. Let me help. Him and you."

"By putting him back in prison for a crime he didn't commit!"

"He's going back to prison," he said quietly. "He was convicted for transporting drugs. The evidence suggests he shot those marshals, but he hasn't been convicted of those crimes yet. He still has a chance to tell his side of things. You want to help him? Do it the way you have been doing. By working inside the law. Anything else is going to end badly and you know it."

She did know it. Jax would never be safe, not la-beled an escaped convict.

"You think he murdered Josiah."

"I can't ignore that as a possibility, but it's a slim one in my mind. And I do give great weight to the phrase 'innocent until proven guilty.'"

She stared at Dylan. Took several deep breaths. Took a couple of steps back to put some distance be-tween them physically even if she couldn't run and hide from what he was saying.

"So don't warn him away. That's all you want from me?"

"Not quite. Let me stay here, on the ranch. Pretend-ing to be a ranch hand. That way if Jackson—Jax—shows up, he won't be suspicious. He'll think I'm hired help. We can take him in easily—no ugliness."

A ranch hand. Dylan was proposing to pretend to be her ranch hand. Right. As if a city slicker like him—a man who didn't even know how to ride Western, for God's sake, could be an actual ranch hand. She snorted.

She didn't need his help. Peter was fine. He'd be home soon and then she'd lock them both inside the house. Away from this man and his ugly accusations. First, however, she needed to get her chores done.

"My answer is no."

Using all her strength, she strode to the barn and raised the iron bar that held the doors open. When sunlight streamed into the darkened barn, the livestock grew agitated. Usually Josiah had fed, watered and turned them out by now.

"Hungry babies," she murmured, then grabbed a pitchfork. First went oat hay to the quarter horses, Anchor and Row. Next she distributed pellets down the alpacas' trough, taking time to ruffle soft necks or murmur to the babies—the crias. All the while she was aware of Dylan following her.

"How much longer will you be?" he finally asked.

She refused to turn around. "I work until sundown. And now that I'm missing two helpers, I'll be working even longer."

Behind her, she heard rummaging and the clanging of metal against metal. She craned her neck to look around a stack of hay bales to see Dylan, feed bucket in each hand.

"Tell me what to do."

"I told you. I'm not betraying my brother by letting you stay here."

"I heard you. I want to help, anyway, okay?"

She stared at him suspiciously. "Sure you do. Do you think Jax is hiding underneath some hay?"

"I think you need to get that I'm just doing my job,

Rachel. If you don't willingly allow me to stay here, I'll go right back to sitting on the ridge on Ginger, binoculars trained on every move you make, my team-mates at the ready to take your brother down by force if he shows up. Before I do that, why not let me help?"

Help. Hanging around ready to nab Jax wasn't exactly what she'd consider help. But if she didn't agree, Dylan and his team would still spy on her. How much of her privacy could she afford to give up? She'd need to call Julia—find out what her legal rights were. Julia's specialty was appellate law, but she'd probably be able to advise Rachel on the legalities of the U.S. Marshals spying on her property. On her every move. Every move her son made.

Peter.

"Weren't you going to call a chopper?" she asked. "I mean, I know Peter's fine. But the sooner he's back, the better I'll feel."

Dylan set the buckets down, then reached into his back pocket and pulled out a phone. Swiftly, he arranged for a chopper to sweep the immediate area around Rachel's ranch.

When he disconnected the call, he stood silent. Waiting.

Rachel cleared her throat. Forced out, "Thank you. I appreciate you doing that."

"I want your son found, too, Rachel. I'm not here to harm either of you. I wish you'd believe me."

But he is here to harm me. How could he think otherwise given what he was accusing Jax of? Her head suddenly started pounding and all she wanted in the world was to lie down, cover her head with something until the world dimmed to nothing and sleep.

That, of course, wouldn't accomplish anything. Not for Peter. Not for Jax.

And not for her.

She could deny and hide all she wanted.

Dylan Rooney wasn't going away any time soon.

She swallowed, then said, "I do believe you. It doesn't change much between us, but I do believe you want to keep Peter and me safe."

"And your brother, too. I want to bring him into custody but I want to do it in a way that's best for everyone. Him included, Rachel. Like I said, the best chance I have of doing that is if he thinks I'm on the ranch helping you out."

"God, you don't give up."

"No, ma'am."

Rachel studied him. "He hasn't been here and he's not going to come here. He didn't kill Josiah."

"I hope that's the case. I really do. Even if it is, you can still use my help. Free of charge. What do you say?"

Rachel hesitated. Struggled with the knowledge that if she didn't give in to Dylan's request, he'd still keep an eye out for Jax. Maybe the best thing she could do was keep Dylan close and do her best to convince him of Jax's innocence.

"Fine," she said. "The alpacas get a full bucket of pellets, sprinkled all the way down the feed trough. There's a hose on the other side of the barn, outside. Empty the water bucket, scrub it out and fill it with fresh water. Then join me back in the house. I'll... I'll think about letting you stay on the ranch and give you my answer then."

"Yes, ma'am." For a brief second, she thought she saw a smile quirk his mouth sideways.

What stunned her most was how, despite everything, she felt that smile in her bones. It made her want to smile back. And worst of all, it made her want to feel the press of his lips against hers.

Chapter 7

Rachel left Dylan to feed the remaining livestock and headed back to the house. She was supposed to be inside, at her computer, paying bills and tallying receipts for the alpaca wool she'd sold over the internet, but instead she responded to the hard tug in her gut and brought her laptop out to the porch, where she settled onto the porch swing.

There, she could see the driveway, the creek and the ridgeline. Keep her eye out for her son. And her brother.

But out in the fresh air, surrounded by the hum of bees and the bubbling rush of the creek, warm sunlight slanting through the chinks in the porch roof, made focusing on bookkeeping near impossible.

Not that she'd have been able to concentrate even if she were inside. Despite truly believing that Peter was fine, she needed her son. Needed to see him, to feel him, to smell the top of his head the way she used to when he was little. Once Peter was back, she'd be able to focus on helping Jax. And how she was going to deal with the U.S. Marshal currently working in her barn.

Briefly, she closed her eyes. Dylan said he'd intended to call a chopper to find Peter whether Rachel helped him catch her brother or not. As much as she wanted to believe he was a heartless monster bent on destroying her life on a whim, she knew that wasn't true. He was here to do a job. He worked hard to protect the public from criminals. He wanted to keep her and Peter safe.

Her instincts told her he was a good man.

He was just mistaken about Jax.

Once again, she told herself that letting him act as her ranch hand would mean she could keep her eye on him and have more time to convince him of Jax's innocence.

Unfortunately she'd also have more time to feel the tingles he inspired whenever he was around. Even as mad as she'd been, when he gripped her arm to stop her from walking away from him, she'd felt his touch in places that hadn't been touched since her husband had died. And even now she could remember the lure of his smile. She could envision them kissing.

Touching.

Caressing.

Exploring and tasting and surrendering to a passion that had nothing to do with anything or anyone but the two of them, naked and hungry.

Those blasted tingles shot through her. Her breath

caught in her throat. *It's been too long,* her body cried. *I want him.*

Rachel's eyes jerked open and she let out a cry of dismay. *Stop!* she told herself. *That will never happen. Never. Never ever.*

She was whispering those two words when she heard the rotor of a helicopter whistling its way up and down the valley and across the ridge.

"You said he's found his way home before."

She jumped at Dylan's voice. He must have snuck up on her while she was daydreaming about them. Although he had no way of knowing her private thoughts, she blushed, anyway, something he apparently noticed given the way his eyes narrowed on her face. What had he said? Oh, right. Peter. "He's been taking off ever since he could walk. At first he'd be gone for about ten, fifteen minutes. Then he started staying away hours. There's not a lot I can do to keep him here. And trust me, I've tried. When he was really little, I built that corral over there—" she pointed at the corral almost abutting the house "—just so he could play without me tethering him to my own body."

Dylan gave the corral a curious look. "And that lasted how long—until he learned how to climb?"

A burst of laughter escaped her. She clapped a hand over her mouth, aghast.

"Don't feel bad for experiencing human emotions, Rachel. You're in grief over your friend, in turmoil over your brother and now you're worried about Peter. You've got a lot to stress you out. But find release where you can."

"Easy for you to say," she responded.

He shrugged. "Maybe. But your brother has a law-

yer, which is good, and my team takes pride in bringing fugitives back alive. He's not in any danger from
us. And as far as your son goes, if he's run off as often
as you say, you're right—he's probably doing fine."

She knew Dylan was right. Peter knew the dangers
of the Texas wilderness better than any kid around.
Precisely because he'd gone on so many of his walk-
abouts when he was little, she'd seen to it he knew
how to take care of himself in the great outdoors. But
she still worried. And hated that she couldn't control
Peter's every move.

"When I first got the diagnosis that Peter was
ADHD, I was scared. But mostly I was relieved. The
more research I did, the more I realized I could help
Peter. Be more understanding. In many ways we've
gotten closer. But being here on the ranch with me
all summer...he's pulling away again. Testing me. I
think it's because he misses Jax."

"Does he know—"

Rachel shook her head. "I told him Jax got offered
a job too good to pass up. A job doing something he's
always loved." Rachel smiled slightly. "Writing songs
for an up-and-coming country star who's planning his
debut. Until then, he's keeping his identity a secret.
The country star, I mean."

Dylan's eyebrows shot up. "Your brother writes
songs?"

Rachel nodded. "Jax plays the guitar. Loves it.
Loves composing."

"Is he good?"

She shrugged. "I think so. But then I'm biased,
right? Unable to be impartial."

At her slightly bitter tone, Dylan sighed. Shifted.

"No one's ever slipped up and said anything to Peter about the real reason Jax is gone? No one from school?"

"Not that I know of. Peter's never said anything to me about it, anyway."

"Right. So when he comes back and finds me here…"

She closed her eyes for a moment, then did what her instincts were telling her to do. "I'll let you stay on as a ranch hand. But I'm only doing it so I can keep an eye on you."

"I understand."

"I'll tell Peter I needed help. You offered it. I don't want him knowing why you're really here or you can leave right now." Her chin tilted up defiantly. "You're not going to use my son to—"

"It's okay, Rachel. I agree with you. We won't say anything to Peter. Not unless there's a reason to. And if that turns out to be the case, I'll talk to you first. I promise. Okay?"

She hesitated. Nodded. "Okay."

"Did Josiah have a trailer somewhere?"

"He has…had…a room in the house. The ranch doesn't have separate quarters for employees." She frowned as she realized for the first time that if she agreed to let him act as her ranch hand, it would only make sense for him to take Josiah's old room. That was a little too close for her. Josiah had practically been family. This man was…not.

"I won't be trouble, Rachel," he said. "I'll give you your privacy. But…"

"What?"

"Will Peter wonder if there's another reason I'm staying?"

"What do you mean?"

"Will he wonder if we're dating? Lovers?"

Her mouth went dry and she jerkily shook her head. "No. He won't wonder."

"Why's that?"

"Because he knows I'm not interested in dating. Jax and Peter and this ranch are my life and Peter knows it. Now I really need to get back to what I was working on."

"No problem," Dylan said. "I'll be as quiet and unassuming as a mouse."

She snorted.

He smiled slightly, then settled his large frame into an Adirondack chair next to the swing. After a few minutes of silence, she relaxed and pretended to work on her laptop.

They sat that way for twenty minutes before a billow of dust down the drive caught her attention. She stood, shading her eyes against the late morning sun. A sheriff's car. Good news, or bad?

The car came to a stop in the drive and she recognized the grizzled head and lanky frame that emerged from the vehicle. It was Sheriff Ryan, hat in hand. He slammed the driver's door behind him and walked toward the house. Alone.

Disappointment weighed heavily on her chest. So he hadn't found Peter.

At the edge of the porch, the sheriff paused, and looked at her then. Gray wrinkles stood out against his tan skin. He caught her gaze, then shook his head.

"Oh, God, no," she uttered, even as her knees buckled.

Two strong arms caught her around her waist.

Knights in shining armor didn't usually get an elbow to their solar plexus. Dylan let go of Rachel, who had used a backward jab to let him know she didn't need his help.

But she was wrong. He could help.

He would help.

He just didn't know how. Not yet.

Before them, the sheriff waved his hat at Rachel.

"Peter's fine. I'm sorry if my expression said otherwise. I'm just unhappy these little escapades of Peter's are costing the taxpayers money."

Dylan cursed softly. He knew what Rachel had thought when she'd seen the sheriff's doom-and-gloom expression. Hell, Dylan had thought the same thing. The sheriff should know better and as he assessed the man, Dylan began to understand that he did. He'd wanted to scare Rachel.

Instinctively, he stepped to her side and put his arm around her shoulders. The sheriff's eyes widened slightly, but as Dylan stared back at him, he knew the other man had caught his silent message. Do not mess with this woman or you will be sorry.

Next to him, Rachel glanced at him in confusion before pulling away. "You found him, though? He's coming home?"

Another shimmer of light moved toward the ranch along the road, dust forming billows behind. The sheriff waved his hat in the direction. "Deputy Loren is bringing him home right now. That chopper you got up in the air—" he nodded at Dylan "—scoped him out down on the tracks, about seven miles away. We got him, but that damn whirlybird probably spooked all the livestock in a ten-mile radius."

And if Jax had made it from Los Angeles to Texas, and was hanging out in the nearby woods, waiting for his chance to come onto the property undetected, he could have been spooked, too, and Dylan and his team might have lost a chance to pin him down. Dylan could only hope that wasn't the case. But at least the kid was safe.

A sheriff's patrol car came to a halt in front of them. Within moments, Deputy Hank Loren let Peter out of the backseat, then handed the kid a backpack and gave him a pat on the back, pushing him toward his mom.

Sullen, the kid walked up the steps of the porch, gaze glued to the ground, averted from his mother, then brushed past Dylan.

No way, no how was this kid getting off that easy. Not after Dylan had called in a chopper to rescue his ass. Not after the kid's mother had spent the past eighteen hours worried sick. Dylan reached out, gently took hold of Peter's skinny arm and turned him around.

"Listen, kid," he said, tightening his grip when the kid made to pull away. "I think you owe me and the sheriff's department a thank-you, and you definitely owe your mom an apology. She's been worried sick." He flashed a glance at Rachel, who stood stiff, arms curled in around her chest. Not as if she was frightened—as if she was protecting her heart.

"I didn't ask anyone to find me," Peter snapped

at him. "I was fine. Caught myself a trout for dinner and ate berries for breakfast. Used iodine in the water to purify it. And I was about to hop a freight train to someplace west."

Kids Peter's age thought they were invincible, but of course, Dylan knew better. He also knew how they could blame themselves for things that weren't their fault. Emotional pain radiated through him before he found control and shoved it back. "In case anyone hasn't told you yet, you didn't kill Josiah. He died from a head wound, not from being shot by a BB gun. His blood isn't on your hands."

The kid's shoulders dropped and his eyes went from bright and snapping to round and glistening. Dylan's heart expanded. The kid had really thought he'd killed a man. Poor thing. That wasn't a weight Dylan would wish on anyone's shoulders.

"But you still owe your mother an apology, and apparently there are a ton of chores to do."

"Sorry, Sheriff. Sorry, Mom." Peter made to move off, but Dylan squeezed his arm tighter.

"Not good enough. A man looks someone in the eye when he apologizes. A man doesn't use a snotty tone. A man accepts his responsibly and carries the burden of blame on his own shoulders."

"I'm ten," the kid threw out. He didn't look at his mother or the sheriff, but at least stared Dylan square in the eye.

"The way I look at it," Dylan said quietly, "you're either young enough for a spanking or old enough to accept responsibility on your own. Which is it to be?" Personally, Dylan didn't believe in spanking, but he wouldn't tell that to the kid.

Rachel cleared her throat and Dylan flashed a glance at her. She stared at him, mouth firm, eyes narrowed. She was obviously pissed at him for interfering with her son, but that was too bad. As he'd thought earlier, he was going to help her whether she liked it or not. He looked back at the kid, who held his gaze for a moment, fight building in his eyes, reminding Dylan of his mother.

Then something changed in his expression. Resignation setting in? Or acceptance? Dylan couldn't tell.

The kid squared his shoulders and faced the others. "I'm sorry I ran off. I'm sorry I made everyone worry. I'm to blame for making you all scared."

Good enough for Dylan. He dropped the kid's arm and turned to Rachel.

"I'm going back to the motel," he said softly, silently communicating that he was doing so to pack up his stuff and move into the house.

Rachel's house.

Where she lived with her son. Peter might not assume she and Dylan were sharing a bed, but an outsider, someone like the sheriff, might.

"Thank you for your help," she said quietly.

He nodded and left Rachel to deal with her kid.

He found himself not wanting to leave her at all, which confused him.

He admired Rachel. He wanted her. He couldn't have her.

The most he could have was her help tracking down her brother.

He knew it.

What he didn't know was why the hell it pissed him off so damn much.

* * *

An hour later, Dylan was packed up and had reported in to his team.

"The fugitive's nephew could be a problem," Marco Hernandez said. "He doesn't know you're a U.S. Marshal, right?"

"Nope. As far as the kid knows, I'm a stranger who raced a horse down from the hill to help when he started screaming. He has no clue I'm with law enforcement," Dylan said.

"I'd like to keep it that way," Marco said. "Could be if he gets wind you're out to capture his uncle, he might warn his uncle off."

Could be, Dylan mentally agreed. Could also be that if Jackson was as dangerous as he appeared, he could use the kid as a human shield. "I'm making progress, but I don't want to push things too far too fast. I'll talk to Jackson's sister. Tell her to send her son to stay with a relative for a while. At least until Jackson is brought in." It made sense. The fact that it would result in him and Rachel being the only two people in her house together was beside the point. He was attracted to her, but it wasn't as if he could do anything about it, even if she wanted him to. Which she didn't.

"Do that. And good job getting the woman to agree to let you work the ranch. Sitting around on a horse pretending to be a bird-watcher has got to be the most idiotic stakeout I've ever heard." With that, the team leader dropped off Skype, leaving Dylan still online with two members of his team.

"But I thought bird-watching sounded plausible,"

Stacy, the team administrator, said. "People do it all the time where I'm from."

Dylan snorted. Stacy Johnson was from Napa, only an hour out from where Dylan grew up in San Francisco. "Texas is not California, and I'm finding that out the hard way. I'll keep in touch, Stacy."

"Take care, Dylan," she said before she terminated their connection.

"So you'll be staying at the gorgeous widow's place round-the-clock." This came from Dylan's partner, Eric, who was holed up in a hotel a few miles from Dylan's—something they'd arranged to avoid attention from small-town busybodies. Even with Dylan staying with Rachel, Eric would remain in town as backup and would continue to scope the ranch from afar. Right now, however, Eric wasn't thinking about the job. Even on the small screen of Dylan's iPad, Eric's smirk showed up bright and clear. "Sleeping under her roof. You always were a glutton for punishment, Rooney. And the luckiest son of a bitch I know."

"Bust my chops another time. The list of chores she has for me is a mile high. And a hell of a lot of those chores have to do with manure."

"Fair trade as far as I'm concerned," Eric said before signing off.

Definitely a fair trade, Dylan thought as he double-checked the room to make sure he hadn't forgotten anything. Having to do some heavy lifting on a ranch was child's play in terms of what he was willing to do to get the drop on Jackson Kincaid.

Of course, he knew that wasn't the kind of trade-off Eric had been talking about. He'd been referring to the fact that Dylan would get to spend more time with Rachel. A smart, beautiful woman who worked too hard and didn't get enough respect from her son or brother. A woman who, regardless of the fact that she'd agreed to let Dylan work her ranch, viewed him as the enemy. She'd been up-front about the real reason she'd agreed to let him help her—to keep an eye on him. Dylan was betting she'd also use their time together to try to convince him of her brother's innocence. Hell, maybe she thought she could work out some kind of deal. Get him to go easy on her brother.

He wondered how far she'd be willing to go. If she'd be sweeter. Friendlier.

If she'd offer him her body.

But as soon as the thought crossed his mind, he dismissed it.

Rachel would never use her body to manipulate him or any man, even if it was to help her brother. He didn't know why he was so sure; he just did.

And while he knew he wasn't the type of man who'd ever go easy on a fugitive even if Rachel did offer him her sleek, tan body to do so, he knew turning her down would be one of the hardest things he'd ever have to do.

Chapter 8

After Peter returned home, Rachel ordered her son into the shower and spoke with a local minister on the phone about Josiah's funeral. She spent the next few hours with Peter, then mentally preparing herself for Dylan's return. By early afternoon, when he returned carrying a single duffel bag, she felt composed. That composure fled when he found her in the kitchen preparing dinner, leaned against the counter and asked if she had relatives Peter could stay with.

He wanted her to send Peter away? She'd just gotten him back.

"The fact is, Rachel," Dylan said, "there is a chance Peter is in danger. There is a chance you're in danger, too, although I doubt I could say anything to make you leave this ranch."

Plus, she thought, he needed her on the ranch to

increase the chances Jax would show up. The same wasn't true for Peter.

"My son is not in danger from my brother."

"He's believed to have shot two U.S. Marshals in cold blood."

"You said you believed in being innocent until proven guilty."

"I do. But I also believe in working with the information we have, and right now the only information we have is your brother escaped. During that escape, two men were shot. The only natural conclusion is that your brother shot them."

"With what?"

"Excuse me?"

"What did he shoot them with? Were the marshals shot with their own weapons?"

"No."

"So where'd he get the gun to shoot them? He was a prisoner, for God's sake. He didn't have a weapon."

He folded his arms across his chest. "Prisoners sneak in contraband all the time, Rachel. Guns and drugs."

She frowned, knowing the point he was making by mentioning drugs. "Yes, my brother had started experimenting with drugs before he was arrested. Yes, he even confessed to transporting them. But he was deathly afraid of guns. He probably wouldn't know how to shoot one."

Dylan shook his head in mock amazement. "You just won't give up thinking your brother is innocent. He's the only one who escaped that day, Rachel. Who else do you think shot those marshals?"

"I don't know. But I know in my gut it wasn't Jax,"

she said quietly, just as she'd promised herself she would the next time she said it. Keep calm. Keep emotion out of it. The less hysterical she acted, the greater likelihood he might actually begin to listen to what she had to say.

"What's that?" Dylan put a strong hand on her arm and looked up the valley, his head cocked to the side. "Do you hear that?"

She listened but heard nothing.

Then she did. Under her feet, felt vibrations. It sounded like a...

Peter stuck his head inside the kitchen doorway. "Stampede!"

"Cattle?" Dylan asked.

Rachel nodded. "Peter," she said. "Stay in your room, okay?"

"But, Mom—"

"Do as I say, young man. Now," she snapped. "Or I promise I'm giving every single one of your video games to charity. I did it before. Do you really want me to do it again?"

With a glower, Peter obeyed her, running up the stairs and slamming his bedroom door shut. Praying he stayed inside the house, she ran outside and Dylan followed.

There had been a couple of times in the past few years when Aaron's herd escaped their pasture and headed to the streambed. From there, they'd take off down the natural pathway, which led through her property. After the last stampede, she had made sure the fence line had been thoroughly reinforced, which should have kept the cattle out even if they escaped from Aaron's property.

Now, however, the vibrations were heavy under her feet and she could already hear the lowing and bellowing of cattle in distress.

Had something startled Aaron's cattle into a wild enough stampede that they'd taken down two solid fences? Were her alpacas in danger of being trampled?

She couldn't take the risk.

Breaking from Dylan's grip, she raced toward the grazing herd of alpacas, which stood between the barn and the creek bed. If the cattle hadn't been turned by the fence line, they would come straight through this area—and the alpacas wouldn't have a chance. Behind her, she could hear Dylan's heavy breathing. Although she ran at full speed, he passed her within seconds.

As he ran, he called out over his shoulder, "Go back! Keep yourself safe! I'll herd them into the corral, get them out of danger."

"You can't do it alone. You're faster than I am—you go around the far side and start herding them out toward me, and I'll cut them off and get them into the corral."

"Damn you, woman, do you have to control everything?" But Dylan didn't stop and kept running full out, waving his arms and yelling at the alpaca herd. One by one, they stopped their grazing to look at him, then communicated together with flashing ears.

"Run, babies," she whispered. They needed to move—now. Dylan put his fingers in his mouth and let out a piercing whistle. At that, the herd shifted, turned and as one, started to run toward the corral she'd once built for her son to play in. From behind, she could hear the herd of cattle growing closer, at a full run, but she refused to move, and instead stood locked in place, her arms out wide, creating a barrier the alpacas would understand.

Smart creatures. She had to bank on their intelligence. They grew closer, still not turning to the corral, but she held firm. Then the herd shifted and streamed into the small fenced-in area, Dylan right behind them. He slammed the gate shut and barred it in place and then turned to look at her. His eyes went wide.

"Rachel, move!" he shouted.

Oh, God. The cattle.

She ran, but could she outrun the thundering herd? Almost at the corral, the swirl of dust from heavy hooves choked her.

"Here, grab my hand!" Dylan reached out and grabbed her, then in one swoop, hauled her up onto the top board of the corral right before fifty head of Texas longhorns crashed through her property.

The two minutes it took for the cattle to pass by seemed like two hours. She sat with Dylan on the wooden fence, waiting for the danger to pass. When the cattle trotted out of sight, Dylan swung himself down. He reached his hands up, an offer of help. A gesture of peace.

Still shaking, she let him help her down, his hands holding her rib cage firmly. But once her feet touched ground, she found she still needed his grip. Her bones seemed to have lost density.

"Rachel," Dylan murmured.

Their faces were so close she could see the small scar at the corner of his mouth. Could see how his nose angled a little to the right, as if he'd broken it more than once. Could feel his heartbeat thudding against her chest. His scent swept up around her, replacing the stench of cattle with the smell she'd come to recognize as being uniquely Dylan.

Again, he said her name. Soft. Quiet. And she didn't back off. Didn't move away. She moved closer instead, hungry for the sensation of a strong man against her. Needy for a man's touch.

His mouth crashed down on hers—his lips firm and warm and velvety. His tongue silken. His breath and her breath combined to make magic. She slid her hands up his back, grasping at his shoulders and pulling him in closer, starving for his touch. For his mouth. For his heat and strength.

And feeling desolate when he pulled away and stepped back, leaving her standing alone, shaking with the release of adrenaline, the rush of desire and the intensity of sexual arousal.

He pushed back a strand of her hair as he gazed into her eyes. "Rachel. Peter...Jax..."

His words instantly snapped her out of her desire-induced malaise. She took several shaky steps back. "Oh, God. I'm sorry. I can't believe..." She stared at the ground, tears of frustration welling in her eyes. "What you must think of me. The sex-starved widow. Ready to take on any man, including the one who thinks her brother is a murderer. You must be laughing yourself sick inside." She blinked furiously. Swiped at her eyes.

"Rachel, look at me."

She ignored him.

He stepped closer until she had no choice but to look up.

"I'm not laughing myself sick. Even if I wanted to

laugh, I'd be too blown away by that kiss to do it. We have chemistry. That's been obvious from the start. The stampede got our adrenaline going, that's all. We'll forget that ever happened. Agreed?"

As easy as that? she thought. Maybe for him. For her, who hadn't wanted to kiss a man in seven years? She doubted she'd forget the feel of his lips and body against hers any time soon. But all she said was, "Agreed."

"Right. So...how'd those cattle get here?" he asked, his voice rough. He stared at a spot over her head.

"I don't know. The fence line is reinforced. At least, it was. They had to have broken through it." Which meant she had to repair the line. And she didn't have the money to do it. She'd have to keep her alpacas in the lower field until she could find another solution.

"Let's saddle up the horses. It's time we go for a ride."

"Where?" she asked numbly.

"Where those cattle came out. I want to look for a break in the fence line."

But she didn't. She didn't want to spend any more time with him. She wanted to hide under her covers in the dark. She wanted to figure out what the heck had just happened between her and U.S. Marshall Dylan Rooney. "Can't it wait until tomorrow?"

"No."

"Why not?"

Dylan's mouth set in a grim line. "I don't think it's a coincidence those cattle ran through your property. I think this was deliberate."

Chapter 9

What on God's green earth had possessed him to kiss Rachel Kincaid? Dylan adjusted his seat on the back of Anchor, one of Rachel's quarter horses, as they rode to the fence line to see how the cattle had broken through.

He knew the rules inside and out about fraternizing with fugitives. You did not make out with fugitives. And you did not make out with the sister of a fugitive. Yet fifteen minutes ago, Dylan had practically thrown her up against a corral and had his way with her mouth. He'd wanted to have his way with far more of her. Had almost given in to temptation.

But then he'd remembered her son was in the house. And the reason why Dylan was even on their ranch to begin with.

One of his fellow marshals was dead because of

Rachel's brother and another was barely clinging to life. He had to keep his mind focused on his mission. Bring in Jackson Kincaid, no matter what. Yeah, Rachel Kincaid's body, mind and heart triggered him in all the right ways, but now was not the time to indulge.

Ahead of him, Rachel had come to a stop and dismounted. He nudged Anchor up to her horse, the one she called Row, and did the same. Then he checked out the fencing.

Was his suspicion correct? Had the stampede been deliberate?

Clean, sharp nips ran down a straight line on two sections of her heavy-duty barbed wire fence. Wire sat rolled up, off to the side.

Deliberate, then.

No way could anyone think the stampede had been an accident.

He flashed a glance at Rachel. The wind picked up, whipping a strand of her white-blond hair into her eyes. She used the excuse of brushing her hair away as a way of wiping away the tears he saw glistening in her eyes.

She had a soft heart. She cried easily. When she was sad. Angry. Frustrated.

She was so tough, but also vulnerable.

Someone had tried to cause her harm. That same someone had probably killed Josiah. He wanted to beat the bastard to a pulp.

"Let's go check out Aaron's line," Rachel said. "After the last property line dispute, we both agreed to put an acre's length of land between our fence lines. His is due west." At his nod, she mounted Row, then squeezed him into a trot. Dylan followed on Anchor, and in a minute, they were an acre west, at Aaron Jacobson's fence line.

Again, the fencing had been deliberately cut. Both Dylan and Rachel dismounted, and Dylan came close to examine the cuts. Aaron's fence line had been older than Rachel's—rusted—but still strong. Dylan ran his finger across a clean slice. Wire cutters. Someone had set up the stampede.

Could that person have been Rachel's brother? After all, causing a stampede was nothing when compared to breaking out of prison and gunning down two marshals to do it. But why would he do it?

Did he know Dylan was on the ranch? Had he guessed he was law enforcement and wanted to warn him off? Warn Rachel off? But if he knew Dylan was a cop, he'd know a stampede wouldn't run him off. And why would he want to get his sister off the property?

No, it didn't make sense.

Chances were the stampede was unrelated to the hunt for Jackson Kincaid. That didn't mean it didn't need to be investigated.

"You said you're in a property line dispute with your neighbor." Dylan bent down and pulled on a section of wiring, taking care not to cut his finger on the rusted barbed wire.

She nodded. "Aaron Jacobson. The guy who rented you Ginger. This is his fence line. His property. But if you're thinking he'd let his cattle stampede all over my property to get me back over wanting the spring, you're wrong."

"How so?"

"He loves his longhorns. Besides, half are pregnant. Running like that, all panicked, could compromise the pregnancies."

"Okay, how about anyone else that might want to cause problems for you? Because if there's no other suspect…"

"No. I know what you're going to say. But this isn't Jax. It's not. He'd never…" Rachel slumped, as if suddenly exhausted—probably too much stress and not enough sleep. She found an old stump and sat, picking at the grass below.

The woman needed a break. He wanted to help—to make everything okay for her. What was it about her that triggered his inner knight in shining armor, just as she'd snidely accused earlier? Dylan came to sit next to her on the stump, then made a zigzag pattern on the ground by flattening new grass with his boot.

Her horses were trained to remain in the same place when their reins were dropped, and now stood nose to tail, swishing flies from each other's faces. Spring in Texas brought beautiful things: bluebonnets, songbirds, green grass…and bugs.

A ladybug landed on Rachel's bare shoulder. Dylan gently lifted it, then held it out on his index finger in front of her face.

"Make a wish and blow it away," he said.

She smiled weakly. "I thought you were supposed to tell it to go back home. Something about its house being on fire and its children alone."

"Seems harsh. I like asking it for a wish instead," Dylan said.

Rachel held the silence for a moment, then took a deep breath and blew the ladybug off his finger.

"What did you wish for?" he asked.

Her face grew clouded. "For this to all be over."

That was what he wanted, too. But probably for much different reasons than the ones Rachel had. He said, "I don't have all the pieces of the puzzle yet, Rachel. But something's going on here." He gestured to the cut fence. "Until I can figure out what, you have to admit getting Peter someplace off the ranch, just like I suggested earlier, makes sense."

Rachel blew out a long, measured breath. Dylan waited.

"I can't," she finally said. "Peter is all I have. I can't be away from him. The safest place he can be is with me."

She was wrong. But she was also right. Without more evidence that Josiah's death, the stampede and her brother's escape were linked, he didn't know what he could say to make Rachel change her mind. "All right," Dylan said.

He stood.

"That's it?" Rachel asked. "You're not going to fight me about Peter?"

"He's your son. You know what's best for him and I can't force you to send him away. You agreed to let me stay with you and that's enough for now. But get used to the fact that I'm going to be staying very, very close to you and Peter, Rachel."

"In case Jax comes by? Because you want to catch him?"

"That's one reason."

"What's the other?"

"You said Peter is safest with you? Well, right now

the safest place for you and Peter is with me. And I'm going to make sure no harm comes to you, whether the threat is from your brother or someone else."

Chapter 10

Later that day, Rachel leaned back in the leather seat that faced Julia's desk and drew in a deep breath through her nose. At the edge of town, tucked in between a bakery and coffee shop, the lawyer's office smelled heavenly. Although at early afternoon the bakery had already finished its day's worth of baking, the scent of yeast and sugar snuck between the walls, reminding Rachel how little she'd eaten. She'd shown Dylan to Josiah's old room, given him a list of chores, driven Peter to a friend's house to play, then come to town to confer with Julia.

And to get away.

"You willingly agreed to let a U.S. Marshal who has every intention of capturing your brother live on your property?" Julia asked incredulously.

"If Dylan stays on the property, I'll know where he

is at all times. I hate that the marshals are watching the house. I'd rather watch them watch me."

"And?" Julia prompted, as if waiting for more explanation.

"And...with Josiah gone, I desperately need help on the ranch."

"And?"

Irritation set Rachel's spine a little tighter. "And what?"

"Your decision doesn't have anything to do with the fact that the man is drop-dead gorgeous?"

"Get serious, J," Rachel snapped out, irritated. "He wants me to send Peter away until Jax is caught."

"It's not a bad idea."

"What?"

"Let's just talk possibilities. If you decided that was what was best for Peter, where would he go?"

Rachel wrapped her arms around her middle, guarding against a hollow ache forming in her stomach. "If I decided that was best for him, I could send him to his father's parents."

"Then do it. I think Dylan is right. Peter could be at risk, especially with a bunch of U.S. Marshals trampling all over your property, the valley and the ridge. And if the marshals are gunning for your brother, you don't want your son in the line of fire."

Again, Rachel's first instinct was denial. But because it was Julia making the suggestion, she forced herself to reconsider. She had to think of what was best for Peter. She hated losing the little bit of control she still had over her son, but his safety came first. And despite what she'd told Dylan earlier, if someone had intentionally caused the stampede, Peter wasn't safe on the ranch no matter how close she stayed to him.

"I'll drive him down tonight," she said. "Tomorrow I'll call the school and let them know where he'll be. I don't want the sheriff's office after me for truancy." She made a face. She'd just about had it with law enforcement.

"And what about you? I don't want you in the line of fire, either. Haven't you considered that you might not be safe? Maybe you should take a few days off—go away for a while."

"I can't. The ranch is the only future I can give Peter. I can't abandon it." Although she had taken online courses and had earned her B.A. in agricultural sciences from a reputable university, she was trained in nothing other than ranching.

She refused to surrender control of her own ranch.

Plus—and she knew this was what was really keeping her from leaving the ranch—Dylan seemed convinced Jax was coming to her. If he was, she needed to be there for him.

Although the drive to Peter's grandparents' house took three hours, Dylan insisted on coming along, which had surprised her.

"Aren't you afraid Jax might show up while I'm gone?" she asked before they left.

"My partner can cover the ranch while we're gone. Like I told you before, I think that stampede was intentional. I'm not willing to risk your safety."

Her heart warmed at his words, but she reminded herself that while he'd admitted he was attracted to her and had enjoyed their kiss, he was probably more concerned with keeping her alive because she was his best bet to getting Jax. Still, he insisted on driving, for which Rachel was eternally grateful.

Twenty minutes into the drive, Dylan surprised Rachel once again, this time by making an obvious effort to engage Peter, who sat between them in the cab of her old Ford pickup. He asked questions about various things, including skipping stones and climbing trees and school-age bullies, which reminded her he'd also been a ten-year-old boy once. That had her imagining what he'd looked like and what kind of mischief he'd gotten into at that age. Those thoughts then led to her wondering what his life had been like since. What kinds of girls (then women) he'd dated. Whether he had family. Where he lived when he wasn't chasing down fleeing prisoners in Texas. More than once she had to quash the urge to join the conversation and ask. She already felt too drawn to Dylan as it was—the more she focused on Dylan as an officer of the law and less as a man with human experiences and connections, the better off she and Jax would be.

At first, Peter mumbled and barely kept up his end of the conversation.

Then Dylan nodded at the BB gun Peter had clutched in his hands.

"Cool Red Ryder. Had one just like it when I was your age. Your mom teach you to shoot?"

Peter actually smiled. "Nah. Josiah did."

Dylan smiled back. "Didn't want you to get one? Afraid you'd shoot your eye out?"

Peter looked at Rachel, and Rachel winked at him. Then he turned back to Dylan. "Your mom worry about that, too?"

"I think it's part of some secret moms' club ritual to worry about that. But just like Ralphie Parker's mom, and my mom, looks like your mom finally came around. She trusts you to have fun, be safe and be responsible. That tells me a lot about you. Good things."

Peter didn't respond directly, but he did say, "We always watch *A Christmas Story* on Christmas Eve. Me, mom and Uncle Jax. But Uncle Jax missed it last year. He's away."

It was the first time Peter had directly mentioned Jax in front of Dylan, and as soon as he did Rachel stiffened. Her tension increased as Peter commenced to tell Dylan more and more about his uncle.

"Uncle Jax taught me how to ride."

"Uncle Jax is great at tracking jackrabbits."

"I want to learn how to play the guitar like my uncle Jax."

Eventually Peter seemed to run out of breath and accolades.

"You know," Dylan said, "your uncle Jax…"

Rachel stiffened and Dylan's gaze caught hers.

"…sounds like a really fun guy," he finished.

"You'd like him," Peter said. "And…" Peter bit his lip and hesitated before saying, "I think he'd like you."

Rachel's eyes widened. In Peter's world, that was a huge compliment.

Dylan seemed to get it. "Thanks, kid. But why do you say that?"

"Because you helped me. You tried to help Josiah. And you're helping my mom."

Again, Dylan looked at her. There was a message there. One she didn't miss. *Your son gets it,* it said. *Why can't you?*

Because you're not trying to help Jax, she thought. And if Peter knew that, you wouldn't be winning him over right now. Not ever.

Of course, Peter also wasn't old enough to truly understand the mistakes Jax had made, her rational side told her. Or how Dylan was just doing his job. Heck, even she had trouble with those concepts.

But Rachel didn't want to deal with logic and reason right now. Not when she was having to send her son away. Not when she didn't know if and when she'd ever see her brother again.

Eventually they arrived at their destination. It didn't take long to drop Peter off. Her former mother-in-law came out front to greet them, but though she gave Rachel a hug, she didn't invite her or Dylan into the modest ranch house. Told that there were warm cookies waiting for him inside, Peter gave Rachel a kiss and ran to the front door, where his grandfather waited. There, he turned back and waved. Then he yelled, "Bye, Mom. Bye, Dylan."

"Love you," Rachel shouted back as Peter disappeared from view. She turned to Maureen and almost winced at the lack of spark in her eyes. Before Phillip's death, this woman had practically glowed with vitality. But after...she looked as if she'd aged two decades instead of seven years.

They spent about ten minutes going over Peter's routine. Although Rachel had told Maureen about Peter's ADHD, he'd never spent more than a few hours with his grandparents since, and even then Rachel had been present.

"Don't worry," Maureen said. "We'll keep a close eye on him."

Rachel nodded. "Thank you for keeping him."

"It's our pleasure, Rachel," Maureen said. She smiled wanly, then followed Peter inside. Her husband, Tom, stood at the front door. He stared at Dylan a long time, his gaze curious. And sad. Then he nodded at Rachel before walking into the house and shutting the door.

Rachel and Dylan drove away. With every mile they traveled, she felt anxiety building inside her as if she were a balloon. She squeezed her hands together tightly, wanting nothing more than to command Dylan to turn around so she could retrieve her son. She reminded herself that she'd sent him away to keep him safe, but now she didn't have her brother or her son.

She was completely alone in the world.

Either Dylan sensed Rachel's need for silence or he was working something around in his own head, because they talked very little on the ride back. When they were about five miles out from the ranch, however, Dylan cleared his throat.

"Rachel, I know we discussed that kiss and agreed to forget about it, but…if you're uncomfortable with me staying in Josiah's old quarters," Dylan said, "I can always borrow a sleeping bag and stay out on the front porch. Your call."

She kept her eyes closed, considering her options.

Keep your friends close and your enemies closer. Wasn't that it?

Years of being a mother had taught her to sleep lightly—she would know if he got up in the middle of the night. Plus, if Jax was to sneak in at night, he would sneak in through the French doors in the master bedroom—where he'd always snuck out of the house as a kid. And where she was now sleeping. She would be able to get to Jax before Dylan could.

Besides, she wasn't afraid Dylan would try to sneak into her bed. Truth be told, she was more afraid she'd try to sneak into his. "I don't mind," she said. "Like you said, that kiss was just the result of adrenaline. I know I'm just a job to you. And you…well, you're nothing to me." She said it despite how harsh the words sounded. She said it to try to convince him but also herself.

She cracked her lids opened and peered at Dylan between her eyelashes. He shifted his seat, and his grip tightened on the steering wheel. Had she insulted him? Or was he taking her words as a challenge and thinking of proving her wrong? Was he thinking of their shared kiss? She hadn't been able to get it out of her mind. In Julia's office, when Julia was interrogating her over her intentions for letting Dylan act as her ranch hand and stay on the property, she had hoped her cheeks had not betrayed her desire by turning bright pink.

"Are you sure?" Dylan asked, his voice sounding tighter than before.

Not at all. But she also knew how alone she felt right now. At least if he was in the house with her, she could pretend there was someone who cared. Someone who'd listen to her if she needed to talk, even if she had no plans of doing so. "Absolutely."

Headlights from a car behind them grew closer, illuminating the cab of the truck. With the added light, she could see the lines framing Dylan's mouth grow deeper.

The headlights grew even brighter, and Dylan

growled under his breath, then flipped the rearview mirror down to dull the glare. "Assholes," he swore.

Odd. Rachel had not heard him swear before, except when he was speaking of her brother. Did the man hate all rule breakers?

A bump from behind jolted them forward. Rachel's seat belt caught her up short, the sudden jerk forcing air out of her lungs.

"Damn it! Rachel, here—" Dylan reached in his leather jacket pocket, pulled out a cell phone and tossed it to her.

"Do you want me to call 911?" she asked.

"No. Just put it on speakerphone and hold down the number one button for a moment." With that, he leaned down, reached into his boot and pulled out a handgun. Steering with one elbow, he released the safety.

Eyes glued to his gun, Rachel held down the number one on his phone. A woman who identified herself as Stacy answered.

"I'm driving Rachel's truck and we're getting rammed." He proceeded to give her their location and instructed her to get them backup.

"Got it," Stacy said quickly. "We'll have help there as soon as we can."

"Right," Dylan said, and Rachel disconnected the call.

Twice more they were rammed. Dylan fought to keep the truck on the road. Rachel fought to breathe.

"Rachel, lean in front of me and take the wheel," Dylan ordered.

She didn't stop to ask why. To question. To snivel or whine or cry. Instead, she leaned in close to his body and grabbed the steering wheel as he twisted, keeping his foot on the gas, and leaned his upper body out the driver's-side window, gun pointed straight back.

"When you have a straightaway, steer a bit toward the left. That'll give me a clear shot."

Copper filled her mouth. Blood. She'd bitten through her lip. "Straightaway coming up. Two seconds."

Dylan floored it, and there they were, in the straightaway. She steered slightly left, heard popping sounds, then a squeal of rubber on pavement. Dylan eased his frame back into his seat and took over the steering wheel from her. She sagged back into her seat as he continued to drive.

"Got both front tires. They won't be going anywhere for a while." He used her cell to call Stacy and confirm the location of the car and the fact deputies would be on the look-out for the men who'd rammed them. After disconnecting the call, he shot her a glance. "You did good, lady. Are you all right?"

Was she all right? She fought back a gag response. Her world had been turned upside down. She'd never be all right again. "Who was that? Why were they ramming us?"

"I don't know."

A thought occurred to her and she grabbed his shirt in a panic. "Were they following us? Did they follow us when we dropped off Peter? Maybe we should head back—"

"They weren't following us, Rachel."

"But how do you know?"

"I'd know if someone had been following us. I'm

trained to pick up on those kinds of things. I promise, we weren't followed. That car only came on us once we got off the main highway."

"So were they drunk? Dumb kids playing chicken?"

"I don't know," he said again.

"Great. You don't know. At least you don't think it was my brother," she snapped out bitterly.

"There were two men in the front seat of that car. Both their silhouettes were all wrong. Neither was your brother."

She sat in silence for a while. Ramming a moving vehicle at seventy miles an hour wasn't a prank. Something serious was going on. But what?

"At least they weren't shooting," she said, trying to lighten the mood.

Dylan didn't laugh.

She looked at him and saw his lips pressed in a grim line. Those lines on the side of his face were deep, and his eyes narrowed. "What is it?" she asked, hesitantly.

"That's why I told you to get in front of me," he said.

"I don't understand...."

"They hadn't started shooting yet. But if I hadn't gotten to them first, that would have been the next thing coming at us. I couldn't see much, but I could see both men held guns."

Dylan had barely parked the car before Rachel was out of it and heading into the house. With a quiet curse, he called Stacy, who told him law enforcement had found the car with its tires shot out, but no sign of the two men who'd been driving it. "Keep me posted," he said before disconnecting.

Slowly he followed Rachel through the front door. He expected to see her climbing the stairs to her bedroom. Instead, she stood inside the foyer, frozen, staring at the kitchen doorway in front of her, her arms straight by her sides. Dylan stepped next to her so he could see her profile. He winced at the blank, almost robotic look on her face.

"Rachel," he whispered. Unable to help himself, he lifted his hand and caressed her cheek with his knuckles. Her skin was soft but cold, as if despair was freezing her from the inside out. "Baby," he said.

The endearment seemed to jolt her out of her paralysis. With a frown, she turned and looked at him. Confusion flashed across her face, as if for a moment she didn't even know who he was. Where she was.

"I'm alone," she said, her voice thin and reedy.

"No," he began, but her bitter laughter interrupted him.

"Yes. I'm alone. No parents. No husband. No Josiah. No Jax. No Peter. Right now I'm alone and weird things are happening, things that scare me, but no one can help me."

He took her by the arms and gave her a small shake. "I'm here to help you, Rachel. I won't let anything happen to you."

She tried to jerk away from him, but he wouldn't let her. "You can't help me," she cried. "Not when you believe what you do about Jax. Not when you want to take him away from me forever, which is what will happen if he's blamed for shooting those marshals."

"I have a job to do, Rachel, but that's not going to stop me from helping you. From keeping you safe."

She placed her palms on his chest as if she wanted to push him away but couldn't bear to do so. She shook her head. "You can't keep me safe. You can't. You can't. You can't."

She kept repeating the words and something snapped inside him. He couldn't take it anymore. Couldn't take the grief and desolation he saw in her eyes. He needed to erase it. Needed to make her forget her troubles and how unsafe she felt. "I will keep you safe, Rachel," he said fiercely. "I know you don't believe me, but I will."

"You c—"

Before she could once more deny what he'd said, he covered her mouth with his.

For a split second, she stiffened.

But only for a second.

Almost immediately she softened in surrender, her body melting into his and her mouth opening to the strong thrust of his tongue. Even so, Dylan wrapped one hand around her neck and one arm around her back, ensuring that she couldn't pull away as he explored her sweet taste. He wanted to fill her up with his strength and shoot his essence inside her again and again until she couldn't help agreeing that she was his. That she wasn't alone. That she'd never be alone as long as he had a single breath left in his body.

His body hardened more and more the longer they kissed. He couldn't remember ever wanting a woman as much as he wanted her. Couldn't remember feeling as if he'd die if he didn't bury himself inside her. His hands went in search of her curves—first, her full, rounded breasts. Then the dip of her tiny waist and the flare of her womanly hips. Finally he palmed her rear, pushing her closer even as he bent his knees slightly so he could rub his erection against the vulnerable juncture of her thighs.

He was lost in the feel and taste of her, so much so that it took a while to register the sound of his own ragged breaths and the sweet erotic cries of pleasure she was making. He wanted to ratchet those cries into screams as he brought her to orgasm. Automatically, his fingers moved to unsnap the button of her jeans. He growled in frustration when her hand covered his and she broke their kiss.

"Dylan. We can't. I want to, but we can't."

Their gazes met, her brown eyes fiery with desire but also clouded with regret. His hand trembled beneath hers. He wanted to argue with her. Opened his mouth to do so. But the words wouldn't come. She was right.

They couldn't give in to their desire. If they did, he knew Rachel would regret it. And the last thing he wanted to do was cause her more pain.

Even though it nearly killed him, he nodded. "You're right. We can't. But I can hold you. Just hold you for a minute more. Can I do that?"

Her eyes filled with moisture before she buried her face in the crook of his neck. Wrapping his arms around her, Dylan did as he'd promised.

He held her. He also stroked her hair. Told her things were going to be okay. That she was going to be okay. And he prayed that he was telling her the truth.

He had no idea how much time had passed before she pushed away from him.

Briefly, he tightened his arms around her, not wanting to let her go. But letting her go was something he was going to have to get used to. This beautiful courageous woman wasn't his.

He let her go.

"You okay?"

"Yes." She cleared her throat. "Are you?"

No, he thought. *This woman is killing me. And all I want is more of her.* "Yes," he said. "But I've got to check in with my team. Find out what they've learned, if anything, about the men who tried to run us off the road."

She nodded. "Do you want to use my office?"

"Thanks, but I noticed I get the best remote internet connection out in the barn. In the tack room. I'll head out there and give you some privacy so you can get to bed."

She stared at him for a moment, probably thinking that he wanted to talk to his team where she wouldn't overhear him, and she was partially right. But he really did want to give her some privacy, as well.

"I'm tired," she said suddenly.

"You're tired," he agreed. "You need to rest. Go to sleep and things will look better in the morning."

She smirked and cocked an eyebrow. "You really believe that?"

Once again, he brushed his knuckles against her cheek. "I hope so."

With a sigh, she nodded and turned away. He watched as she climbed up the stairs, looking as if she were carrying the weight of the world on her shoulders. At the top, she paused and looked over her shoulder at him. "We keep complicating things," she said.

"Yep," he agreed.

"I know in the morning I'll regret it, but right now I don't. Because for a moment, I didn't feel alone, Dylan."

He wanted to say he didn't regret kissing her, either, but he couldn't. Complications, he reminded himself. Instead, he said, "I'm glad, Rachel. Now go to bed."

Her smile indicated she understood what he *wasn't* saying.

She lifted her chin and said, "Good night, Dylan. I'll see you in the morning."

"Good night, Rachel."

He watched as she walked into her room and softly closed the door.

He waited almost twenty minutes before checking in on her. He knocked softly on her door. When she didn't answer, he peeked inside. He didn't enter her room, but from the doorway he could see she was asleep. In slumber, her face wore an expression of serenity, as if all the worries of the past two days had been erased. Rachel in sleep was as beautiful as Rachel awake. He fought the urge to climb into the bed beside her and simply hold her again.

With a sigh, he closed the door and headed out to the barn. Even though he knew Eric had eyes on the ranch, Dylan still made sure he had a clear view of the house, however, so he could see anyone coming or going.

Five minutes later, Dylan was talking to Stacy over Skype.

"Wish I could tell you more," she said, "but all we

know so far is the SUV was stolen in Hartford, about forty miles away."

Dylan swore. "So no way to tell if they're related in any way to the Jackson Kincaid case?"

"I can't find the link—but that doesn't mean there isn't one. I have local law enforcement on the lookout for two Caucasian males, about six foot two, and weighing around two hundred pounds. Bodybuilder types, is that right?"

"We were driving at least seventy and it was night, so I couldn't make a positive ID, but they had the dome light on in their SUV, so I'm confident of the description I've given you."

"So neither man was Jackson Kincaid?"

He shook his head. He wanted to capture Jax, sure, but he also didn't want Rachel to get hurt, either physically or emotionally. She seemed unable to believe her brother capable of any wrongdoing. Although the facts suggested otherwise, he harbored a small hope in his heart that somehow Rachel was right—at least, right in the fact that her brother would not hurt her.

"Dylan?"

He brought his attention back to the screen. "Kincaid doesn't have gang tats on his neck. Those guys did." He blew out a breath. "There have been two threats against Rachel Kincaid and a suspicious death on her property, all within forty-eight hours, and I don't like it. I'd like to get her out of here. Force her to leave."

Stacy tilted her head. "No can do. Boss man wants her on the property and there's really no reason to think the incidents are related. Not yet. The death of her ranch hand has not proven to be a murder. She admitted to having a feud with her neighbor over the property line, so that cattle stampede you told me about could have been prompted by that feud. And as far as the SUV ramming you goes?" She shrugged. "I'll admit, that looks hinky, but since neither man in the SUV was Jackson Kincaid, we cannot link the incident to him."

He knew she was right. Without more, there was no reason to move Rachel off the ranch. Especially when it was still possible Jackson Kincaid might be heading to Texas to get to his sister. "Got it. No convincing Rachel to leave her property." He didn't like it, but between him and Eric, Rachel would be safe. He'd make sure of it.

"It's 'Rachel' now, is it?" Stacy gave him a leering wink. "I think someone's got a crush on the widow Kincaid."

More like a hard-on, he thought, then forced himself to be honest. He was insanely attracted to Rachel, yes, but there was more than that when it came to his feelings for her. Despite the fact that she was just like his mother—always blaming herself for the mistakes her family made—she was also stronger in many ways. And it hadn't escaped him that when she ordered Peter into his room to keep him safe from the stampede, she'd shown a maternal background inconsistent with the excuses she constantly made for her brother. He liked her. Hell, he more than liked her. By the way he'd stared at her while she was sleeping, he knew he *was* crushing on her.

"Any sign of Kincaid from the others?" he asked.

"Trying to change the subject?"

Trying to get Rachel out of his mind and focus on

the job. He did not need the distraction. "Just answer the question."

"No sign of Kincaid."

"Right." He sighed. "Thanks. I'll check in tomorrow."

"Sounds good," Stacy said. "Now go play cowboy. Gotta say, I'd love to see you in spurs and a whip."

He managed to smile but just barely. Dylan was a city boy, born and raised in San Francisco. No matter. A whip and spurs weren't what it would take to bring down Jax Kincaid. If Kincaid showed up, however, his ass would belong to Dylan. He just had to keep Rachel safe in the meantime.

Chapter 11

Good God, Dylan thought the next morning. How tight could a pair of shorts get on a woman? In the barnyard in front of him, Rachel chopped wood—the round moons of her butt peeking out at him from under the frayed denim of her shorts every time she finished a stroke of the ax.

Last night, he'd dreamed of her. At first, the dreams had been dark. Her in danger. Him trying to protect her. Her refusing to believe she was in danger and running to her brother instead. Eventually the dreams changed because *he* changed. He no longer asked to help her; he simply refused to leave her side. That meant they fought. But it also meant sex. The Rachel in his dreams loved to give over control to him, but she loved taking it, too. There wasn't a position she shied away from, but her favorite was when he powered into her from behind, fisting her hair with one hand while the other played between her legs. Her second favorite was riding him, teasing him with tender shallow thrusts followed by fast deep ones that had him shouting her name.

By the time he woke, he felt her in every pore of his body. He swore he could smell her. Taste her on his tongue. In the shower, he'd tamed his erection, dressed and gulped down the coffee Rachel had prepared. When she'd come in from outside and she'd seen him, his hunger must have been reflected in his eyes, because she blushed. For a second, her eyes ate him up and he could plainly see reciprocal desire reflected in their depths. She stood there, cheeks flushed, mouth parted slightly, breath exhaling on quick puffs. Then her expression went blank. She told him she'd talked to Peter, who was doing fine with his grandparents, and then she told him to meet her in the barn.

Where she handed him an ax.

And handed him humiliation on a plate.

He'd admitted to never having chopped wood before. Now she was giving him a demonstration. One he liked very, very much. Those cheeks triggered his fantasies from the night before. Fantasies involving him on his knees behind a naked Rachel and—

"Are you paying attention?"

Rachel's voice brought him out of his reverie. So much for fantasizing over the widow Kincaid. There was wood to chop. And his manliness to reclaim. "Yeah. I got it. Left hand holds close to the bottom of the ax handle. Right hand holds the top. Sling the ax back, then over your shoulder and start sliding your hands together at the apex. Then—smack."

She handed him the ax.

He grabbed the wooden handle and imagined giving it a sudden tug, pulling her off balance. And against him.

Heat rushed to his crotch. Another hard-on formed.

Damn, but he wanted to kiss her again. Wanted to drop the frigging ax and take her in his arms. Unbutton her shirt and unhook her bra and let his hands wander over her breasts.

Instead, he did none of those things. He simply stepped forward to the chopping block and placed a quarter round on top, then backed up, visually measuring the distance. He lifted the ax, sensing the weight and heft of the wood and iron, balanced between his widespread hands. Then, following Rachel's directions, he slung the ax back, high and down, in one swoop.

He hit the log dead center, and two pieces shot off the chopping block. He let a grin slide to the surface, and turned and faced her. Inane pride filled his chest. "I did it!"

She smiled, wide and full, and Dylan thought it again—Rachel smiling full-out was a thing of pure beauty.

"If you were eight years old," she said, "I'd tell you how proud I am and pat you on the back. I took Jax out for ice cream the first time he chopped wood, and bought Peter a video game for his first. Instead, I'll just ask. Think you can chop all those quarter rounds there?" She pointed to the side of the barn, where a good fifty quarter rounds sat piled high.

"Yeah, I can do it. No choice, since it has to be done. There's so much to do around here. I can hardly believe you've been getting by, even with Peter and Josiah's help."

Rachel sighed. "None of this is easy. Jax used to help until he started getting into too much trouble. Peter helps—has done so since he was a little one. Josiah—" her voice caught "—Josiah put in a good forty hours a week on the ranch work. Now it's just me."

So she was back to that again. He wondered if she said it to remind him to keep his distance. To remind herself. "I'm here now," Dylan said knowing that wasn't enough for her. Wishing he could give her more. But he couldn't. She was cooperating with him, but in her heart, Rachel still believed Jax was innocent. She refused to accept his true nature, just as his mother had refused to accept his brother's. And for that reason, she wasn't what Dylan needed, no matter that she was what he wanted. Even putting all that aside, he had no doubt that once her brother was back in prison, whether Dylan was the one who actually brought him back there or not, she'd be done with him.

The knowledge made him want to take the ax to the waiting quarter rounds and keep going. And how crazy was that? He'd known Rachel a couple of days, but the way his body reacted to her, it was as if they'd not only kissed but spent weeks exploring each other's bodies and trading intimate secrets.

"Well, when you're gone, I'll have to figure out how to either manage this place on my own or pay for a ranch hand. Heck, maybe this time instead of an elderly man like Josiah, I'll look for some young handsome thing to muck out my stalls." She said it with a twist of her mouth, probably meaning it to be a self-deprecating comment rather than the challenge his body heard.

Ignoring the spark of jealousy that immediately ignited at her words, Dylan said, "Whoever you get, I'm glad you'll have help. That you won't be counting on your brother to come home anytime soon."

She folded her arms over her chest and set her jaw. "He'll be back soon enough. Julia will prove he's not a murderer. And as for the fact that he ran? Maybe he had a good reason."

Same old song and dance, he told himself, but then something Rachel had said drifted into his head—that her brother didn't like guns. That he composed music. Did that really sound like someone who'd be able to get the drop on not only one but two U.S. Marshals to engineer his own escape? So far there'd been no evidence that anyone else had been involved in the prison escape, but it wasn't as if the marshals had a lot of witnesses to interview. Their only one was still in a coma fighting for his life. If he woke, what would he tell them? That Jackson Kincaid had indeed had a good reason to run? Or that Rachel didn't know her brother as well as she thought?

And why was he even considering the possibility that Rachel was right about her brother's reasons for running? She couldn't even accept that he'd been involved in the drug deal to which he'd confessed. She was beautiful, but she preferred to walk around blind to the flaws of those she loved.

He just hoped that tendency didn't end up killing her the way it had killed his mother.

* * *

Rachel left Dylan outside, chopping wood, and headed indoors to her office to pay bills. As she did, Dylan's handsome visage haunted her. In his soft and faded jeans and a plaid button-down rolled up to his arms, she didn't know what she enjoyed feasting her eyes on the most: Dylan's tight butt or his wide shoulders.

Both.

She entered her office, sat down at her ancient rolltop desk and turned on the computer.

And then promptly turned around to stare out the window at a wood-chopping Dylan.

She wanted him. Well, at least her body wanted Dylan's body. Her mind argued firmly against the idea.

Run, her mind told her. *Take him,* her body screamed.

She listened to her mind and turned away from the window to once again focus on her computer screen. Enough of dreaming about a man she could never have. Would never have.

A few clicks and hits of the return button later, and her emails popped up. Bill. Bill. Another bill. A reminder from her veterinarian's office that it was time to order vaccines for her alpaca herd. And an email without a subject in the subject line. Spam, most likely. She hit Delete, then froze. There was something familiar about the return address.

Hurriedly, she opened her Trash folder. There, at the top of the dumped emails, sat the one she'd just deleted.

An email from her brother.

Tears filled Rachel's eyes and pain radiated outward from her chest. She hunched forward, almost cradling the computer monitor, and read the email from Jax.

Sis. By now you probably know about the jailbreak during transport. How I ran. I swear I didn't shoot those men. As long as you and Peter are safe on the ranch, I'm coming. We can work out a deal. I'm coming home, but promise on the memory of Mom and Dad you won't tell anyone. Love, Jax.

Fear, relief and confusion slammed into her all at once. Dylan was right. Jax was headed home to her. But Dylan was also wrong. Jax hadn't shot those U.S. marshals. Yet she knew how much detail he took in composing his music, and the odd wording of his email suggested they'd been deliberately chosen, as well. That he was sending her a message. But what? That she and Peter would be in danger if they left the ranch? Or that they'd be in danger if they stayed on the ranch? Did he know the marshals were here?

Rachel closed the email and filed it in a folder labeled Taxes.

Her first instinct was to call Julia, but Jax had begged her to promise on the memory of their parents not to tell anyone. What was Jax involved in? Why, after all this time, had he finally decided to contact her again, as if the past year of silence and rejection hadn't happened?

She propped her elbows on the scarred desk and sank her head into her hands, suddenly weary. The desk wobbled, the loose leg in the back one of the many items in need of repair. But she didn't have the money.

That was what had landed Jax in this mess in the first place. If he really had transported that package knowing it contained drugs, he'd done it because he'd been trying to make money to help her out.

Maybe history would repeat itself and Jax really would come to the ranch, just as he'd said in his email. If that happened, she knew which trail he'd use to come up to the house. Which door he'd use to sneak in. What time he'd try to sneak in.

She hadn't been his mother for ten years for nothing. She knew most of his secrets, even if she didn't know them all.

The question was who'd be here when Jax arrived. Just her? Or her and U.S. Marshal Dylan Rooney.

"Rachel, are you okay?"

At the sound of Dylan's voice, Rachel jerked in her chair and raised her head. She blinked, noting the light sheen of sweat that covered him, making him look even more sexy than normal if that was possible. A man like that who could work so hard outside bed? He'd only have that much more stamina in bed.

And what a silly thought for her to have when she knew her brother was on his way and might be walking directly into Dylan's waiting hands if Rachel allowed that to happen.

That might be the best thing for everyone. Dylan had said he wanted to take her brother into custody without anyone being harmed. It was always better to face problems head-on, within the confines of the law, than to make matters worse. "Dylan—"

"I've finished the wood and was about to move

on to my next chore, but I wanted to check in on you first. Make sure you're okay."

"You mean because of Josiah and the stampede and someone trying to run us off the road. Those were just weird coincidences," she said.

"That's what you've decided to tell yourself?"

"Unless you can prove they're connected somehow. Can you?"

"You know I can't. Not yet. But I don't like the sight of you sitting in here, head in your hands, radiating weariness and vulnerability, either."

She raised her chin. "We all need to take a break sometime. I'm fine. And I can handle myself. I've done it long before you were around, and I'll continue to do it when you're gone." When his mouth tightened, she sighed. "I'm not trying to be difficult, honest. But, Dylan, I just showed you how to wield an ax, remember? I'm not exactly a fragile flower."

"No, but you remind me of a wildflower. Delicate. Beautiful. But strong enough to withstand the elements, too."

Her mouth parted at his unexpected compliment. A flare of something in his eyes made her want to stand and go to him, as if she were a moth and he a flame. Instead, she looked away and gripped the edge of her desk tightly, praying for the willpower to withstand temptation.

"You taught me how to wield an ax. How about I teach you something now?"

Her gaze met his once more. "What's that?"

"You said your brother doesn't know how to shoot a gun. Do you?"

"I can shoot a rifle. On an isolated ranch, it's important to be able to protect my family and livestock."

"Right. But can you shoot a handgun?"

"You mean, like the kind of gun you carry around in your boot? No."

"Want me to teach you?"

"Because you think I might have to shoot my brother to protect myself?"

"Because you've never shot a gun before, it could be fun and maybe, just maybe, it might come in handy someday."

"You're serious?"

"It's better than sitting in here feeling sorry for yourself, right?"

She narrowed her eyes. "Now you're just trying to make me mad."

He grinned. "Is it working?"

In the field acres from Rachel's house, Dylan put a soda can on a wooden fence post, then moved six feet down and placed another can on the next post. Headed in the opposite direction, Rachel did the same.

"How many cans are we putting up?" he called out.

"As many as you want to shoot." She finished placing her last can on a post and returned to Dylan.

The sun caught the light in her hair. Running his fingers through it suddenly seemed so appealing, but that wasn't why they were here. He was here to teach Rachel how to shoot a gun. Because whether she wanted to accept it or not, weird things were happening around the ranch and he liked the idea of her being able to protect herself if need be. Not that he was going to hand her a loaded weapon to carry around after one shooting lesson, but it would be a start. He could teach her a little every day, and when he left, she could continue with the shooting lessons.

He frowned at the idea of leaving the ranch. Her. He knew it was coming. That he couldn't stay here indefinitely on the chance that her brother showed up. But one thing was for sure, he wasn't leaving until he knew she and her son would be safe. And hopefully by that time she'd be on her way to feeling better so that he wouldn't walk in on her and find her looking beaten and defeated the way he did when he'd walked into her office earlier.

On her way back to him, Rachel stumbled but quickly corrected herself, her hips swaying as she regained her balance. Her incredibly sexy hips, with her firm, tight butt held by the soft, well-worn denim. When she reached him and turned to face their targets, he came up behind Rachel. "Ready?" At her nod, he placed the handgun in her hands. He'd already gone over the basics of the gun's mechanisms with her. "Feel the weight?"

"Yes."

"Good. Now here. Take the safety off."

"Am I standing correctly?"

Shooting a gun wasn't like playing golf. A marshal never knew what position he or she would be in when having to discharge a weapon. Assuming a perfect position wasn't necessary. But Rachel didn't know that. He stepped right behind her and slid his arms around hers, covering her hands with his. Her backside fit perfectly against his front—molded to him. He breathed in her scent, that breathtaking mixture of rose and cinnamon and nutmeg.

"Are you planning on smelling my hair all day, or will you teach me to shoot?"

He chuckled. Spunk. With her world falling apart at every corner, Rachel still had spunk. He dropped his hands but stayed behind her, their bodies maintaining a subtle connection. "Okay, then. Sight down the barrel. See the target?"

"Shiny red, dead ahead."

"Squeeze."

A shot sounded and the can popped off the fence line. The energy dispelled from the weapon sent Rachel back somewhat, against his chest, and he held firm. Chemistry radiated outward, almost visible. He ran his hands across her shoulders. "Sore?"

"Somewhat."

"Want to try again?" he asked.

"Absolutely!"

Even though he'd wanted to give her a distraction from her pain, the flippancy of her tone gave him pause. He gripped her shoulders tight. "Rachel, you were raised on a ranch. You know guns aren't a game. Just like how you treat the rifle and shotgun with respect, you need to treat a handgun the same way. It's not a toy."

She pulled away from him. "I know that. I'm not an idiot."

"I didn't say you were."

At that, she turned to face him. "No, you were just playing the big, bad law enforcement dude. I don't need a lecture."

"What's with the 'big, bad law enforcement' part of that statement? Do you have issues with authority?"

"Both my brother and my son seem to keep getting

in trouble with the law. So yeah, I guess I do have an issue with authority."

"Christ, Rachel, I'm here to do a job. Your brother's the one who escaped. My job is to be here when he shows up. I haven't given you any reason to mistrust me, have I?"

She tilted her head down, studied the thin shoots of new green grass at their feet. "You're right," she murmured.

He resisted the smile that seemed to want to tip the corners of his mouth up. "What was that?" he asked, knowing full well he was goading her.

Rather than growing irked, Rachel instead looked back up at him and flashed a grin. "You're right. *R-I-G-H-T,*" she said, spelling out the word. "I can't fault you for how you're handling your end of things."

He reached out and gripped the handle of the handgun, twisting it to point back at the target. "Another?"

A quick nod, and then Rachel was lining up another shot. That one went wide, as did the next, but over the course of twenty minutes, Rachel ended up hitting a good 90 percent of all shots she took. The ones that didn't hit the soda cans weren't all that far off. Dylan found her accuracy a relief.

"That's it," he said after she emptied the last chamber. "I'm out of practice ammo."

Rachel gave a tight nod, then handed him the empty handgun and looked around, as if she'd suddenly recalled where they were. "We've still got a lot of chores to do. But thank you. This was fun."

When she turned away, he grabbed her elbow, unable to help himself. He didn't want their time together to end just yet. "Was it just firing the gun that was fun?"

"What else is there?" she asked.

As he stared at her, her gaze dropped once again to the ground...only to rise a second later to rest on his—

Oh, yeah. The widow Kincaid was checking out his crotch.

Heat flooded him, and he fought back the desire to grab her and cover her mouth with his. Palm her breasts. Slide his knee between her legs and press against her mound. Nope, wasn't gonna happen. Not again.

"I'll go get the horses," he said tightly, not allowing himself to say more. After all, what could he say? That her mouth tasted like heaven? That the way she softly exhaled while squeezing the trigger was enough to make a lesser man come? That he'd woken up with an erection because he'd been dreaming of her naked body? He stomped over to Anchor and Row, who refused to so much as look up at him as he gathered the reins. Each horse kept its muzzle buried in the soft new grass, munching away.

Five hard tugs on the reins later, coupled with a few curse words on his end and a soft giggle that came from Rachel, Anchor and Row both lifted their heads and reluctantly stepped in line behind him.

"I'll give you a lift up," he said when he finally came to a stop in front of Rachel.

She reached out, slid the reins over Anchor's neck, then grabbed the saddle horn. "Thanks," she said softly, placing a hand on his shoulder as he bent before her.

Anchor shifted, and Rachel stumbled against him.
He grabbed hold tight, holding her steady, his head
now pressed tight against her belly. An audible gasp
slipped out from between her lips. Under her thin
button-down shirt, he could hear her heartbeat. One-
two. One-two. One-two. The pace rapidly increasing.

"Dylan," she whispered.

And suddenly his shirt was being bunched up in
her fist, and he was rising to his feet, and Rachel was
bending underneath him like a strong sapling in the
wind, and then his lips were on her neck. For a moment, the earth faded away into a shimmery gray, the
crickets' hum evaporated and all he could hear was
Rachel's heartbeat. All he could feel were Rachel's
fists against his shoulders and her hips pressed hard
against his. All he could see was Rachel's hair, her
ear, the line of her jaw, the lush red of her lips.

He kissed her then. Hard. Wrapped one arm around
her lower back to wedge her tight against his hips and
the other arm around her neck to hold her head in
place as he teased her lips, asking without words for
her to open to him. His own heartbeat matched the
rhythm of hers and suddenly they were one—tongues
sliding, lips touching, teeth nipping.

The kiss seemed endless. As did the others that
followed, each kiss a universe of its own. Again and
again. And again.

Hiding his erection became a thing of the past. Instead, he ground it against her and felt a rush of desire
tugging deep within him as she met his movement
with a heady groan. He drew his hand from behind her
head and palmed her breast, her heat soaking through
the thin layer of cotton. With dexterous fingers, he

unbuttoned her blouse, tugging it free from where she'd tucked it into her jeans, then slid his fingers under the wispy lace of her bra. Her groan turned into quick pants as he rolled her nipple between his thumb and finger. Hungrily, he bent down and sucked the tightened bud into his mouth, nearly coming undone when she ground her crotch against his knee, which he'd shoved between her legs.

Just the way he'd fantasized.

He slid his hand lower to cup her butt and pull her hips in tighter. She mewled and torqued, twisting as if to climb up his body and settle her crotch on his erection. He met motion with motion, bending at the knees to dig the head of his erection against the apex of her thighs, seeking to connect their heat. He sucked, hard, drawing her breast deep into his mouth. Her body, wrapped in his arms, shook, the vibrations growing stronger with each pant emanating from her lips, until finally she shuddered and cried out his name.

Damn. She'd just come. From nothing more than the pressure of his mouth on her breast and the press of his body against hers. He pulled his head up but kept his arms wrapped tightly around her. She kept her face, which was flushed a blazing pink, averted.

"Are you okay?" he murmured, stroking her hair.

She closed her eyes, but nodded just before straightening. He remained close, his hips nudging hers to provide support, sliding his hands up to her shoulders to keep her steady.

"God, I'm sorry. We keep… I keep…" Her voice quavered with tears. "I don't know why…"

"I know why. Because we're attracted to each other. And you're a beautiful, passionate woman. A woman I want desperately. Don't feel embarrassed because of the pleasure I gave you, Rachel. I don't. And I know you don't believe me right now, but everything is going to be okay. You're going to be okay."

Her eyes flicked open and she stared at his chest. "Nothing will ever be okay again," she said in a small, tight voice, "but I appreciate your concern. Really, I do." She released the fabric of his shirt that she still held in her fists and slid her hands down until they rested on his belt, slung low around his hips.

"Rachel?"

Her chin rose, and slowly, so did her gaze, until she made visual contact. She cleared her throat, the sound delicate yet deliberate, then spoke. "Like you said, we're attracted to each other. I thought my reaction to you was a fluke. But this…"

"But this was real," he finished for her. "No aberration. No fluke." He knew not to press her, but rather to let her draw out her own conclusions.

She shook her head, sending her hair flowing in the gentle evening breeze. "I want you and you want me."

He wove his fingers under her hair and stroked the soft skin covering the back of her neck with the pads of his thumb. "That's a truth I would never deny. But my job. Your brother. Our feelings complicate things, Rachel."

"I know." She took a step back, breaking their contact, and blew out a sharp breath. "So, while this was fun…" She waved her hands in the air, as if gesturing to their momentary lapse of judgment.

"So, while this was fun, it's over now," he said firmly.

"Exactly."

Yeah, they could both wish that were the case. But he knew in his bones it simply wasn't true. This wasn't over between him and Rachel, but it had to be.

He couldn't be like Rachel, hiding his head in the sand from the realities of life. Some people were bad and deserved to be punished for their bad deeds. That was the case for her brother, just as it had been for his. She wanted to make excuses. He couldn't.

He knew what kind of tragedy came with continually making excuses for another. So no excuses about what he and Rachel had done. He'd take full responsibility.

But he'd also have to make sure he had the strength to keep it from happening again.

No matter how damn bad he wanted it to happen again.

And over and over and over again.

Chapter 12

Two hours after Dylan's impromptu gun lesson, Rachel sat in Julia's office, staring at her friend. After their wild make-out session, both Dylan and Rachel had gotten back to working on the ranch when Rachel's cell buzzed. Her friend's voice mail on her cell phone had sounded urgent, so she'd dropped paying the bills and headed out without telling Dylan where she was going. She did, however, leave him a note so he wouldn't worry.

He had a list of chores as long as her arm—he'd stay busy. Wasn't as though she needed to give him her itinerary, anyway. As he'd reminded her, anything between them personally was impossible. So then, he was just a guest on her property. She owed him nothing.

"So I got some new information today," Julia said. "That's why I called you in."

"And?" Rachel prompted, fingering the brass studs on Julia's leather office chair.

"I'm sure I've never mentioned this before, but I have a friend…my college roommate…her father was a bigwig with the U.S. Marshals in Colorado. Retired now, but I gave my friend a call and asked if her father could put an ear to the ground about Jax's escape."

Rachel leaned forward. "And?"

"And he couldn't find out anything more than we already knew. At first. But he kept digging. And it turns out he has a friend who's a bigwig with the DEA. He asked questions about Jax and the drug raid last year and discovered something that's been kept under wraps this whole time. About the man who Jax delivered those drugs to in L.A."

"Lou Parker?" Like Julia, Rachel had gone over Jax's trial transcripts hundreds of times during the appeal process, so she knew the major players that had been identified during the DEA's raid. "He was arrested on a bunch of outstanding warrants. He was sent to prison before Jax was."

"Right. Only he never gave up information about who he was working for. If he was working for anyone. What we never knew was the DEA believes he was working for the leader of an American drug cartel. A man named George Evans. Big into cocaine, Ecstasy and heroin. High-end stuff. The kind of stuff celebrities get caught smoking or snorting."

"I'm not seeing how this is related to Jax."

"The DEA believes Evans was at the raid but escaped before he could be apprehended. Just like Jax. The big question is which one of them left with the money."

"Money? What money?"

"The million dollars Lou Parker was supposed to pay Jax in exchange for the drugs he delivered. The drugs that Evans never got. But the DEA thinks Jax took his money, anyway."

Rachel lifted her hand to her temple. She felt disoriented. As if the world was spinning around her. "Jax never said anything about any money. And they arrested him at the ranch. He didn't have any money on him."

Julia just looked at her until Rachel understood what she was silently communicating.

"You think he hid this money on the ranch before he was arrested? That *that's* the reason he's heading home?" Not for family. Not to make sure that she and Peter were okay. But for drug money? "And this is what Dylan thinks?"

Julia shook her head. "According to my friend, the DEA hasn't shared the information about the missing money with anyone, including the marshals."

"Maybe that's because they know Jax didn't take it," Rachel said. "There were all kinds of criminals arrested that night. And you said yourself George Evans got away. He probably took the money with him."

"That's a possibility," Julia conceded. "But it's not the only possibility, Rachel."

Rachel's mouth tightened. "You're Jax's attorney. You're supposed to be focusing on the possibilities that can help him, not hurt him." *You're not supposed to be focusing on the possibilities that will hurt me.* Why was Julia doing this? She had to know how much it would hurt Rachel to think that Jax would come to her only because of money. It was on the tip of her tongue to tell her about Jax's email—that he only wanted to make sure that she and Peter were safe—but she held back. She felt she couldn't trust anyone anymore—even Julia.

"Rachel," Julia said, her tone soft, "I know you love your brother as both a sibling and a parent. And I know that love can go deep. But consider the facts. Jax has just escaped federal custody, and during the escape, two U.S. Marshals were killed. Whatever happens, you need to protect yourself. If Jax comes home, turn him over. Do *not* harbor a fugitive. Do you understand? Because if you do, and you're caught, you could get a prison sentence yourself. And who would raise your son then?"

Dylan stood, one hand on the pitchfork and the other on his hip, watching as Rachel drove up to the ranch, twin clouds of red dust following her beat-up pickup truck like two Tasmanian devils racing after her back tires. She hadn't told him she was leaving, and when he first realized she was gone, he'd been pissed. Beyond pissed. But only because he'd been worried. Someone had tried to drive them off the road last night and she was off on her own doing God knew what. But then he'd found her note just before he got a call from Eric that he'd seen her leave the ranch and had followed her into town. She'd indeed stopped to see Julia, and her drive into town had been uneventful. Eric had promised to follow her until she got back home safely.

Knowing Rachel was safe, Dylan had worked most of his anger off doing the chores she'd asked him to do. The entire time, he told himself Rachel wasn't his and he had no right to expect her to check in and out with him.

At least Rachel had a friend during all this. He couldn't imagine her not having someone to talk to, to confide in. Had to be so lonely for her, out here on the ranch, miles from town, with only her son and her ranch hand to share her day with.

He grimaced, thinking of the ranch hand, and wiped a hand over his brow, swiping off the rivulet of sweat that had started to pour. Fifteen minutes earlier, Stacy had called with the coroner's preliminary findings of Josiah's death. He had to speak with Rachel, although this was yet another conversation he didn't want to have.

He resumed shoving the pitchfork into the pile of discarded hay the alpacas had left behind after their morning feeding. Rachel had told him to pitch the remnants into a wheelbarrow and dump the load off at a compost pile covered by a tarp at the edge of the barn. He hadn't realized how many wheelbarrow loads were involved. Apparently Josiah only cleaned up the remnants once a week, and this was his fifth and final wheelbarrow load. How on earth Rachel would keep the ranch running after he returned to California, he didn't know.

And if it involved the young stud she'd talked about earlier, he didn't *want* to know.

Rachel drove up parallel to him and slowed the truck, putting it into idle. She rolled the hand-cranked window down and stuck her head out the window, gazing at the area he'd already cleaned up. She smiled tightly. He knew immediately she was upset but trying to hide it. "Wow," she said, her voice dripping with false cheer. "Can't believe how tidy you've made the corral. Josiah does—*did*—a good job, but he always left quite a bit behind. It's almost as if you've taken a broom to the place. Were you in the military once?"

"Nope. This is just what you get when you put law enforcement on the job. We're pretty damn thorough." As soon as he said the words, he regretted them. Her attempts to look cheerful gave way to a pinched expression that made her look as if she'd just licked a lemon.

He'd take it. At least it was honest. Real. He didn't want her hiding her troubles from him. And by the same token, he couldn't hide what he knew from her either.

"Rachel…" He stopped speaking. What could he say? That he was sorry he was out to get her brother? He'd be lying if he voiced the words. Jackson Kincaid was a fugitive who'd confessed to his crimes. He deserved to be behind bars, not gallivanting about the countryside, worrying his sister and costing the taxpayers loads of money trying to get his sorry ass back in prison. But he was sorry her brother, and by necessity his job, was causing her pain.

"I have things to do," she said quickly, taking her gaze away from his, staring straight ahead through her dust and bug-spattered windshield, and grinding the gears as she put the truck into first. Suddenly she frowned, then turned her attention back to him.

The intensity in her eyes caught him off guard, and his heart skipped a beat. How beautiful she was. God, he needed to keep his damn focus—this was not a pickup in some bar. This was a woman whose brother had done a very bad thing, and he had a job to do.

And part of his job was to inform her about what had happened to her ranch hand.

"I know you need to get back to work," he said, as a way of apology. He was about to continue, but she cut him off with a wave of her hand.

"I just realized...did you do the list of chores in order, the way I asked?" she said.

He nodded, unsure where the conversation was headed.

"Wow. That means you've already stacked a cord of wood, repaired the broken board on the side of the barn, dug the ditch for the new watering system *and* mucked out the chicken coop, right?"

This time instead of nodding, he grimaced. That chicken coop had been no pretty picnic, that was for sure. He wasn't sure he'd ever forget that particular stench. "Yes to all the above," he said, swinging the pitchfork onto the now-full wheelbarrow. He picked up the wheelbarrow handles, ready to resume his trek to the compost pile. A pile he was becoming far too intimate with, in his mind. "This is the last of it. What else do you want me to do today?"

For a moment, Rachel simply stared at him in silence, her brow furrowed, her eyes narrowed, as if taking in the very measure of him. Finally she spoke, saying, "Color me impressed." She blew out a quick breath. "It would have taken me a week to get all those chores done. I owe you."

"You don't, though. I'm just doing my job."

"Right. I remember. But you could have dinked around, pretending to do your job. But you didn't. You actually did the work. I'm...I'm grateful."

He knew by the way her throat bobbed up and

down that the word *grateful* had been a difficult one
for her to squeeze out. He appreciated it. She didn't
have to like him, and certainly didn't have to be nice
to him, but here she was, telling him she was grateful. There was more to Rachel Kincaid than met the
eye, and her complexity intrigued him. Probably more
than it should.

Too bad she couldn't have instilled more values in
her criminal brother.

The air shifted, bringing with it the pungent odor
of the compost pile he'd left uncovered. Damn. He
needed to hurry up and get the tarp back on it before
the entire ranch was drowned in the nasty scent. "I
need to talk to you."

She looked wary, then resolved. "I'll go park the
truck and can meet you on the back porch with lemonade. Just give me about ten minutes, okay?"

He tipped his head in agreement, and watched as
Rachel gave the truck gas and eased past him, the
open window letting the breeze toy with her near-
white hair.

Fifteen minutes later, the compost pile thoroughly
covered by the tarp, and his hands washed in the outside faucet, Dylan strode onto the back porch. Rachel
was already seated, a magazine illustrating heavy
equipment open on her lap, a pitcher of lemonade, a
bucket of ice and two glasses on the small table by
her side. For a moment, he simply enjoyed the picture
she made and imagined he was coming home to her.
That she was his. That there was nothing between
them but desire and affection.

His core stirred, and he allowed himself the in-
dulgence of picturing her naked in his mind's eye.

Of covering her with his own naked form. Penetrating her. Stroking her with his shaft and his hands and his tongue...

She glanced up at him and he clenched his fists even as he drove his lustful thoughts from his mind. Every time he saw her, it was the same thing. He wanted her. And not just her body. Her company.

She was a good woman. She stimulated his mind and his body. She wasn't like the sophisticated city women he normally dated, and to him that was nothing but good. She was real. Fresh. Sensual in a Mother Earth kind of way that made him want to take her on the ground, surrounded by trees and wildflowers that couldn't begin to compare to her beauty.

He could easily see himself falling in love with her. In fact, sometimes it felt as though he was already halfway there....

No, he mentally growled. *Do not go there.* So she was good. Sexy. So damn beautiful. He couldn't love her. He wouldn't. First, he didn't believe true love could form in such a short amount of time. Second, how could he love someone he didn't totally respect? He respected a lot about Rachel, but her inability to see the truth of her brother's flaws? Her willingness to bury her head in the sand so that she was endangering not only her life, but her son's?

No.

How many times did he need to remind himself that he couldn't have her before it stuck?

He lowered himself down onto the empty Adirondack chair next to hers, then filled both glasses with ice and poured what appeared to be fresh-squeezed lemonade until the ice bobbed to the surface. Handing one to Rachel, he gave her a soft smile. At least he tried to. But given his recent thoughts, combined with the type of news he was about to deliver, he was betting his smile was strained.

Damn, but he hated having to tell her about Josiah. So he'd wait. For a few minutes, anyway. No need for him to hurt her right off the bat, not when she'd gone to the lengths to squeeze lemons for fresh lemonade.

"You and your brother have the same last name. But you were married," he commented. "You kept your maiden name, then?"

Rachel sipped from the glass in her hand and made a sour face. "I should have put more simple syrup in. The lemons are extra tart this year." She twirled a lock of her long, straight hair with her fingers, the sliver of sunlight that hit the back porch causing shimmers to glint off the highlights. "When I got married, it wasn't really out of love, but more to provide Jax a good home. I'd known my husband for years—we'd gone to school together." She gave a light laugh. "He was the kid who pulled my pigtails, you know?"

"Cute."

"Clichéd," she said. "But still, he was sweet. And when my folks died and I needed help with Jax, he stepped up to the plate. Offered to marry me and help out on the ranch. Only problem was, he was still a kid himself. When he discovered I was pregnant, he freaked out and started partying with his friends. Wouldn't come home all night sometimes. Ended up driving drunk and killing himself by the time Peter was three."

Some of the story he'd known by researching Jackson Kincaid and his sister. But the sorrow in Rachel's eyes spoke of something research could never tell him. She hadn't loved her husband—not the passionate, "in love" kind of love you would expect from a marriage—but she'd cared for him. That was clear.

"And your name?" he prodded. He didn't know why the fact that she used her maiden name intrigued him, but it did.

"Peter has his father's last name, but I felt like I'd never really been married, so taking his name would have felt like a lie."

Interesting. She'd exchanged vows with a man, had signed a contract before God and the law, had made a child with the man, but never considered herself married. Warmth suffused his chest, then spread down to his belly, where it transformed into a tingle.

Despite his best intentions, she was worming her way inside him again. Making him want her. Making him think he could love her....

Once again, he pushed those feelings away.

It was time he shared the information he'd been holding on to. Information he knew for certain Rachel wouldn't want to hear.

After a few more minutes of idle chitchat about the weather—unseasonably hot and oppressive—the alpacas—sweetly humming in the distance—and the tractor Rachel wanted to buy—expensive—she finally gave him a flat glance and let out a deep sigh. "You haven't said what you wanted to tell me yet. Is it bad?" she asked.

"Bad enough."

"Is it about Jax?"

"It's about Josiah." He waited, watching her expression go from guarded and worried to sad and concerned. She toyed with her drink, pushing one ice cube around in circles with the tip of her finger, staring at the lemonade as if it held the secrets of the universe.

"He was murdered," Rachel said, not asking a question, but rather making a statement.

"Yes," he said, in confirmation. No sense skirting about the issue. Not when Rachel already knew the answer.

"Oh, God," she said quietly, almost to herself, and stared off into the distance, not meeting his gaze. She set her glass of lemonade down on the table and folded her hands in her lap, staring down at her entwined fingers. He didn't press forward, but instead gave her space to process the news.

A loud snort caught his attention, and he turned to gaze at a few of the alpacas Rachel had put in the corral by the barn. These five were expecting any day now, she'd explained, and she wanted them nearby, not out in one of the bigger pastures, in case they went into labor. They'd seemed agitated, being cut from the rest of the herd, and he'd suggested they could maybe be let out on the far pasture with the remaining herd, let nature take its course. Rachel had responded almost angrily, insisting that they needed to be close, where she could control the situation in case something went wrong. He'd backed off but still felt a pang of empathy for the penned-in fuzz balls.

It wasn't lost on him that she had a thing for control. Of course she did. She'd had to take control of her brother after her parents died. Had to take sole control of this ranch and her son. Taking control was her way of making sure everyone stayed safe.

But she couldn't control everything.

"How?"

Her single word startled him. No wailing, no moaning, no gnashing of teeth. No hysteria. Just the quiet, factual question. If it hadn't been for her glistening eyes, or the way she clenched her arms tightly around her chest, he would have thought she didn't care. But that pulse at the base of her delicate throat said otherwise. Rachel was grieving. In pain. But keeping it to herself. He had to admire her resolve.

"He died from a cerebral hemorrhage, as we already knew, but what we didn't know was that it was brought about by a heavy, sharp object hitting the top of his head."

"The top of his head," she repeated dully.

Damn. She was beautiful, compassionate, loyal to a fault and shrewd. She'd caught the clue he'd unwittingly handed her. "Yeah. There was no way he could have fallen and hit himself on the top of the head that hard. He'd have to have fallen from a height and landed on a rock straight on top of his head."

"But why would someone kill Josiah? The man was a simple ranch hand. Everyone around town knew him. Loved him." She turned suddenly in her seat and speared him with a sharp look. "And don't go saying my brother killed him because Josiah somehow stumbled across Jax. First, Jax would never, ever kill anyone. And second, Josiah would have helped Jax hide from the law—from you, if he'd known about you—and Jax knows that. Josiah was like family to us, Jax included."

He held up a hand. The woman was a force to be reckoned with. He eased forward, the deck chair squeaking under his shifting weight, and said, "I won't tell you I think your brother killed Josiah. I can say, though, that I've seen family members kill one another over the most trivial of things— I once had to track a woman who'd run off while out on bail who was accused of killing her husband because he didn't put away their kid's LEGOs the night before."

Rachel winced involuntarily. "Ouch. Stepping on a LEGO in the dark—I've been there. If you don't have kids, you don't realize how murderously painful that can be."

Her words suggested she was trying to lighten the mood, but her expression was tense and unsmiling.

"I don't have any evidence as to who killed your friend, Rachel. And I'll give your brother the benefit of the doubt. My job here is to bring him back to face justice, not to try him for a theoretical crime."

"I know that. I like that you're at least willing to give him the benefit of the doubt. Some people aren't. Hell, even Julia—"

She stopped speaking abruptly.

"Even Julia what?" he asked.

"I don't believe it," she said. "And I don't want you to, either."

Whatever it was Julia had told her was eating at her. Would she trust him enough to tell him? Was it possible she was beginning to see him as more than the enemy?

Dylan reached out and took her hand. "Do you remember what I said about keeping you safe, Rachel?"

She bit her lip and nodded.

"I meant it. I can't tell you what's going to happen to your brother, but you can trust that I want to help."

"I don't know why, but I can't deny it. I do trust you."

"Then tell me what Julia said."

Chapter 13

An hour later, in the tack room in the barn, Rachel sat on a Western saddle, supported by a saddle tree, using it as a seat. After she told Dylan about George Evans's missing money and the DEA's ludicrous theory that Jax had taken it, Dylan had looked ready to explode. Instead, he'd stood, thanked her for confiding in him, then told her he needed to get in touch with his team.

Twenty minutes later, he'd come back to the house and asked her to join him in his makeshift office. She'd obeyed, but only after taking her time to slide her arms into the sleeves of a chambray shirt and button it up. A breeze had picked up, and even in the barn a chill prickled goose bumps along her arms. She shivered, but whether from the sudden cold or from the way Dylan gave her a sidelong glance, his

eyes smoldering with what she'd swear was posses-
siveness, she wasn't sure. But then he turned his attention back to his tablet, and she continued to stare at
him, and any cold she was feeling disappeared under
a spreading heat.

It had felt good, confiding in him about what Julia
had told her. The fact that he clearly hadn't known
about the DEA's theory and was angry about being
kept out of the loop had made her relieved he hadn't
been keeping a secret from her and had made her feel
that they were finally on the same side for a change.
Maybe that was why she couldn't seem to take her
eyes off him. His strong jaw. His blue eyes framed
by such thick lashes. The soft dark hair she wanted
to run her hands through. The ears she wanted to lick
and nibble...

She sucked in a breath. *Focus,* she told herself.
Stop gaping at the lawman as if he were an ice-cream
cone on a hot summer day. Shifting in her seat, she
brought her focus back to the situation. She'd told
him about the DEA's theory. Maybe she should tell
him about Jax's email. Let him know that Jax was
coming so they could talk about the best way to help
her brother. Only she was too used to protecting her
brother to make that leap. Not yet.

Dylan's tablet buzzed, startling her. Again she
wondered why he'd called her out here.

"Here we go," Dylan said, even though she had no
idea what he was talking about.

She nibbled a lip. "Are you sure you want me in
on your meeting? Isn't this top-secret stuff, or something?"

Dylan flashed a grin. "We're U.S. Marshals, not CIA. Get back in the saddle and stay awhile."

Dylan leaned to the side so Rachel could get a good look at his tablet's small screen. A woman's face filled the screen. She didn't seem surprised to see Rachel seated behind Dylan.

"Stacy, have you checked into what Rachel told me?"

"I certainly have," she said. "Marco's still reaming our contact with the DEA, but he's fessed up. George Evans. Age fifty-two. He's a known high-end drug dealer but has never been caught. Rachel's friend is right. The DEA thinks he was present during the raid, but they didn't know it at the time. He got away. They never found the money that was supposed to be given to Jackson in exchange for the drugs. They acknowledge Evans might have taken it. They think the more likely scenario is that Jackson grabbed it, fled to the ranch and hid it before he was apprehended."

Dylan turned to Rachel. "When they picked up your brother, how long did the DEA agents stay on the ranch?"

"Hours."

"Did they search the entire place?"

"I don't know. They could have. I—I was so upset and focusing on Jax at the time, I didn't really pay attention."

He turned back to Stacy. "So they searched the place. Came up empty. But now that Kincaid has escaped and is heading back to the ranch for the money?"

"They figured they'd wait until you captured him,

then try to talk to him again. Which they've tried doing several times in the past. All with poor results."

"And in the meantime, they didn't think we needed to know this? They didn't think the fact that Kincaid stands to gain not only his freedom but upwards of a million dollars was relevant to the danger he might pose to others in trying to get here?"

Rachel had been listening to Dylan's conversation with Stacy, but it took her several minutes for what Dylan was saying to sink in. Her first clue was that he was referring to her brother as "Kincaid" again. "Wait a minute," she said. "Are you—are you saying you *believe* Jax took the money and hid it on the ranch? That he's heading here because of that? Are you back to thinking he killed Josiah…for money?"

Dylan frowned. "I'm back to considering those are possibilities, of course."

"Of course? So nothing I've said about my brother, about him being good, about him not being capable of hurting Josiah, has sunk in?"

Dylan stared at her, deliberately reached out and turned off his tablet, then stood. "Rachel, I thought I explained that while I believe in the theory of being innocent until proven guilty, that can't stop me from considering the evidence as it stands, too. The evidence suggests your brother might have hidden a million dollars on this land. That's a huge motivation for him to come back here and to not get caught. Besides, even putting aside how I view the evidence, that's irrelevant to my job. I'm a marshal. My job is to bring your brother back into custody. It's not to interpret or gather the evidence. Even if I believed your brother was innocent, I'd still need to bring him in."

"But you don't *believe* he's innocent, do you?" She jumped off the saddle and began backing away from him and toward the open barn doors. "And I don't know why I believed *you* when you said you wanted to help me. The fact is you're too blinded by Jax's past mistakes to do that. Why aren't you considering that George Evans took the money?"

"Because if he did, there'd be no reason for him to hurt Josiah. Or to try and hurt you, and we both know…" A weird expression came over Dylan's face as his words trailed off.

Rachel wondered about it for a split second, but then all she could think about was escape. She felt as if everyone in the world was against her, and she was all that stood between herself and the total annihilation of everything she loved.

She'd forgotten that Dylan was her enemy for a short time.

She couldn't do it again.

She whirled and ran toward the house. Once inside, she flew up the stairs and locked herself in her bedroom. She knew she was fleeing. Hiding. But she didn't care.

Thank God she hadn't told Dylan about Jax's email.

Tomorrow would come soon enough. She'd take some time to hide and think of a way to help Jax.

And hope that as she did so, she purged every trace of the desire and building affection she'd started to feel for Dylan from her mind, body and soul.

Chapter 14

The next day, Rachel dealt with her frustration and anger with Dylan quite simply—she *didn't* deal with him. Instead, she kept a detached manner as she detailed the chores she wanted him to do, and she busied herself with her own chores, making sure to keep plenty of space between them. Any time she wanted to give in to her urge to see him or talk to him or daydream about the kisses they'd shared and how good the orgasm he'd given her had felt, she simply pushed herself harder.

She was a mother. She wasn't supposed to be running past third base and about to slide home with a man she barely knew. She was supposed to be making a living for her and her son. Most important, she was supposed to be considering what was best for Jax: continuing to keep his email from Dylan or trusting that despite his prejudices against her brother, he would do what he said, and treat him right.

By the time she'd finished her chores, it was evening and just starting to get dark. When she caught sight of Dylan dismounting from Row and walking the horse toward her, she said, "The alpaca herd has headed into the barn for the night," swinging off Anchor. "If you could take the tack off the horses and brush them down, I'll bring in the pregnant ones from the corral, then do one last count and make sure all alpacas are here. Put the horses in the far corral, then head on into the house. You get first dibs on the hot water—I'll whip up some dinner while you shower. After we eat, I need to spend time on the accounting, and I'll need you to pull nails out of old boards. There's a stack about shoulder-height in the barn."

Dylan reached for Anchor's reins. "Rachel, things don't have to be this way between us."

"What way?"

"Back to treating each other as enemies."

"You're here on my ranch, Dylan. Obviously I don't think of you as an enemy. But as we discussed yesterday, you plus me equals complication. I'm just playing things the way they need to be played. We keep our hands—and lips and bodies—and our opinions about my brother—to ourselves, no problem. That's all."

Without waiting for his rebuttal—and she was certain he'd come up with one—she turned tail and headed to the corral to bring in the pregnant alpacas.

Five minutes later, she returned, concern worming its way through her veins.

Dylan looked up from running a body brush over Row. He frowned. "What is it?"

She shook her head and nibbled her lip. "Two of the females are missing. There's a board missing on the corral—it looks like it was broken and dragged away. I brought the other three into the barn, but the rest of the herd seems nervous."

"Coyotes?"

"Alpacas are good at fighting off coyotes. I've lost crias to the varmints, but no adults. In fact, when I first got the herd, there were a few times when I actually watched as they fought off coyotes. The local pack knows to stay away from the adults now."

"Would they have run off?"

She nibbled her lip. "I don't think so. Alpacas are herd animals. They feel safest when they're together. It doesn't make sense that they would have gone off on their own, but I suppose it's possible."

He put down the brush and came over to her, the warmth of his body a comforting sensation. "I'll grab a flashlight and go look for them. Just tell me where to go."

"I wonder if they headed down the trail to the creek." Nerves twisted her belly. The two missing females were worth seven thousand dollars each, and both were carrying unborn crias that could fetch up to nine thousand dollars so long as their conformation and coats turned out perfect. She'd insured her herd, but not for the full value, the cost being prohibitive. She'd take a hard hit if anything happened to either of the females.

"I'll go," she said. "They're my responsibility. But if you want to come with me, I'd appreciate the company." And she would. Dylan was no Josiah, and he didn't have a clue about ranching, but he was a strong man and she was about to head out into the dark. Coyotes might not tangle with one of her adult alpacas, but that didn't mean she was without a healthy sense of fear of things that went bump in the night. As Dylan had pointed out, strange things were happening on the ranch, and while she didn't believe her brother was involved, she wasn't going to risk her life on her theory on coincidences, either.

She led the way, Dylan a step behind her, lighting the path with his flashlight. After reaching the trail, he swept the beam of light in cross sections as they moved forward until she heard a noise. She reached out and grabbed his hand to still the movement of the light.

"Listen," she breathed.

A rattling, bubbling sound came from not too far away.

"Is that the sound of alpacas?" Dylan whispered.

"No. At least, not a sound I've ever heard."

He twisted, breaking her contact on his wrist, then stepped in front of her. "Stay close, but be ready to run back to the barn."

She didn't argue. Sure, he'd be putting himself at risk if anything dangerous was out there, but she was a mother and that came first.

Slowly, Dylan swept his light in the same crosshatch pattern, but this time further ahead and off to the right. "There," he said. "What are we looking at?"

Squinting, Rachel looked to where the faint beam of light shone. There, lying on their sides, were the two missing alpacas. It took a moment for her to recognize that something wasn't right. Instead of lying still, both alpacas were writhing on the ground. Bur-bling, gasping sounds came from them.

"Oh, God!" she cried out. She moved to race for-ward, but Dylan grabbed her wrist and held her firm. "Let me go—something's wrong!" she shouted.

"Rachel, I know. I can see that. But I'm going first. Keep behind me." He pulled the handgun out from his boot holster and with one hand held the gun up and with the other held his flashlight against the gun as he stepped forward, slowly.

After sweeping the flashlight around, he beckoned for her to come closer. "It's not good, I'm afraid," he said as she stepped up to her stock. He focused the light on the two alpacas.

Both females still lay on the ground, but the one on the right had ceased writhing. As Rachel stood there, she could see it could barely breathe. Its eyes rolled in its head until they met hers, panicked. "Oh, no…" The words spilled from her mouth before she could stop them. A sob followed. Dylan placed a warm hand on her shoulder and instinctively, she leaned against him.

"No blood," he observed.

She swallowed several times, words sticking in her throat. The truth hurt. Ached. "No, they haven't been injured."

"They aren't giving birth, right?"

She shook her head. "No. Something's horribly wrong here."

"Do you know what it is?"

Her insides churned. She'd seen an animal look like this before when she was young—a neighbor's dog who'd gotten into some rat poison. She swallowed against the rising bile in her throat, then managed to get out, "I think they've been poisoned."

"We need to get them into the barn."

The alpaca on the right had grown too weak to do more than flick its ears at Rachel. Froth bubbled on its muzzle and a deep moan came from somewhere inside. Pain scratched its way through Rachel's chest. "This one's too far gone," she murmured.

Stepping heavily, she made her way to the other alpaca, then bent down and lifted the hundred-plus-pound weight up in her arms. After staggering briefly, she turned and faced the barn, deliberately keeping her back to Dylan and the dying alpaca.

"Have any bullets left?" The words nearly choked her.

"Rachel?"

"This is a ranch, Dylan. Out here, we do what we have to. Shoot her."

The ache in Dylan's chest threatened to explode. Watching Rachel stumble to the barn, a poisoned and pregnant alpaca dangling limply in her arms, recalling the anguish on her face and the words she'd spoken— *shoot her*—had something inside him all twisted up and tangled. Getting turned on by the sexy widow he could handle. But this aching inside? This he could not handle. This emotion went well beyond what he expected of himself as a marshal. He needed to curb this connection he felt to Rachel Kincaid. Because no matter how many times he reminded himself she wasn't the type of woman that was good for him—no matter that she refused to let her brother take responsibility for his mistakes—he knew deep down that if push came to shove…

He'd be lost if somehow he ended up having to choose between her and his duty. He wasn't sure what that meant—if he'd actually let her brother go instead of taking him into custody. He hoped not. He prayed he'd still have the willpower to do the right thing. But he had to admit that the "right thing" was beginning to become less black-and-white to him.

He'd told Rachel that even if he believed her brother was innocent he'd still take him into custody. Would that really be right thing to do? Could he overlook his own gut feeling just to fulfill his job?

Wouldn't that be the opposite of justice? Of integrity?

And Rachel believed her brother was innocent. What if…just *what if*…she was right and the rest of them were wrong?

It took only a moment to put the soft, fuzzy creature out of its misery. After, he swept a hand over its face, shutting its eyes. He'd killed before—twice, actually. Both times in the line of duty. Both times someone else's life had been on the line and he'd had to take the shot. Both times he'd walked away from the shooting without regret. Left the bodies for the CSU team to photograph and dispatch. Now? His hands shook as he put his gun back in its holster. Something had edged its way under his wall of defense, and he needed to get a grip.

He followed the path Rachel had made in the dark, and entered the barn to see Rachel in a stall, the alpaca on a bed of sweet golden hay. "Will it make it?" he asked.

"This one seems better than the other, but only time will tell." Rachel kept her back to him as she spoke. She tucked more hay around the alpaca's heaving rib cage, then stood and pulled her phone out of her back pocket. "I'm going to call my vet. Not sure there's much we can do tonight, but I have to try everything."

He nodded, understanding. As he listened in on the conversation, it became clear the vet agreed with Rachel's assumption: the alpacas had been poisoned. The vet felt that the poison had probably entered the bloodstream and nothing could be done, but he'd promised to come over in the morning and gather blood samples to test for poison.

Phone conversation over, Rachel sank down to her knees in the hay. Without thought, Dylan came to her side and lowered himself down, next to her. She wrapped her arms around her knees and tucked her chin between her arms, hiding her face from him, but the sharp shakes of her shoulders told him all he needed to know: Rachel Kincaid was crying.

"Come inside," he murmured, stroking her hair off the back of her neck. Softly, he massaged the tight muscles there. "Soak in the bathtub while I make you something to eat. I think both the accounting and those nails can wait."

"I hate being such a crybaby," she said, the words sounding choked. "I hate falling apart."

"You've had a number of shocks over the last couple of days. And this isn't falling apart. This is a woman at the end of her rope, releasing some of the tension that's eating her up from the inside out." He realized he was stroking her skin, making small circles with the tips of his fingers along the line of her spine.

He rose, brushed hay off his rear and took a step back. "Let's go. There's nothing more you can do here tonight, but if you don't get some food and rest, you won't be good for any of your stock or business tomorrow. Bath, food and bed. In that order."

An hour later, he'd managed to get Rachel into a bath, fixed her a meal of soup and corn bread, made sure she spoke to her son and ensured that she was thoroughly tucked into bed. Only when her breathing settled into a deep rhythm, which he could hear from standing in the hall by her bedroom door, did he returned to his established headquarters in the barn and ping his team. One by one they all logged on until the faces of the entire team showed on the screen.

"Status update?" he asked.

"One of Eric's informants contacted him," Stacy responded, then frowned. When he tipped his head, she continued. "Said he heard a big-time American dealer is on the hunt for the guy who escaped prison transport."

"George Evans." The dealer present at the shoot-out in which Jax had been nabbed.

"We're pretty sure that's the one. And we're pretty sure he's after Jackson Kincaid. Eric's informant said the guy was headed to Texas. Maybe even put a hit out on the escapee."

"Not good." George Evans was out to get Jax.

It had to be because of the money.

Good news: if Evans wanted that money, he probably hadn't put a hit out on Jax. George Evans would want Jackson Kincaid alive to talk.

Bad news: once George Evans caught Jackson, her brother would be tortured into revealing the whereabouts of the money if he didn't do so readily. And then he'd be killed.

He also had to consider something that he'd only started to consider yesterday, when he was telling Rachel that if George Evans had taken the money, he wouldn't have a reason to mess with her or Josiah. That was true. But if George Evans suspected Jax had taken the money and knew where the money was and was now in a position to lead him to it, it could be that Evans was messing with Rachel and her ranch, hoping that news of it would reach Jax and be interpreted as a message: get Evans the money or watch your family die.

Now that they suspected Evans was after Jax, it made all the more sense.

"You know about the scares Rachel has had over the past few days," he said quickly, drawing the attention of Stacy, Marco and Eric back to him. "We found two of her stock poisoned earlier tonight."

"You think that's linked to George Evans rather than her brother now?" Stacy asked.

"It's possible," he said definitively. "It's also possible Jackson is trying to get his sister off the ranch just like I once thought. So he can get the money. The question is, does he want it for himself or to hand over to Evans?"

"You really think he'd put his sister in danger just so he can beat Evans to the money?"

"I have to consider the possibility."

"And the fact that his sister won't."

He twisted his mouth into a frown. Stacy was exactly right. Not only wouldn't she believe that about her brother, but if she knew Jax was being hunted by Evans, she'd do anything she could to protect him.

And in doing so, she'd be putting herself at even more risk.

That was why he was tempted to keep what he'd just found out from her.

The only thing that swayed him to a different course was Peter—and his belief that not even for her brother would she risk her son.

When she was young, Rachel would pretend to fall asleep in order to sneak on a flashlight under the covers and read her book. Her parents had been strict about bedtime—no reading after dark. So she'd steady her breath until she heard the creak of footsteps in the hall, then down the stairs, then the faint sound of the TV in the living room, and only then would pull out her flashlight and her book and tuck the covers securely around her.

Seemed the old falling-asleep trick had worked equally well with Dylan. She'd heard him creep away from her room and head outside to the barn a good fifteen minutes ago. She rose from her bed and padded across the room to unlock the double French doors leading to the balcony. Dylan had checked to make sure they were locked after sending her to bed. Now, if Jax came home in the dead of night, he'd at least have an open door to sneak into.

She returned to bed, sliding in between the cool, crisp pima-cotton sheets, and twisted her pillow under her head, staring into the darkness, willing the hot tears to stay in her eyes. Some alpaca owners named each and every one of their stock. Not her. She'd been raised to ranch the old-fashioned way: animals were stock, not pets. But even with a herd of thirty, the alpaca who'd died had been as familiar to Rachel as if she'd been given a name. The brown-and-cream five-year-old had been a good mother and a loyal member of the herd. She hadn't deserved to die.

To be murdered.

Because that was what had happened. The poisoning hadn't come from a wayward plant. Nothing grew in Rachel's fields or anywhere near that could have caused such a violent death. No, someone had deliberately poisoned at least two of her alpacas. But who? She gripped the soft coverlet in both fists.

Dylan would suspect Jax.

And God help her. For the first time, a flash of doubt sparked in her mind.

It was the information about the money that was causing her to doubt him.

She'd never thought Jax would have transported drugs for money, but he'd confessed to doing just that. She hadn't wanted to believe it, but what if she was wrong?

What if money could motivate her brother to do stupid things? Why couldn't it also motivate him to do even more horrible things?

Like cause a stampede? Kill alpacas? Kill Josiah? Try to kill her?

She rolled over and buried her face in her sheets. *No, no, no.*

This wasn't right. She was letting her feelings for

Dylan mess with her head. And if she allowed herself to see Dylan as anything but her enemy, she'd open herself up to a world of hurt.

Chapter 15

Morning dawned bright and cheerful, a far cry from the dark mood that had settled over the house because of the poisoned alpacas. By the time Dylan had woken, stretched his aching back and taken a shower and dressed in faded jeans, cowboy boots and a white T-shirt, Rachel had already commandeered the kitchen, cooking up a hearty breakfast and brewing tar for coffee.

He'd half expected her to spend the morning in bed, grieving what had happened to her animals. The fact that she hadn't reminded him that while she might be felled low for a while by bad news, she never stayed down for long. In that way, she was very different from his mother. Watching her carefully, he poured a cup of coffee, swallowed, then grimaced.

Catching his expression, Rachel snorted. "Need

cream with that, city boy?" she asked, turning away from him and busying herself at the sink.

He snagged a strip of bacon from the fry pan and brushed past her, coffee mug still gripped in his other hand. "Nope. I promised to be your handyman. And I'm assuming Texan handymen drink their coffee black." He paused and gazed at the liquid sloshing in the cup. "Maybe I should get a fork, though," he added under his breath.

"It's not that bad. A little dark, maybe...."

"Rachel, if you think this coffee is a 'little' dark, you and I definitely don't see things the same way." As soon as the words left him, her face fell and he regretted what he'd said. Somehow a veiled reference to how she viewed her brother had wormed its way into what he'd thought was going to be a casual statement.

"I've checked on the sick alpaca several times. She's about the same. I'm not sure what time the vet will be coming by, but I'm thinking I'll take a drive and go see Peter afterward."

He cleared his throat. "Rachel, I'm not sure that's a good idea right now." Not when he and his team thought George Evans was after Jax and bent on using Rachel to get to him. "We need to talk."

Speaking around a clenched jaw, she said, "About my brother. You think he poisoned the alpacas. You're wrong." She kept her back to him even as she said, "But I want to thank you for what you did last night. Both for me and my alpacas. I—I was worried about the other one, or I would have taken care of it myself. I *should* have taken care of it myself."

God, he hated it when she blamed herself, considered herself weak, when she'd just been accepting help. He stepped up to her and laid a gentle hand on her shoulder. He frowned when he realized she was shaking, holding her spine straight, her shoulders stiff. The woman had been through a lot in her life—and even though sometimes she succumbed to tears, in no way did he see that as weakness.

No, Rachel Kincaid was one of the strongest women he knew. No matter what he threw at her, she'd keep her spine straight. Of that he was sure.

The house phone rang, and Rachel jerked, startled by the sound. She moved away from Dylan's touch and he let his hand drop away. After picking up the line, she listened for a moment, then handed the phone to him.

"It's the sheriff. He wants to speak with you," she said.

He took the handset. "U.S. Marshal Rooney."

"Good morning," the familiar sound of the sheriff's voice carried across the line. "I have news I figured you and your team might want to hear. Local police found the bodies of two men off the highway."

"And?"

"And…these men didn't die of natural circumstances. They've been murdered. Shot three times in the head, execution-style. But that happened after they'd been tortured."

Tortured. He pushed away from the kitchen counter and stiffened as tension crept up his spine. "Description of the vics?"

"Bodybuilder types. Mid-twenties. Shaved heads, multiple tattoos, with gang tats running along their necks. We don't have an ID, but we ran a trace on their tattoos, and we figure they're members of an exclusive gang from L.A.—one specializing in moving high-end drugs for the rich and famous."

Damn. Had to be the two men who'd tried to drive him and Rachel off the road. And if the sheriff suspected they were linked to an exclusive gang from L.A.—that had to mean they'd been working for George Evans.

He thanked the sheriff and hung up. Rachel watched him with a worried expression on her face.

"It's okay. Nothing's happened to Peter or your brother. They're fine."

Her expression and body relaxed substantially. "Then what is it? You look like something bad has happened."

"The two men who tried to run us off the road have been found dead. I have to check in with my team. I won't be able to get started on the chores right away, but I'll catch up, okay?"

She smirked, as if him asking her for permission for anything was the height of hilarity.

He went out into the barn and as soon as he had his team up on the monitors, he didn't waste time with pleasantries or bantering, but instead got right to the point, relaying the sheriff's information about the two gangbangers found tortured and dead.

"George Evans," Stacy said quickly. "Has to be. Hold on…" She focused on her keyboard and a second monitor by her right elbow for a few minutes. "Here," Stacy said. "I'm emailing you info. I got into the sheriff's database and found the photos of the victims' tats. Ran them through a couple of databases I have access to and came up with positive IDs. Both men were part of the Hurricane Gang—that's George Evans's crew. And there's something else, Dylan. Something we just found out."

"What's that?"

"Those are also the two men we believe were responsible for busting Jax out of custody. Against his will."

What the hell? Not only was Jackson Kincaid busted out of prison but it wasn't his own doing? Dylan felt shock at the news, but he also felt a healthy bit of relief. Rachel had been right about this at least. If her brother hadn't tried to escape from prison, that meant...

"The second marshal that was shot? He just woke up from his coma last night. He's still weak, but he told us what he saw. Jax fought against two men who stopped the prison transport by force. They're the ones who shot the marshals, not Jax."

"So that can only mean, since word on the street is that Evans is hunting Jax..."

"Jax escaped from his own escape. He got away from Evans's two goons, and..."

Dylan closed his eyes as the worst possibilities filtered through his mind. "And Evans punished them for it." It made sense. "He killed and tortured them because they'd failed to bring him Jax. Failed to scare away me and Rachel. Probably failed to find the money after searching for it," he said, remembering the stampede and the cut wires of Rachel's fence.

George Evans wouldn't allow failures in his crew. Dylan knew the type. Evans wouldn't just fire a crew member. No, he'd make sure no one else on his crew ever screwed up by making him an example. And that meant torture and death.

Hell, forget death. Nothing kept a crew tighter than the threat of torture.

And if Evans found Jackson Kincaid, the same would happen to him. And anyone who tried to get in his way.

His team.

Him.

Rachel.

The image of her being hurt in any way made his stomach roil.

Dylan finished his talk with his team, then went inside, where he found Rachel still in the house. He fought against the urge to reach out and stroke a wayward strand of hair off her forehead. To rest the back of his fingers against her cheek. To wrap her up in his arms and hold her tight as he shared what he knew she needed to know. Instead, he kept his hands fisted at his sides. "Your brother is in trouble. We need to get him back into custody."

"That's why you and your team are here. Tell me something I don't know," she said, bitterness snapping the words out of her mouth.

"No, Rachel. He's in *trouble*. Jax is at risk of being killed. And tortured first, just like the two men who tried to run us off the road. This man we've been talking about, George Evans," he continued. "We have reliable information that he had two of his men, the same men the sheriff reported were killed, break your brother out of prison. The only reason that makes sense is that he wants the money your brother took from him. Only your brother must have escaped, and now Evans is hunting him. He's out to get your brother, Rachel. And when he catches Jax? He won't be satisfied until he tortures him and then kills him."

Damn her weak knees, wobbling underneath her like those of a just-born cria. Rachel reached behind her and grabbed the counter to steady herself. What the hell had Jax gotten himself into? Being an idiot and transporting drugs across state lines had been bad enough. Now her brother had a major drug dealer who tortured and murdered his crew members out looking for him. Dylan was right: Jax would die. But how could she help the U.S. Marshals? More to the point—*should* she?

Instead of pressing her for an answer, Dylan pulled out a chair from the kitchen table, then indicated she sit down. She did. He eased himself into a chair beside her. And sat. Waiting. Waiting for her to make a decision.

Because she needed to come to a hard realization. She needed to face the terrible reality.

Even though she disagreed with Dylan about Jax—in her heart, she knew her brother wasn't a criminal—she also knew at a deep level that Dylan was trustworthy. He cared. About her, about her son, about her livestock, even. And oddly, he seemed to maybe even come to care for Jax, who he'd been so derisive about when he first arrived. She might hate how Dylan had viewed her brother, but she knew without a doubt that he would do everything he could to protect the innocent.

Not that Dylan thought Jax was innocent, but he seemed to understand that her brother needed protection. Needed help.

"Can you guarantee he'll be placed in solitary when he gets back to prison? Not in the general population?" she asked.

Dylan nodded, holding her gaze with his.

She nibbled her lip. She wanted to talk to Julia, but she could almost hear her friend's voice in her head, telling her to get her brother back into custody. She didn't need to talk to a lawyer or a friend to know what her decision had to be. She was operating on mother instincts. And those instincts told her to protect her brother. The first child she'd ever raised.

"I'll help you," she said, straightening. "The way I see it, at this point, the best thing I can do for Jax is to make sure he goes back to prison alive. And the way I'm going to start is by confessing Jax sent me an email. He's on his way here to the ranch."

Surprise flickered along Dylan's expression and was swiftly followed by a myriad of emotions that Rachel wished she couldn't see—disappointment, anger, even betrayal. She tried telling herself that Dylan had no right to feel any of those things, that the only duty she'd had was to her brother and not to him, but it didn't matter. Guilt ate at her. And not just because she'd hurt Dylan by keeping such important news from him. Guilt that if she'd told him about the email right away, something might have been done to get Jax to safety sooner.

Instead, now he was out there. Scared and alone.

And with a madman after him.

Chapter 16

For the rest of the day, Rachel went about doing her ranch work as if she was in a daze. Dylan had stuck close to her, telling her he wanted to make sure she stayed safe, but his expression and body were distant and disapproving, suggesting the more likely reason he stayed close was that he no longer trusted her and wanted to make sure she didn't do something stupid like receive and hide another email from her brother. By quitting time, defeat had spread through Rachel's limbs like a thick miasma, rendering her almost immobile.

After cleaning up and calling Peter to say goodnight, she headed to the stairs, intending to go up to her bedroom, but the trek seemed impossible. How had her life come to this? She'd always obeyed the rules—never bucked the system. Had given and given and given of herself—letting go of her dreams to provide for her orphaned brother. Putting her own grief for the death of their parents on hold for so long the pain had long ago faded without commemoration. Working above and beyond what she needed to in order to pay for Jax's legal fees.

And what had her brother given her for all her sacrifices?

Guilt swept over her. She didn't hate Jax. No, that wasn't the case at all. She loved her brother as both a sister and a mother. But she couldn't help acknowledging that had Jax not made such foolish, stupid choices, she wouldn't be in this situation.

And her brother wouldn't have a death threat hanging over his head.

In the kitchen, after telling Dylan about Jax's email, she'd confided that if Jax showed up in the dead of night, he'd most likely try to sneak into her bedroom. Dylan had asked if he could sleep in the room to be there to catch Jax when he slipped in. He'd asked her to sleep in her son's room for the night, but she'd refused. If she was going to help trap her brother, she wanted to be there and make sure Dylan handled the situation correctly. Figuring Dylan would argue, she'd been surprised when he hadn't, and instead simply told her he'd sleep on the floor in her room. Although she'd agreed, and although she knew getting Jax back into custody was the best thing for him, regret still stabbed at her.

Now, with one hand on the balustrade, she placed a foot on the first step, but her other foot seemed to refuse to move.

And suddenly Dylan was behind her. Sliding one

arm around her rib cage. Sweeping another behind her knees. Lifting her. Carrying her. Cradling her. Seconds seemed to spread to minutes, as Rachel's senses took in Dylan's presence. His scent—fresh hay mixed with some sort of evergreen—filled her nostrils. His heat radiated, spreading across her skin. And his breath fell on her face, the sharp puffs of breath a reassurance.

How was it this man could reassure her? This man who thought her brother the scum of the earth because he was a criminal. This man who was about to send her brother back to prison.

But she knew. She knew in the core of her heart that this man, U.S. Marshal Dylan Rooney, was one of the good guys.

"You're angry with me," Rachel said.

Dylan shook his head. "No. Not angry. I know you did what you thought was right for your brother."

But not for us, she thought. Even though there was no him and her that she could speak of.

"Stay down," he said, gently laying her on her bed.

"Can't," she mumbled. "I need to shower and brush my teeth."

He backed away, then headed to the bathroom. Without looking at her, he called out over his shoulder, "I'll draw you a bath. You're staying down until your mind settles down. You're emotionally exhausted, Rachel. I've seen this before—stress can trigger a total collapse. And I won't have you collapsing on my watch."

She couldn't argue. Not that she didn't want to, just that she had no strength. A moment later, the sounds of rushing water out of the faucet came from the bathroom, followed by the sweet scent of blood orange and verbena. Warmth flooded her chest—how sweet. Dylan had found her secret stash of bubble bath.

As tough as the man acted, inside he was a marshmallow. Not that she'd tell him.

Just as she'd never tell him she was falling for him.

The bubble bath was a bit of heaven in the midst of a chaotic storm. Dylan let her alone to undress and ease herself into the suds. She just about fell asleep then, lulled by the gentle motion of the water and the warmth that sent her bones to liquid. She relaxed for a good quarter hour, then ducked under and got her hair wet. Five minutes later she'd shampooed and rinsed her hair and was realizing she had no desire to exit the bath and enter the real world again.

Dylan knocked at the bathroom door. "Rachel, I have food for you. Do you want to come out and eat in the kitchen or do you want me to bring it in?"

She stared at the door. Decorum and sense told her she should get out, dress and meet him in the kitchen. But she didn't want to. Maybe it was because she was so relaxed, but she was suddenly haunted by the memory of him cradling her in his arms and carrying her without effort up the stairs. That, of course, brought memories of his kisses. His touch. And the way he'd lit up her body, making her shudder as her first orgasm in years had coursed through her.

Unconsciously her hand strayed to her breast. Down her stomach. Between her thighs.

She gasped softly, then bit her lip.

On the other side of that door lay danger. Temptation.

Pleasure.

For all his talk of duty, she knew Dylan felt the way she did.

That he wouldn't fight her if she asked him for what she wanted. What she needed.

But she couldn't. It wouldn't be right for either of them.

She knew it, but that didn't stop her from doing what she did next. She took a quick peek down to make sure the bubbles covered everything she thought needed covering. Ranching meant she kept her body in shape, but motherhood had caused stretch marks on her belly and her breasts no longer held their shape the way they had when she was a teenager.

Funny, how her thoughts had drifted from her worries over her life to stretch marks.

"You can—" She took a deep breath, then called, "You can come in."

Was it her imagination, but did it take him a few more seconds to open the door than he should have? He entered, bearing a tray with herbal tea and graham crackers. He paused after a few steps and stared at her, his eyes flashing darkly before his expression went blank. It didn't matter. She'd seen the desire he hadn't been able to hide. The man did something delicious to her very core even when her world was falling apart.

"You didn't have much in the form of comfort food," he said, setting the tray down next to the tub.

She reached for a graham cracker, trying to act cool. "Not exactly Ben and Jerry's Chocolate Therapy, but should do the job."

He turned toward the door. "You ready to get out yet? Because we should probably talk about…what's going on." He sounded a little desperate to get away from her.

She sighed. It was good he could be sensible, she told herself. One of them had to be. "In a minute. If you hand me the comb on the vanity, I'll get rid of my tangles before climbing out."

Dylan reached for the comb, then stood there, his back still to her. He didn't move and she could see the tension rippling through his body.

"Dylan?" she whispered.

He turned and she gasped yet again. This time, he didn't bother banking the heat in his eyes. He stepped closer until she was craning her neck to look up at him. Then he crouched down beside the tub. "Can I do it?"

Again, she told herself she should say no. But his question had been tinged with something...that same desperation she'd sensed earlier, but this time it was a desperation to touch her rather than to get away from her. Her heart was now beating so fast she was sure he must be able to see it causing ripples in the water.

Too shaken to speak, she simply nodded. He shifted closer, reached out and took the weight of her wet hair in one hand, then with the other began to work the comb through her wet tresses.

Oh, God. The man was combing her hair.

When had a man ever combed her hair before? Never.

Tingles shot through her body—from the gentleness of his touch? From the way his breath brushed her wet shoulder? From the knowledge this honorable tough marshal was as tender and caring as a lover in a romantic movie?

"You...you don't have to do this, you know," she said, then bit her lip, mentally willing Dylan to continue.

"I know."

"This feels like a complication to me."

"It is."

"Then..."

"Then nothing, Rachel. We're in the realm of complicated now. No sense in denying it." He tugged gently, the action releasing a knot in her hair.

"But what about your job?"

"There are strict rules about getting involved with a suspect. That's a no-go zone. I'd never compromise my job or my responsibility to my country. But this? This thing between us? It's not a professional issue."

Just a personal one. She wondered who this man was—what made him tick. What his story was. The way he acted, how seriously he seemed to take his duties, gave her the sense Dylan Rooney wasn't the type to cheat on a woman. But still...

"You're not married, are you?"

His hand, the one holding the comb, stilled. "Not married. Not dating anyone, either. I wouldn't do that—see one woman and come on to another."

Was that what he was doing? Coming on to her?

She shifted, the movement sending the water into motion and washing away some of the bubbles covering her chest. A sudden sharp intake of breath from Dylan had her realizing one of her nipples was now exposed.

"Sorry," she whispered, sinking lower under the bubbles until her breasts no longer showed.

"I'm not. You're beautiful." The words had come

out of his mouth tight, almost strangled. As if he were holding himself back from expressing emotion.

"Dylan…"

Behind her, he released her hair and stood, then came around the front of the tub to face her. "I'll get you a towel," he said gruffly. "Leave you alone for a bit. I'll go check emails, then will come back and make sure you got into bed okay."

"Okay," she said.

"Okay," he echoed.

But he didn't go.

And she didn't tell him to.

No. She was done denying to herself the fact that something existed between them. He'd been clear about the fact that he wanted her. Thought she was beautiful.

Heck. He'd even combed her hair.

She wanted him. Needed him. Even if only for a night. The lawman had somehow worked his way under her skin, and the drive to have him claimed her. Rode her. Drove her.

She stood, water and bubbles streaming down her body, and enjoyed the sensation of power and pure womanly joy that spread throughout her as Dylan gaped at her naked body. As he swallowed. As his heartbeat sent the pulsing vein in his neck into over-drive.

He wanted her.

As she wanted him.

"Dylan…"

This time, when she uttered his name, he didn't back off. Didn't turn and leave her alone. Instead, he reached behind him for the fluffy white towel hanging on the towel rack, still holding her gaze with his, then sucked in a deep breath.

"Are you sure?" he asked.

"I know what I want. And you know what I'm asking for. For tonight. It can't be for more than tonight, but..."

He nodded, then stepped closer. With both hands, he stroked the towel across her face. Then down her neck and against her body. By the time he was done, her body was dry, but she was still dripping between her legs for him.

After dropping the towel, he cupped her face in his hands. "Fair warning, Rachel. If all we have is tonight, I'm not going to go easy on you. I'm going to sate myself on your body. I'm going to make sure you sate yourself on mine. I'm going to give you so much damn pleasure you're going to remember the feel of me inside you forever. I want that, because I know I'll never forget you. Or stop wanting you. Not in this lifetime. Maybe not even in the next. You okay with that?"

"More than okay," she whispered back.

Just as he'd done before, he lifted her into his arms. He carried her to her bedroom and laid her down on her bed as if she was precious. He stared at her, taking in her body with heated eyes that didn't miss a thing. She could feel herself blushing but refused to cower or cover up.

She wanted him to look at her. Want her. Pleasure her—just as he'd promised. But she hadn't forgotten his vow that she'd sate herself on him, as well.

So she lifted herself up on to her elbows. Waited until he bent, cupped the back of her head and kissed her for several long, wonderful minutes. When he reached down and caressed her breast, she almost forgot…almost lost sight of her goal because his touch felt so amazing. Somehow she managed to pull his wrist away.

He frowned. "What is it? Have you changed your mind?"

"Not at all. But you've looked at me. Before you touch me, before you make me lose my mind completely, I want to look at *you*. Take your clothes off, Dylan. Please?"

Dylan felt burned by the intensity of Rachel's gaze. Deaf to her pleas. Blinded by the sight of her naked body splayed out in front of him. Her endless curves and valleys made his mouth water as if he were a starving man presented with a buffet of the most decadent desserts imaginable. He wanted nothing more than to take her mouth again. Suck on her breasts. Plunge his fingers and tongue and more into the moist, tight cavern between her thighs. He wanted to ignore what she was asking so he could focus on *her,* but he'd promised this night would be a two-way street. With shaky hands, he unbuttoned his shirt. Before stripping it off, he removed his shoes. As he exposed more and more of his body, he watched her pupils dilate. Her breathing accelerate. Her nipples tighten. Her gaze roamed over him hungrily and she licked her lips more than once, urging him to move faster until he was practically ripping at his clothes. In under a minute, he was as naked as she. He stepped forward, but she shook her head again. "No. Wait. I want to look at you. Let me look at you."

She sat up and slid her legs over the side of the bed. Then she stood but didn't come closer. He wanted her to come closer.

Her gaze was a trail of fire that moved over his body, one that was almost painful as he anticipated her touch only to be denied. He wanted to preen and pose, flex his muscles and tempt her to touch him wherever she looked. His throat. His shoulders and chest. His abs. His…

His shaft jerked, growing harder and longer as she stared. Unable to help himself, he reached down and wrapped his fist around himself, making her gasp. "Come closer, Rachel. I'm dying for you." To give her added incentive, he began to stroke himself with slow, hard pulls. Without taking her eyes from his hand on his body, she moved closer. He released himself when she stopped within a foot of him.

"You're beautiful," she whispered. "So, so—" she raised her hands and rested her palms against his chest "—beautiful."

At that initial, gentle touch, he groaned. Clenched his fists. Trembled once more with the effort of remaining still. "Yes," he hissed out. "Touch me wherever you want. However you want. I want to give that to you. But in a minute, I'm going to take over, Rachel. And I don't know how long I'll be able to hold back."

Her hands smoothed over his chest to his shoulders, cupping and caressing. To his delight, wherever her hands went, her lips soon followed. The dual torture threatened to snap his control as she did exactly what he said. Touched and kissed him everywhere she wanted, however she wanted. It was a toss-up which he liked best. Her smooth hands or her soft lips and wet tongue. Thank God he didn't have to pick, because she gave him both. On his throat. Then his chest and shoulders. Then his abdomen. Soon she was kneeling in front of him, her hands on his butt, but her gaze, her focus, her *breath,* on his erection.

She looked up at him from beneath her lashes, a mischievous smile playing on her lips. "Is my minute just about done? Or can I continue without worrying that you'll take over?"

He loved her teasing even as it was killing him. "Why don't you come up here?" he suggested, moving to help her to her feet. "You'll like the way I—"

She resisted and he groaned as she circled her fingers around him. She pumped him once. Twice. Several more times. And it felt better than any woman's touch ever had. Unable to help himself, he buried his hands in her hair. Caressed the silken strands that reminded him of diamonds. Even though he wanted to, he didn't push her face closer. Didn't demand that she take him in her mouth. But then again, he didn't have to.

She'd been following up every caress with her mouth. And this was no different. He sighed in relief and utter pleasure when her lips brushed the sweetest of kisses against him. He groaned as she licked and nibbled at his shaft. Then yes, God, yes—he nearly shouted when she opened her mouth and took him in by degrees. Sucking him in before releasing him. Licking him before sucking him in again. Her hands stayed on his butt, pushing his hips closer as if she were afraid he was going to pull away at any moment, which was ridiculous. He was helpless against her. All he could do was moan. Encourage her. Call her baby. Plead with her to take him deeper inside her mouth. And she followed his instructions to a tee. Giving him pleasure as if she were born to do it. As if she'd been made just for him.

Before he knew it, his muscles were tightening all over and he could feel that familiar tingling at the base of his spine, warning him that he was close. That he'd let her take him further than he'd ever intended. That he was about to come and that was unacceptable because even as he relished the fact that part of him was inside her mouth, he knew he needed to be inside her in a different way altogether.

God, she was amazing. And he loved that she knew the power she held over him. He could see it in her eyes as she looked up at him. For once, they were clear of worry and shining with a single-minded determination to pleasure him.

Only he wanted to pleasure her first.

"Stop," he said.

She didn't listen. Gritting his teeth, he tightened his fingers in her hair and pulled until she reluctantly released him.

"I want you to come," she said.

"Not yet," he said. He helped her to her feet. "Not until I make you half as crazy as you make me."

The promise in Dylan's eyes and voice made her shiver. Before she could respond to his vow, he pulled her against his body and covered her mouth in a deep kiss. Her senses were immediately on overload. His tongue plunged into her mouth, robbing her of speech and breath and reason. Her breasts pressed into the hard muscles of his torso, stimulating her nipples to even greater tightness when she'd thought such a thing would be impossible. His shaft poked her belly and she arched her hips, trying to maneuver him to the V of her thighs so he could rub against her. Sensing what she needed, he cupped her rear and lifted her slightly even as he nudged his thigh between her legs, giving her not what she was aiming for but something fabulous nonetheless. She rocked against his thigh even as he broke their kiss.

"That's right, Rachel. Use me. Whatever part of me you need to make you feel good."

He kissed her neck, then trailed his lips down to her collarbone. As if she could lure him where she wanted him, she cupped her breasts, lifting them as an offering.

"You want me to kiss your pretty nipples, baby?"

"Yes," she moaned. "God, yes, Dylan."

"Shh," he said. "I'm going to give you my mouth, baby, just like you need. But keep moving on me. Don't stop."

She didn't stop. In fact, when he sucked her nipple into his mouth, hard, then harder still, her hips jerked frantically before picking up speed. "B-bed," she managed to say. Then when he didn't move fast enough, she pushed, actually catching him off balance so he went down on his back on the mattress. Of course, he pulled her along with him.

She braced herself on her hand and knees until she was straddling him. His mouth was still playing with her breasts, and his hands smoothed over her hips, but not for long. One hand gently gripped her thigh and tugged her legs apart even farther. Then he touched her between her legs with his other hand.

She gasped, closed her eyes and threw back her head. His mouth briefly left her breasts so he could stare up at her. "God, I love that expression on your face. You look like you're dying with pleasure. Only I know I haven't even begun to pleasure you." His fingers, which had been gently sliding across her cleft, touched her with greater purpose. His thumb rubbed against her. His fingers probed. Spread. Then he slid one finger deep inside her. "Oh, yeah," he breathed when she cried out. "That's so hot. But I want more. I want to give you more."

He slid another finger inside her, making her feel almost too full, and she tensed for a second, remembering how big and hard he'd been in her hand. Trying to imagine how deep he'd go inside her body. She didn't know if she'd be able to take it. She already felt on the verge of insanity. How had he gotten her to this point? Past reason? Unable to think about...

For a moment reality intruded.

Control. She needed to stay in control, didn't she? As good as this felt, she had responsibilities. People who were counting on her. And Dylan, he was here to—

"Rachel."

Dylan's voice came to her from a distance, then seemed to grow louder as he continued to call her name. She blinked when she realized she was now on her back and he was hovering above her, frowning. "Baby, don't. Don't go there. Stay with me. Here and now. Give us tonight. I can't predict the future, but

I'm here for you. I'm going to take care of you. You can count on me."

She stared up at him, at his beautiful face. She focused on the heat that still coursed through her body. She tightened her thighs, which were on either side of his hips, as he kneeled between her legs. He was braced above her, not touching her, yet she still felt him everywhere. In that moment, she knew it was too late. They hadn't had intercourse yet, but she'd already let him in. She didn't want to lose him now. Didn't want to trade the full experience of being in Dylan's arms for a control that she didn't need—not tonight, at least. Tomorrow would be different.

Tomorrow she'd focus on her responsibility to others.

But he was right. Tonight was hers.

It was theirs.

She reached down and caressed him between his legs. Then she guided his shaft between her thighs and rubbed him against her, covering him with her moisture even as she arched her hips in an unmistakable plea.

"Take me, Dylan. Now. Make me forget everything but tonight with your touch. With your kiss. With your co—"

His eyes flared a second before his mouth crashed down on hers. His mouth was voracious. She tightened her arms around him, rejoicing in the fact that she seemed to have pushed him past *his* control. Because she'd be damned if she'd surrender control without him doing the same. When he lifted his head and moved away from her, she moaned in protest but then he said, "Protection."

She lay there, stunned, as he swiftly retrieved something from his pants pocket. A condom, which he slipped out of its wrapping and on himself so fast that he was back in position, crouched over her, before she'd have thought possible. "I didn't think—" she said.

"It's okay," he said. "I told you I'd take care of you and I meant it, Rachel." He cupped her face with his hands. "Now I want to watch your face as I take you. I want to see everything you're feeling."

She nodded, wanting that, too. She didn't take her eyes off him as he reached down and guided himself to her entrance. Then he pushed into her slowly. Steadily.

It had been seven years for her, something that her body wasn't hesitant to communicate. Her muscles resisted him at first. He was patient. Working himself in a bit at a time. Giving her a few inches, then sliding out before starting in again.

"You're so tight," he said. "You feel so good."

"You're so big," she responded. "And you feel so good. Keep going. Give me more. Give me everything you have, Dylan."

His eyes narrowed at her words and his hips thrust, planting himself to the hilt inside her. He rested his forehead against hers and they both groaned. She wiggled, trying to adjust to the overwhelming feeling of being filled to capacity and then some. Pleasure flared, making her gasp. And wiggle even more. Soon she was arching, thrashing, rotating her hips, urging him to move, not understanding why he remained still.

Then she looked at his face. His eyes were closed.

His expression one of agony. The muscles in his arms bulged and his whole body trembled with the effort he was making to hold back. He was waiting for her to get used to him. Holding back to make sure she was ready.

True affection flooded her, combining with the respect she'd already grudgingly given him and the lust she'd already surrendered to. He'd taken her, but he wasn't taking *from* her. Just as he'd stood naked in front of her, urging her to touch him, he was making her give herself to him. And whether it was intentional or not on his part, she was being moved to give him not just her body, but her heart, too.

"Dylan," she said.

He opened his eyes and she saw what she both hoped and feared she'd see. He was giving her more than his body, as well. And right now, for tonight, she wanted it.

She arched her hips and this time he followed her lead. Slowly, carefully at first, he thrust in and out of her. Swiftly, his hips picked up speed so that her cries of pleasure grew steadily louder and louder, and her arms around him got tighter and tighter. He used his mouth and hands, too, driving her closer and closer toward climax with everything he had. And when he pushed them both over the peak of pleasure, he didn't say a word, but she still heard them. Words that could have been just her imagination. But words that made her feel loved nonetheless.

Afterward, they lay in bed, both recovering from what had to have been the hottest sex Dylan Rooney had ever experienced. He wanted more. More of Rachel. But more of what?

What they'd just shared had been more than sex. He'd felt emotionally connected to her in a way he'd never felt before in his life. And he knew she'd felt it, too.

Unsure of what to say or what to do, he held her close for a long time, stroking her hair and back, trying to tell her without words how much he liked her. Respected her. Wished things could be different for them.

Finally, when she said nothing, he pulled back. As he did, he saw the emotion flit over her face, changing from relaxation to wariness.

"I don't have meaningless sex, Rachel," Dylan said.

"Me, either," she said.

"Of course not. It's just…"

"What?"

"As clichéd as this sounds, I want to make sure you know where we stand. This thing between us isn't meaningless—at least, not to me—but I can't see it going anywhere. I don't want to set you up with false expectations."

A light laugh bubbled out of Rachel. She shifted, turning onto her belly and raising herself up to rest on her elbows to smile at him. "You're such a good guy, Dylan. No wonder you're a marshal. Such a sense of duty and responsibility." Her expression sobered. "But you're forgetting one thing. I said tonight, remember? Tonight only."

"Yeah, I know. But that was before."

"Before you gave me another orgasm, you mean? You expected me to be so dazzled by your sexual prowess that I immediately fantasized about riding off into the sunset together?"

He grimaced. "Something like that."

"Well, don't worry. No matter what happens, my brother is going to be in my life forever. That means things would never work out for the two of us. Right?"

"Right." An image of his mother's face, two black eyes welling with tears as she tried to justify his older brother's abusive actions, rolled into his mind. Following quickly was a more sickly image—him at fifteen, his mother in the bathtub, the water around her tinged red from the blood that dripped from her slit wrists. And finally his brother's pleas for understanding and forgiveness as he was taken away by the police that final time. Pleas for forgiveness that Dylan had never granted.

Oh, he knew his brother hadn't killed their mother. He wasn't technically responsible for her death any more than Dylan was. But technicalities didn't matter when emotion was involved. Their mother had failed them by taking his brother's abuse and making excuses for it. They'd both failed her in different ways—his brother by abusing her and failing to curb his lawless ways, and Dylan for not stopping his brother sooner or being able to make up for his brother's failings in time to convince his mother she had a life worth living.

Tension twisted his gut. Damn it—he didn't need to remember his past just now. But maybe remembering was what kept his heart safe.

Jackson Kincaid was between the two of them.

Rachel couldn't know in what way, but the fact

remained that she, like his mother, instinctively took victimhood on as a shroud.

Dylan couldn't give his heart to her.

Doing so would only hurt them both.

Chapter 17

The next morning, after she headed downstairs to make breakfast and found an empty house, a surge of relief washed over Rachel when Julia walked into the kitchen a short time later. Sex with Dylan had been amazing, but now it was over. It had to be. For her brother's sake.

"You going to tell me what the text you sent me this morning meant?" Julia asked, plopping her purse on the wooden kitchen table. "I mean, cryptic much?"

"Sorry," Rachel said, ducking her head to let her hair hang in her face. "I wanted you here, but I didn't want to say too much in case anyone got a hold of your phone, or mine."

"Because 'J, come here now. Things U need 2 know' was way so descriptive," Julia scoffed.

Rachel peeked out at Julia, taking in her high heels,

black pencil skirt and blush pink silk button-up blouse with lace insets. How could a country attorney look so pulled together? She glanced down at herself. Her jeans molded nicely to her form, but that was due to the years and years of wear and washing. Her white T-shirt had a stain on the right breast, which she'd conveniently covered with an old plaid flannel shirt of Jax's. She couldn't help thinking that if Dylan was here right now, he must see the differences between Julia and her. She had a feeling Julia was more like the women he dated than she was. But she also knew she was more than an easy lay to him. The fact that he was a marshal—he took that seriously, which meant his feelings for her had to be pretty strong for him to sleep with her in the first place. "Jax needs help. He needs protection," she said. She told Julia about George Evans and Dylan's certainty that Evans was after her brother.

Julia asked a few questions, which Rachel answered as best she could. Then she sighed and picked off a piece of fuzz from her brother's shirt. "You were right—I can't keep protecting my brother from everything. But this? Torture? I can protect him from that, at least. I only hope he'll see it that way when the marshals take him back into custody."

"He'll understand. I know he will. He loves you, Rachel. Don't forget that."

She would never forget. But until Dylan had come into her life, she never would have doubted how pure her brother's love was. Now? Now she had to wonder about that purity. How could he have not shared with her about this George Evans man, or the hidden money?

"How are things with the lawman?" Julia asked.

Unprepared for the sudden shift in conversation, Rachel felt heat rush up her neck and into her cheeks as memories from the night before swam into her mind's eye. "Um…"

"Oh, God," Julia said, clasping a hand over her chest, "you're blushing. What the heck, Rachel? I was curious about how the two of you are dealing with the fact that he's pretending to be your ranch hand while he's on the prowl for your brother. Looks like something else entirely is going on." She sat on one of the kitchen chairs, delicately placing one knee over the other. "Spill. You know you have to. I won't leave this alone."

And she wouldn't, as Rachel well knew. Huffing out a breath, she joined Julia at the table, then fiddled with a crumb she found there before speaking. "We had sex but it's over. He'll catch Jax, then will head back to L.A. or wherever he's from."

"But you like him. Despite everything you like him."

"It's not hard to like him. Dylan's a good guy—I know that. But he sees Jax as a criminal. Someone who is bad to the core. He lumps people like my brother—who was a stupid idiot but not a bad guy—in with all the other criminals. Even if he was interested in more with me—which he's not—I can't have someone in my life if that person views those who make mistakes with such contempt. We all make mistakes. I certainly have."

. "What kind of mistakes are you talking about, Rachel?"

"I wasn't a good enough mother to him," she murmured, focusing on the multiple crumbs she'd created by crushing the original crumb.

"You're wrong. You can't blame yourself for Jax's mistakes. He's a grown man, responsible for his own actions. He made the decision to carry what he had to have known were drugs across state lines. You didn't make that call—he did. And he's to blame for everything, not you."

How easily the words seemed to come from Julia's mouth, Rachel thought bitterly. Julia hadn't been thrust into being a parent, or had her own dreams stolen from her. But instead of arguing, Rachel instead said, "You're right. I shouldn't have said that. I get it. I'm not responsible for Jax's dumb decisions."

"You're not responsible for Jax, period. It's time he accepts his responsibilities, to himself, to you and Peter and to society in general."

"But he didn't plan that escape, Julia. George Evans broke him out. He's not responsible for that— surely you can understand that."

"But according to what you've told me, he escaped George Evans's men. He had every opportunity to turn himself in to the law by now. But you're right, now you have to focus on keeping him safe. So what are you going to do?"

"I'm going to email him," she said simply. "Tell him to call me so we can set up a time to meet. That way, Dylan can be prepared to take Jax in safely." One simple email to her trusting brother and Jax would be back in jail. Jax would trust her to keep him safe, the way she always had. She had to hope and pray with everything she had inside that her decision to set him up to get taken into custody was the right one.

Or else she'd just signed her brother's death warrant.

Rachel's backbone had stayed stiff and strong while she drafted and sent the email to her brother. The decision hadn't been an easy one for her to make, nor had the actual email been an easy one to write. Dylan had to hand it to her—Rachel was one strong woman.

"Jax—I'm so glad you're coming home. Please call me so I know you're safe. I've been worried sick," was all the email had said.

It took several hours, but eventually Jax replied to Rachel's email. The response had been short—simply stating he was on his way but didn't have a phone to call her. Dylan's team had tracked the location of where the email had been sent from. Although they didn't have an exact location, Jax was in town—close by. Thinking he was communicating only with his sister, Jackson Kincaid had agreed to meet Rachel in the master bedroom at midnight. As Rachel had anticipated, Jackson planned to enter the house through the second-story French doors. Dylan prompted Stacy to pull in extra manpower, but made it clear that Jax wasn't to be detained until after he'd entered the house.

Now all they had to do was wait. In less than twelve hours, the team would have their charge in custody and would be headed back to California.

And he'd have to say goodbye to Rachel.

Rachel's phone rang, jerking her attention from the window she was staring blankly out of. She checked the caller ID, then clicked to take the call.

"Peter?"

Dylan couldn't hear what the kid had to say on the other end of the call, but whatever Peter was telling his mother wasn't sitting well with Rachel, whose face grew more pinched as she listened.

"It doesn't matter if Nonna and Papa are strict. It's their house, so you need to follow their rules," she said, then stood and paced the length of the kitchen and then back again. "Peter. I expect you to be respectful of your grandparents. I don't care if they won't let you play video games on a weeknight the way I do. Please listen to them. Please."

Irritation crept up Dylan's spine. The kid was upsetting Rachel. Her voice had gone from frustrated to pleading in a matter of seconds. She spoke with Peter a little longer, then ended with a quick "I love you, too" before hanging up.

When she was done, she wouldn't look at Dylan. "I'm going to check on the alpacas."

In the corral, alpacas nuzzled up against Rachel, who moved through the herd, picking up hooves to check for embedded rocks or the need to trim the one large nail the camellike creatures had, and plunging her hands into the soft fibers. In a few weeks she'd need to hire a shearer—her ranch hand had always shorn her herd, but with him gone, that would be an expense she'd have to figure out in her budget somehow.

After all, Dylan was going to be gone.

Jax was going to be in jail.

Peter was going to be back, butting heads with her.

She closed her eyes, so tired. Talking with Peter on the phone hadn't been a big deal. He was ten years old—of course he was going to complain that his grandparents were too strict. But as she talked on the phone with him with Dylan watching her, it had struck her how she wished she and Dylan had more than one night together. That they had night after night. That she had someone to share her life with. To share raising Peter with.

To share her bed with.

Dylan would be a wonderful life partner.

Sexy.

Sensual.

Excellent in bed.

Willing to do hard work and good with her kid.

Damn. The lawman checked all her boxes.

He just had a closed mind when it came to viewing flawed people as still worthy.

But she couldn't even fault him for that.

She struggled with the same thing when it came to herself.

She did blame herself for Jax's problems sometimes. But the truth was, she wasn't a bad mother. Sure, she'd made mistakes, both with Peter and with Jax, but she wasn't a failure. Parents who were failures beat their children. Starved their children. Abandoned their children. They did drugs and got drunk in front of their kids—they didn't get them to school on time or dress them or bathe them or show them any love.

That hadn't been her.

No, for the past ten years, she'd made sure the two boys she loved the most always had a roof over their heads, clean clothes on their backs, food in their bellies and were clean—except when catching frogs in the mud, of course. She'd read their favorite books to them, had helped them with their homework, had taught them how to ride horses, shoot, fish and even bake. She'd been on the PTA and a parent volunteer. Had stayed up all night with both when Jax brought home strep throat from high school and then gave it to Peter.

She'd been a good mother.

She only wished Jax and Peter could have had the benefit of a good father, too.

A good father would have raced down the ridge on a horse to rescue her son, the way Dylan had. A good father would have insisted she get her kid to safety, the way Dylan had. And a good father would have insisted his son act in a respectful manner…the way U.S. Marshal Dylan Rooney had with her son.

A strange sensation wormed its way up her body, a sensation full of tingles and accompanied by the sound of buzzing. She suspected what it was. It was a beautiful feeling—one that held both calm and excitement all at once.

A feeling she didn't want to experience. Not now. Not like this. Love.

"No!" she said, realizing after the alpaca herd scattered that she'd spoken the word out loud. "It's okay, babies," she crooned, but the herd was already reforming into its little group at the far side of the corral. The peace had been broken.

The way her heart would be if she kept down this path.

In her pocket, her cell buzzed. She pulled it out and noted an unfamiliar number. Climbing to the top of the corral to sit on the railing, she clicked the phone on and said hello.

"Sis?"

Her heart thumped against her chest and she sat straight. Jax. Sounding as if he were about to cry. Why was he calling now? He'd said he didn't have a phone—or had he just been worried she was trying to have someone track him? "What is it? What's wrong? Where are you?" she asked, the barrage of questions plummeting out of her mouth. "You said you didn't have a phone with you." In other words, he'd lied...

"I'm in town. Don't want to say exactly, but I'm nearby."

"You're still coming home tonight, right?" she asked.

"I have to. I don't have an option."

"You'll be safe," she promised. "I won't let anything bad happen to you." Like being caught by George Evans's men and tortured and killed.

"I didn't set up the jailbreak, sis. You have to believe me. There's this guy—a really bad guy. He hired people to break me out of the transport."

"I know," she said. "I knew you'd never arrange something like that. It's not in you. But why would he break you out, Jax?" She knew why, but she needed to hear it from her brother. Needed to hear the truth.

Jax choked out a few sobs before saying shakily, "Money. The money I was supposed to bring back to Texas after I delivered the drugs. I found it after the bust and hid it. But that Evans dude? He figured it out, and he had my cellmate killed when the guy couldn't get the info out of me. And he set up the jailbreak so he could get me to tell him where the money is."

"You could have told him, Jax. Just told him where you hid the money."

"No! It's my only leverage to keep you and Peter safe. He wants it. A lot of people do. So long as they don't have it, they won't kill me, and you and Peter will be safe."

"But we haven't been safe, Jax. Weird things have been happening on the ranch. Josiah is dead, and it seems suspicious. There was a stampede. Someone poisoned my alpacas. And someone tried to run me off the road. We think it was Evans's men."

There was tense silence on the phone before Jax asked, "Who's we, sis?"

Rachel cursed herself for her slip up. Now what did she say? She decided to tell the truth—at least partially. "The law sent some U.S. Marshals after you. They've been in touch with me, Jax." She quickly shared with him what she knew about the two murdered and tortured members of Evans's crew. When Jax started crying, loud, choked sounds, she wanted to comfort him. To tell him everything would be okay. But she couldn't. "Jax, I don't understand. Why don't you just tell Evans where the money is and be done with it? Peter and I won't be in danger if the guy gets his money back."

On the other end of the line, Jax's breathing grew more ragged, his voice rougher, as he said, "If only it were that easy. I'm doing this all for you, Rachel. I want to make sure that the money is there, where

I hid it. And yeah, I hid it on the property. The only problem is that it was dark and I was freaked and I can't remember where the hell I buried it."

A gasp caught in her throat. "We don't have that big a property, Jax. How could you not know where you buried one million dollars?"

"I don't know, okay! I just know it's somewhere along the perimeter fence, the one that separates our property from Aaron Jacobson's. That's why I need to get onto the property without anyone knowing—so I can find where I buried the cash. Because there's no way I could tell anyone where to go—I need to get out to the fence line so I can figure out what's familiar."

"You have to remember, Jax! We have to get Evans the money."

Another moment of silence stretched between her and her brother before he responded dully. "I—I'll try Rachel. All I can do is try. Maybe there's another way—"

"There's no other way, Jax," she began.

But the call had been cut off.

A few hours later, Rachel had finished most of her chores, including grooming the alpacas, and had turned the herd out into the far pasture to graze. She'd decided not to share the phone conversation with Dylan. After all, Jax hadn't told her anything new and what more could be done? Jax was in town, nearby, and would be at her place at midnight. All would be over at that point. Dylan would catch his fugitive, Jax would be safely tucked away in protective custody and they'd find the money hidden on her property and turn it over to the authorities.

George Evans would have to find another way to get his cash back.

She made her way back to the barn, where she checked on the poisoned alpaca, who seemed to be doing better but still struggled with breathing. Rachel could hear Dylan in the tack room—his makeshift office—speaking to his team members. Although his words were indiscernible, the low rumble of his voice somehow reassured her. Just having Dylan around as her world caved in on her gave her some semblance of strength.

Gathering up saddle soap, a bucket of warm water, a sea sponge and Anchor's and Row's bridles, she set to work cleaning the tack.

"Rachel?" Dylan's smooth, warm voice came from behind her.

She swung around, shoulders tensing at the frown on his face. Did he know Jax had called her?

"Rachel, I'm sorry, but your alpaca…she didn't make it."

"What?" she breathed out. "I just checked on her not only an hour ago. She was breathing then."

He shook his head gently. "I was just in there. She's gone, Rachel." With the pad of his thumb, he traced the path of a tear that ran down her cheek, his touch soft and cool and comforting.

God, she wanted so much to fall into his arms. To let him caress her, to take care of her. To comfort and care for her.

"I'm here for you," he said. "Let me hold you, Rachel. Please let me hold you."

How was it possible for her heart to ache in so

many ways at the same time? For Jax. For Peter. For her alpaca. For this man.

He wanted to hold her. And suddenly she couldn't imagine anything that would feel better than being in his arms.

She placed her hands on his chest. "Please," she said. "Hold me, Dylan. Make love to me."

Chapter 18

"This isn't some fly-by-night hookup, Rachel," Dylan said, his words sending puffs of breath into her hair. It surprised him how content he was to hold her in his arms after their passionate lovemaking. He wasn't normally into cuddling.

How lovely she looked, covered by only the filtered light of the afternoon sun coming through the open window in the barn roof above. Lying on a bed of blond-colored straw and their clothes, her legs entwined with his and her fingers tracing a path across his chest, she'd never been more beautiful.

And Rachel was beautiful. Inside and out. From her slightly off-center nose to the fierce way she loved her son and brother, beauty radiated from her. If only their lives were different. If only they'd met under circumstances far removed from the ones they currently were living in. But life wasn't made up of "if onlys." Something he knew all too well.

"We've been over this before. I get it—you don't sleep around. But there's no future here," she said.

"Neither of us knows what will happen. But you need to know something. I care for you. Deeply. I—" Holy hell. The words *I love you* had been about to roll off his tongue with such ease it shocked him.

He'd imagined he was falling in love with her. Apparently there was no falling about it—he was there. That was what he'd been feeling when they made love in her room. He'd felt it again just moments before.

Against all reason, despite the fact that he'd wanted to keep his distance from her, a woman who couldn't accept the mistakes her brother had made, he loved her.

And he didn't want to let her go.

He blew out a breath. Talk about a complication.

She shifted, and the movement sent a shaft of light over her breasts. A few stretch marks gleamed silver on her tummy—marks of bravery.

Of life…

Of love.

Once again, the words swelled inside him, and this time he couldn't keep himself from saying them. "I love you, Rachel Kincaid," he murmured.

Shock rounded her eyes. Automatically she shook her head.

"Yes," he insisted. "I know it sounds crazy. That our situation is crazy. But I love you. I don't know if I can make things work out between us, but…"

"But what?" she said with a small smile.

"But I want to try. Do you?"

She twirled her fingertip around the copper circle of his nipple, her smile fading. "I do. But with Jax…I don't know if it's possible."

Dylan was silent for several seconds before he said, "I have a brother, too, you know. A brother who made mistakes in his life."

At that, she sat up, coming up on one elbow to look down upon him. "You do?"

Dylan nodded. "He's older. A good ten years older than me."

"Is he alive?"

"Yeah. At least, I'm assuming he is. We lost touch when he started his fifteen-year sentence."

The warmth that had been in her face evaporated, and her expression grew cold. "Your brother's a convict?"

"He was arrested multiple times throughout his childhood. Was convicted as an adult five days after he turned twenty-five."

"What did he do?"

A wave of nausea built in his stomach. God, he hated the memories. Tried to shove them away any chance he got. But Rachel deserved to know. He swallowed, shoving the nausea back where it belonged. "When he was twelve, my dad took off. Brandon at first turned inward, but then he started acting out. In response, my mom tried to gain control of him."

"And?"

"And then he got bigger. Grew taller. And started beating her."

At Rachel's sudden intake of breath, he held up a hand. He needed to get through this. To tell her, to explain to her. So that she knew and understood him.

"My mom took all the blame. She thought if she'd been a better wife, my father wouldn't have left. And she always said that if she'd been a better mother, my brother wouldn't have gone ballistic. According to her, it was her fault he hurt her."

Rachel shook her head. "Typical victim response, taking on the blame of the abuse. But not the truth. That's why you get frustrated with me when I shoulder the blame for Jax and Peter's actions," she said quietly.

He shrugged. Looked away. And she could tell there was more to his story.

"What happened to your mother, Dylan? Did he…"

He closed his eyes. "He didn't kill her. But he might as well have. She was so immersed in her guilt over everything, over what our father and my brother had done to her, that she killed herself. Slit her wrists in the bathtub. I'm the one who found her. I was fifteen years old."

"Oh, God," she cried out. Just like Jax, he'd found his parent dead. "I'm sorry, Dylan. So sorry."

He opened his eyes. "My brother…after my mother died, he just kept getting worse. He went on a downward spiral. Got drunk. Picked fights. Started using drugs. He beat a man so badly he put him into a coma for weeks. He was arrested, convicted and I haven't seen him since."

The story he was telling her was ugly, so ugly, yet part of her couldn't help herself—she couldn't believe that he'd abandoned his brother so totally. Yes, what his brother had done was horrible, but they were still blood. Didn't that matter to Dylan?

"Rachel, if I have any advice to share, it's this.

Give Jax and Peter the freedom to make their own
mistakes. Don't take on their actions as your own.
You'll only end up creating monsters...and getting
hurt."

Rachel sucked in a deep breath. Her mind spun—
dizzy with all that had transpired in just a few moments. Dylan had confessed he loved her. Heady stuff.
Was she ready to accept it as truth? Or did a part of
her secretly wish he'd kept his heartfelt expression to
himself? Complicated was an easy word at this point:
convoluted, impossible...those were words that now
came to mind. She almost wished they could go back
to just "complicated."

And what he'd just shared? The story about his
mother and his brother? How painful a past that
must have been. He'd been ten years younger than
his brother. Without a father, watching his mother
being beaten by someone she loved...that had to have
churned something up inside him that he'd never been
able to settle. His suggestion to let her son and brother
make their own decisions spoke to that. Dylan saw the
situation as a wounded son, not as a mother.

"We've been over this before, Dylan. We won't
ever see eye to eye. I appreciate all that you've shared
with me, but my instincts tell me that when they get
into trouble, I need to tighten the leash, not loosen it."

Dylan rolled away from her then, placing a hand
over his eyes. "I think you're making a mistake."

"I know you do." She hesitated. Touched his arm.
"I realize that I've been blind to Jax's faults. He confessed to transporting those drugs. He's never told me
otherwise. I need to accept he made some bad deci-

sions. But they're nothing we can't work past. I can't abandon him the way you did your brother. If that's a mistake...it's my mistake to make."

"I know. That's one thing that's become perfectly clear over the last few days. You're strong. Independent. Willing to take risks. And I admire you for that."

She shifted, coming up onto her elbows, slightly buried in the fresh hay. The sunlight streamed through the window to cover Dylan in a swath of warm gold. Emboldened, she reached out a finger and traced a line down his chest, lower even, past his belly and followed the path lower still. When he groaned, she pulled her hand away. She wasn't quite yet ready to follow up on what they'd just experienced. And she had questions still.

"You admire me, even though I still believe in Jax. Even though I stick up for him the way your mother did your brother for so long?"

Dylan captured her hand and entwined her fingers with his, lightly stroking each of her fingers with the side of his thumb. "I admit...it's hard for me when you try to take responsibility that isn't yours. When you refuse to acknowledge the possibility that your brother has done wrong. But at the same time, you're not a victim. I see you as someone who loves fiercely, who protects with everything she has, and who makes tough choices. Between what the U.S. Marshals have brought to the table and what your brother has added into play, you haven't exactly been given many options. You've been doing the best with what you have."

"And so are you," she said softly. "I know you don't believe in Jax the way I do, but why would you? I'm his sister. You don't know him the way I do. And you're trying to do your job. So where does this leave us? I—I care about you, Dylan, but—"

Her phone buzzed. She thought of Jax. Hesitated. Then rooted through her clothes to find her phone. Even with Dylan here, she couldn't risk not answering. When she looked at the screen, she recognized the caller ID: Peter's grandparents.

She answered, "Hello?"

Maureen, her voice wobbly, said, "Peter's run off."

Shocked, Rachel looked sharply at Dylan. "When did he leave? Why did he leave?"

"He must have taken off sometime this morning, after he spoke to you. We're not sure why he left, but we assume it had something to do with the fact that we wouldn't let him play video games."

Disappointment tangled with worry in her gut.

"He's spoiled," Maureen said.

Spoiled? Maybe. Sure, she did allow Peter to play video games and watch TV, but only after he did his homework and finished his chores. And on a ranch, there were a lot of chores.

"And, Rachel," Maureen continued, "we're not pleased. This kind of behavior isn't acceptable. You need to get control over your child before he ends up like his uncle. You need to be a better mother."

Anger stabbed her in the gut. "I'm trying," she snapped out.

"Apparently not enough. Try harder. Or better yet—"

"Give me the phone, Rachel," Dylan said.

She stared at him, hesitated, then gave him the phone. He looked at her as he spoke into it. "This is Dylan Rooney. I'm a U.S. Marshal. Please tell me what you know about Peter." He looked at Rachel. "No, you can't talk to Rachel. Now tell me what you know."

As Dylan talked to Maureen, Rachel stood, swiped at the tears trickling down her cheeks, then swiftly dressed. As soon as Dylan disconnected, he dressed, as well. He hadn't gotten his shoes on yet when Rachel fell apart. Dropping to her knees in the hay, she covered her face with her hands and sobbed. "Oh, God. Now he's completely vulnerable."

She sensed Dylan drop down beside her. He held her shoulders, then pulled her close. "He's going to be okay, Rachel. He's done this before."

"This isn't a night out in the local woods—he'll be in towns, cities, crossing freeways. What if he tries to hitchhike? What if I lose him?" Her body wouldn't stop shaking. "This is my fault. I should have kept him with me. I could have kept him safe."

"Stop it," Dylan said roughly. "You know that's not true. You were protecting him."

"*Trying* to protect him. But now my son is out there, alone, and maybe afraid."

"He won't be for long. We're going to find him, Rachel." He gripped her chin and made her look at him. "Look into my eyes. Tell me you believe me."

She stared into his eyes. Saw the determination and truth there. He'd said he loved her. She hadn't said it back, but that didn't mean she didn't feel it, too. She loved this man. She'd trusted him with her body. Now she had to trust him to find her son.

She took a shaky breath, then nodded. "I do. I believe you. Find my son, Dylan. Bring him back to me."

Twenty minutes later, Dylan ended what was the

latest in a number of telephone conversations and turned to her.

"Our sheriff will be coordinating the search since we think Peter's going to be headed here. We'll get all law enforcement officers on the lookout. The sheriff is calling a community meeting to help find Peter," he said. "There should be a number of people gathered in twenty to thirty minutes, including news crews."

"Where is the community meeting going to be held? Here?"

"No, they're gathering at the town square, according to what Stacy gleaned." He reached out and brushed a strand of hay from her hair. "Let's get you in the shower and changed into something more presentable. You're going on TV."

"On TV?" she said, her voice filled with trepidation. "But why? I understand why we need to gather volunteers to help look for him, but why go on TV?"

"It'll put more eyes and ears on the lookout for him. It's a basic press conference. You simply state that your son might be lost and headed home. Give a description, hold up a picture of his latest school photo and encourage people to keep an eye out and call the authorities if they see him."

Dylan's face had gone tight, the way it did when he didn't want to say something.

"What aren't you telling me?" she demanded.

"Nothing. Truly, I have nothing new to add. My team has great control of the perimeter of your ranch, but I can't forget that Evans it out there."

She should have thought of that, but she hadn't. Now the fear that rose inside her threatened to suffocate her. "Evans is out there. Putting Jax and now Peter at risk," she said, her voice flat.

"Putting you all at risk," he corrected.

The rest of the afternoon was rushed and hurried, with Rachel being so busy she felt she hardly had a moment to breathe. True to his word, the sheriff had organized a community gathering at the town square. There, a tearful Julia came up to Rachel and gave her a brief yet reassuring hug before Rachel had to step in front of the news cameras and microphones.

Before she made it to the media swarm, she heard a search party had been organized. Some of the ranchers planned to ride the range, where they figured Peter would head toward, and other townsfolk were calling friends and family members between here and Rachel's in-laws and sending out messages through Facebook and Twitter to keep an eye out for her son.

"Ready?" Dylan said. When she nodded, he pushed her forward to stand in front of the cameras, the microphones and the gathered crowd.

Her knees trembled as she looked at the multitude of faces—many familiar, but some strangers to these parts. The media, she figured. Peter would hate this, Rachel figured, but she had to protect him. She had to do her duty.

She cast a glance back at Dylan, who gave her a reassuring smile. Yes, she could do this. "My dear community," she began, and held up the picture of Peter. "Earlier today, we were notified my son had left his grandparents' home, and would most likely be trying to make it home." She continued speaking, laying out what Dylan had told her to say. After she gave her statement, some of the media asked questions, which she answered smoothly until she noticed Dylan had taken a call on his cell phone. She faltered in giving an answer, squinting to better take in Dylan's expression.

His pinched and tight expression.

No. That wasn't good. Oh, God. What had happened? "That's all," she said quickly into a microphone, then stepped down from the temporary dais and headed to Dylan, who ended the call just as she walked up to him.

"What is it?" she demanded. "Tell me."

He flicked his gaze at the crowd, then cupped her elbow and gently tugged. "Let's talk where no one can hear."

And she'd thought her knees had been shaking earlier. Now she could barely make them swing forward and hold up her weight at the same time. Something had happened to Peter; otherwise Dylan wouldn't look so concerned. At the alley between the bakery and the bookstore, he propped her up against the rough brick facing and braced his arms on either side of her shoulders.

"I have something to tell you, Rachel. Think you can remain standing, or should I find us somewhere to sit?"

"I want to stand. Whatever you have to say, I need to be strong enough to hear it if I'm to be strong enough to deal with it. Is Peter…" She choked on the words.

"No," he said quickly. "He's not dead. But it's bad, Rachel. Really bad."

His warmth and the scent coming off him and rolling over her brought her strength. Stability. Made her knees solid under her. "What is it, Dylan?" she whispered.

A muscle on the side of his jaw twitched as he switched his gaze from her eyes to her mouth, then back up to her eyes again. He swallowed, the action made visible by the long bob in his neck; then he spoke. "We believe Peter didn't run away. We believe he was kidnapped."

Her knees started their wobbling again. "No," she gasped out. "God, no." Thank God for the strong wall behind her. For Dylan's arms on either side of her. She wouldn't fall. She wouldn't allow herself to crumple.

"Rachel..."

She didn't have time for compassion. Or for herself to fall apart. She gathered her strength and willed her knees to keep supporting her. Her priority now was to find her son. Get him back from the kidnappers. Keep him safe. "Why do you think that? Was there a note? A phone call?"

"No. A witness saw Peter being taken from his grandparents' front yard by force."

"Why didn't this witness come forward sooner?"

"Remember, it's just been a few hours, and the guy was saying Peter had to come with him and go to school, so she didn't suspect anything. She just read about Peter being lost on a friend's Facebook and re-alized everyone had it wrong. He hadn't gotten lost—or even run away. He'd been taken. She contacted the police and they forwarded her to my team."

She looked at the media, most of whom still milled around the town square, some of whom were putting their equipment away in news vans. "We can use the media. Let them know about the kidnapping. They're out there looking for Peter—we can shift their focus to look for the kidnappers, right?"

"Wrong. We have to keep this quiet, at least for now."

"But why?" she argued, running a hand through her hair and coming up with tangles.

"Because we have to assume the person who has Peter is George Evans, who's proven himself to be a dangerous man. He seems to have a pattern of holding people who he thinks could be useful. He's using Peter as a pawn. Trying to draw out Jax."

The panic inside her increased, making it difficult to breathe. "And so long as we don't go after George Evans, Peter is safe."

"Right. We let Evans contact us first. Find out what he wants. We wait."

"Wrong!" All the logic Dylan was giving her wasn't sinking in. "My son is going to die!" Her heart flung itself against her rib cage, hatred making her strike out at Dylan and pound against his chest. "And your stupid 'let people make their own decisions' approach to life is going to kill Peter."

"That's not fair."

To his credit, even though Dylan had just about spat out the words, he hadn't backed away. In fact, he'd come in closer, almost touching his hips to hers. Reached out and grabbed her fisted hands. Held tight but stroked his thumbs over her clenched fingers. God, she wanted the comfort. The strength. She wanted to believe he was right. She wanted…she wanted him.

"At the risk of sounding like a wimpy female,

would you..." She couldn't finish. Couldn't admit her weakness.

"Hold you?"

She swallowed back tears. "I feel so stupid. So weak."

Dylan wrapped his arms around her shoulders, supporting her weight with his strength, and kissed the top of her head. "Spine of steel. That's what you have. You're a mom, Rachel. Moms go into shock when their kids are threatened. You're just in shock, not weak."

The words were somehow reassuring. Released some of the tension cording around her chest. Brought her back to reality, back down to earth. She let out a shuddering breath, forcing herself to rationalize and not stay wallowed in the pain and drama of the moment. "I'll bet your knees have never threatened to dump you in an alley," she joked halfheartedly.

"I peed my pants when the neighbor kid sicced his dog on me."

She gave a hollow laugh. "Yeah, but you were probably like, eight. I'm a grown-up."

"Grown-ups get scared, too." He kissed her forehead, then bent a bit to give her a light kiss on the lips. "And if you weren't scared, you wouldn't be a good parent. You care, Rachel. You just take too much responsibility for the actions of others."

"You're right. I do," she said quietly. "Sometimes I get mixed about what's mine to feel guilty about and what's not."

"Why?"

She shrugged. "You have your past...I have mine."

He raised his head and gazed down at her, his expression full of tenderness and care. "Want to tell me about it?"

"I'd gone away to college," she began, then hesitated. "Shouldn't we be talking about how to get Peter back?"

"My team's contacting the FBI and setting up a plan. For right now, I need you to get calm. In control. Maybe telling me about your past might help ground you."

She nodded, understanding what Dylan was trying to do. By putting her attention on her past, she could get those damn knees to stop wobbling under her. Then she'd be able to be rational and could deal with the fact that her son had been stolen by the very man out to kill her brother.

The thought made deep shudders rack her body. Damn. She needed the focus. She started again. "My parents wanted me to go to a local community college for two years so I could help on the ranch. They'd just transitioned from sheep to the alpacas, and the herd needed constant care. They were exhausted but couldn't yet afford to hire a ranch hand."

"But you say you went away...."

She stared vacantly at the empty alleyway, barely seeing the hundred-year-old brick of the building facing her. Empty. That was how she felt. Empty. Depleted. Sucked dry. Her son was in the hands of a killer. How could she survive?

But her knees were still holding her up. Dylan's arms were still braced on either side of her. The rough texture of the brick wall was a reassuring strength behind her back. She'd get through this. She had to. There was no other option.

"Rachel?" Dylan prompted.

Struggling, she worked to bring her focus back to his face. What was it he was asking? Oh, that's right. They'd been talking about her brother. How they'd ended up in this situation because of one stupid, idiotic choice made in her youth. A choice she'd made.

"If you don't want to continue," he said, "that's fine. I'm just glad to see you still standing."

She shook her head. "I want you to know. I want you to understand how it is we came to be in this place—or at least, how I came to be in this place. It's my fault Peter was kidnapped. My fault Jax made bad mistakes and ended up tangled with a drug lord. My fault my parents—" The words wouldn't come, lodged in the back of her throat. Casting her eyes upward, she caught Dylan's reassuring gaze with hers.

"Your parents wanted you to help on the farm. You wanted to go out and live your life," he prompted.

She could do this. Tell him the full story. Then he'd understand. He might not like her much after, but he'd at least understand what made her. What kept her driven to help her brother. "Yeah. I refused to stick around. Fought with my mom and dad about it, then got a scholarship to my dream college back East. For the first semester, things were great. I rarely called my family. Just partied, had fun, enjoyed learning and college life."

"Sounds normal."

"If you're not a rancher, maybe. But this ranch goes back to just after the Civil War. Peter's the sixth generation to work this land. We don't just take off...not when the ranch needs us. But I did. And because I did—" Tears pricked her eyes as they did every time she thought of that day. That horrible, horrible day.

"You don't have to tell me. Or you can wait until another time. Sometime when you're not so vulnerable over your kidnapped child."

"I need to get this out." To her relief, he didn't argue with her, but instead stayed silent, rubbing his thumbs in little circles against her back. She cleared her throat, then managed to speak. "Because they were overworked and had no cash, they didn't remember to get the house heater checked, even though they knew it needed maintenance. Jax came home from school and found our mom and dad dead in their bed."

"Carbon monoxide poisoning?"

She nodded. "There was a warning alarm, but the coroner thought they were so exhausted from working the ranch that both were sleeping too soundly to have been woken by the sound. They died. Jackson became an orphan at age ten. He lost his childhood. And it's all my fault."

Dylan swore inwardly. No way was the death of Rachel's parents her fault. How could she even think that? But she'd been young when they died—just eighteen. Still almost a child herself. She'd probably see the situation through a child's eyes, rather than the eyes of an adult. Of someone with balanced reason and capacity of logic. He knew too well what it was like to create a belief system as a child and to fight to get away from that belief system when it was no longer working.

Rachel's belief system had been broken for some time now, but she hadn't been able to pull away from it. Not yet. And as much as he wanted to tell her she was wrong—dead wrong—now wasn't the time. She wouldn't be open to shifting the paradigm of her beliefs. Not when her son was kidnapped and her brother had a death threat hanging over his head. Not when she was so very vulnerable. Now was the time for him to be supportive, no matter how much he disagreed with this beautiful, amazing woman in his arms.

A sudden shout off in the distance caught his attention. Pulling away from the exterior wall, he lightly stroked Rachel's arm as he craned his neck to see what had caused the ruckus.

One of the TV newscast vans had backed into a bench, was all. But he noted how many newscasters remained next to his truck, presumably waiting to get an exclusive with her. Damn. There was no way he could get her out of town and back home without her encountering microphones shoved in her face. So far the kidnappers weren't aware anyone knew Peter had been kidnapped. And if the reporters had included him in any of their coverage? As far as anyone knew, he was just Rachel's ranch hand, albeit one that acted more like a lover than an employee. Nothing too surprising there. So he was a man comforting a mother worried about her son. It worked with the message they wanted to send. Keeping the ruse that Peter had run away would be of benefit to his team. With the kidnappers thinking the public believed Peter had run away, they could become lax in their actions.

And he knew all about being lax—that's when people can take advantage. And he'd take any advantage he could to get Rachel's son back.

Chapter 19

"Need help getting out of the truck?"

Dylan's voice cut through her mental fog, and she looked about. They were back at her ranch. The late afternoon sun had lowered even more, casting a wide, dark shadow when it filtered through the willow tree.

"No," she murmured. "I can walk on my own."

"Ready to meet with the team?" Dylan asked. "I have a meeting set up—it'll start as soon as we're in the headquarters in the barn."

On the drive, she'd overheard him on the phone with Stacy, filling her in on the latest turn of events. She was invited to the meeting? "Isn't helping find a kidnapped kid completely outside a marshal's job description?" she asked.

Before answering, Dylan hopped out of the truck and came around to her side just as she opened the door. He held out a hand in a silent offer of assistance, which she took, welcoming the warmth of his touch.

"Officially, we're treating this as part of getting Jackson Kincaid back into custody. The FBI handles kidnapping cases—we're here as support. According to Stacy, the FBI has asked us to continue working on the issue until they can show up here."

They walked the few yards to the barn, then entered. Diffused light filtered through the windows, and a few streaks of light illustrated the need to repair holes in the roof. So much work, so little time.

"What do you want from me now?" she asked.

Dylan held open the door to the tack room and gestured for her to sit on the saddle—her makeshift chair. "Just listen. Stacy will fill you in on what we're going to do."

He went to the computer and flicked it on, as well as the monitors. Stacy's face appeared on one, and the other monitors slowly filled up with faces of the other team members. Rachel sat on the saddle and placed her hands on the pommel, the warm leather soothing to the touch. She'd listen, if that was what would get her baby back.

"How are you doing, Rachel?" Stacy asked, compassion in her voice and expression.

Rachel cleared her throat. "This is a nightmare. Tell me you have a plan to get my boy back."

Stacy nodded. "At the moment we're keeping the information that Peter has really been kidnapped to just us and the FBI, in case there are any leaks at the sheriff's office. Everyone is still out looking for Peter, and we're tracking down the leads. We figure George Evans will get one of his underlings to call you with a ransom demand, and we're assuming that ransom demand will be the missing money your brother made off with."

Rachel choked. "But I don't know where the money is. Jax is the only one who knows where the cash is hidden, and he's not even sure where he put it on the property. We won't be able to trade the cash for my son."

Even as she said the words, she saw the confused look Dylan shot her. His confused expression quickly turned into one of laser-eyed focus. And suspicion.

"How do you know that, Rachel?"

"Earlier," she whispered. "He called me on my cell. He told me about the money. Confirmed he escaped from Evans. But he said he didn't know where the money was. Just that he needed to get back to find it so he could keep Peter and me safe."

"And you didn't tell me this because— Damn!" he clipped out. "Never mind." He turned back to Stacy and snapped, "Go on."

Rachel wanted to whimper at the anger on Dylan's face.

But damn it, she was going through hell here. How dare he judge her?

"The FBI has assured us that the money isn't important," Stacy said. "Finding Peter is—and we're going to find Peter before we have to do any kind of exchange. So again, don't worry."

But she would. Not having the money when the ransom call came went against every grain in her body. This didn't feel right. She had started to voice her concerns when Stacy interrupted her.

"I've already got a tap on your phone and can trace

the call when it comes in. You've watched TV and movies—you know the drill. Keep whoever calls on the line for as long as you can. We'll track the call and get a location. Ask to speak to your son. We have a program where we can tell if he's there at the actual site of the phone call, or if he's been patched in to the call. If he's been patched in, we can track that location, too. Remember, ask for proof of life."

Proof of life? Rachel's mind spun and the room seemed to float around her. Her stomach heaved and she fought to hold back the rising need to vomit. Oh, God. No. She reached out and placed her hand on the wall next to her, trying to connect back to the earth. Peter couldn't be dead. Not her sweet, spunky little boy. Dylan's firm hand on her shoulder brought her back to reality. She looked up to catch his gaze with hers.

"My team will do everything we can to get your boy back," he said. "I won't rest until he's in your arms, safe and sound."

The reassurance of his words and tone helped calm her system. He might be angry she didn't tell him about Jax's call, but he was still going to be here for her. She breathed in through her nose, controlling her intake, settling down the carbon dioxide overload that threatened to make her faint.

"Rachel." Stacy's voice interrupted her thoughts. "Keep your phone on you. We expect a call at any time. But we do want you to rest. Dylan, can you get her to take a nap or something?"

"Will do," Dylan said.

Rachel grew aware of the gentle caress he was giving her shoulder. His hand moved up to stroke the back of her neck. She shuddered, leaning back into the warmth of his hand. God, how she wanted his touch.

But she wanted her son back even more.

And to get Peter home safe, she needed to be stronger than she'd ever been before.

Rachel sat on the edge of her bed, wondering how she'd make it through the next few hours. After the meeting with Dylan's team, he'd brought her up to her room and told her to rest while he made her a snack to keep up her strength. She'd kicked off her shoes and propped the pillows up against the headboard so she could look out the French doors to the verdant land below. Nerves had her stomach knotted up. So far she hadn't received a ransom call from George Evans, nor had she heard from Jax. So she had to wait. And wish. Wish that her son was safe. Wish that this all would be over soon, and her life would get back to normal.

But she knew nothing would be normal again. Her life would never be the same.

"Rachel?" Dylan's soft voice came from her doorway.

She looked up to see him leaning on a hip against the doorjamb, one foot hooked over the other, one hand shoved deep in his pocket and the other holding a plate of cheese, crackers and grapes. A deep frown marred his handsome face.

"You okay?" he asked.

"I'm not sure how to answer that," she whispered, glancing away. She fingered the patchwork quilt that lay under her on the bed, tracing a line of hand stitching. Stitching her great-grandmother had made eighty years ago, back in a time when the Dust Bowl was the greatest thing to fear, not murdering, torturing drug dealers who wouldn't hesitate to hold a child in captivity to get what they wanted.

And yet the thick thread of the stitches under her fingertips somehow reassured her. Her great-grandmother Betsy had survived the terrors of seeing her family's ranch decimated by the drought and subsequent dust blizzards and had sewn this quilt by hand as the family had packed up and driven off to a new home in the hill country. Betsy had made it through the death of their entire herd of cattle and the plow horses. Rachel could do the same. She could make it through this day.

She had to.

Dylan entered her room and placed the cheese tray on the dresser, then came to stand before her. This close, his scent penetrated her senses, his body heat caressed her skin. Desire curled around her insides, making her quiver deep in her core. Wetness dampened her panties. Guilt suffused her. Her son was being held by a kidnapper, and here she was, wanting sex. Was it the distraction she needed? Or the strength Dylan exuded?

"Would you like to eat anything?" he asked.

Shaking her head, she patted the quilt, indicating for him to sit next to her. "I know I need to keep up my strength, but I'm not hungry. At least, not for food." She caught her breath in the back of her throat and let the words hang in the air, wondering what Dylan would do with what she'd said. Had she been too brazen? Inappropriate?

He sat next to her, his weight causing the bed to squeak, then took her hand in his, turning it so he could trace the lines of her palm with the tip of his index finger. "That was suggestive, Rachel," he said, not skirting the issue. "Are you sure it's what you want?"

"I can barely breathe, can hardly keep my mind focused on one topic for longer than a few seconds. I think maybe I need the distraction." She waited, hoping her blunt answer hadn't been taken as rude. Or crude.

Dylan let go of her hand and traced his finger up the underside of her arm, curving the arc of the path when he reached her biceps and circled her breast. She caught her breath in her throat, aware of the sudden increase in her heart rate. Without looking at her, he palmed her breast, then leaned down and placed his mouth on her other breast, sucking gently through the thin fabric of her T-shirt and lace bra. Her nipple pebbled under his tongue and a groan fell from her lips.

Soon those groans turned to screams as Dylan gave her exactly what she needed.

Pleasure and a few blessed moments of forgetfulness.

Rachel sucked in deep gulps of air. Enjoying sex had never been an issue for her. She never had problems coming to climax, had never found the act to be a chore. Had always enjoyed herself. But this? This thing that she'd experienced with Dylan? Could she even consider the heady sensation to be sex? No. Just like the past two times, this hadn't been about sex. It was about passion but so much more than that.

"You okay?" Dylan whispered, pulling her to him

in spoon fashion. He kissed her spine and she shuddered.

Okay? That was hardly the word to describe how she felt. A quivering had started inside her belly and had moved upward to her chest, filling her, stretching her, making her feel lighter than air. She was floating. Untethered. Ethereal.

In love.

But she didn't want to be in love with this man. They were like two puzzle pieces from completely different puzzles—they'd never fit together. Ever.

The sun shifted, a shadow falling across the bed and illuminating her phone on the bedstead. As great as sex had been, it still hadn't completely distracted her from the horrendous situation they all were in. She'd been aware even as Dylan stroked her from the inside that her phone remained silent. When would George Evans call and arrange a ransom?

She shifted, pulling away from Dylan's naked body, and checked her cell phone again. Yes, the ringer was on and turned up to the highest volume. Yes, she had all four bars. Yes, the battery was fully charged. And no, she'd not received a ransom call.

How had this happened? How had she gone from being a plain old single mother struggling to make ends meet to a woman whose son had been kidnapped? Tears pricked the back of her eyes, the sensation gritty and painful. How had she failed?

"I just wish I'd done better by Jax and Peter," she said, choking back the unshed tears. "Maybe neither would be in this situation if I'd known what I was doing."

"Growing up is tough. And parenting is tougher.

I get it. But you have to let Peter and Jax make their own mistakes and learn from them."

Irritation crept up her spine. "No. I refuse to believe that. I need to teach them how to not make mistakes. And to do that, I need to guide them."

"What you're talking about is controlling them, Rachel. Not guiding. If your brother or your son is never allowed to make mistakes and suffer the fallout for what they've done, they'll never get that understanding of what works and what doesn't. Don't you get it? You've been so busy protecting them from life and all its pain, and justifying reasons for their failures, that you haven't been teaching them about how to actually live."

"That's not true," she said harshly. "Don't think that just because you have a particular way of looking at the world, that way would work for anyone else's life."

"I don't think you're really hearing me." Frustration laced Dylan's voice. He pulled away and sat up, the bed squeaking loudly in protest at the sudden movement.

The bedsprings, which minutes before had squeaked in response to their passionate lovemaking, now grated in her ears. "I do, though," she responded. "You think I should have just let Jax and Dylan make their own decisions so they could learn through their mistakes. But that's stupid. It was Jax's decision to transport drugs across state lines. I didn't make that decision for him. And it's not like Peter chose to get kidnapped."

"That's interpreting my words literally. I'm trying to point out that if you hadn't taken the blame for the mistakes your brother made as a youth, he'd have learned his lesson by now. Instead, the minute he gets free from Evans's men, instead of going to the police, he heads for this ranch, bringing danger to his sister and nephew for stolen money and giving some story that he doesn't know where he buried it."

Bastard. Rachel barely kept the word from slipping out between her lips. He was blaming her, saying that it was her poor parenting that had resulted in this situation. Shaking, she reached out and grabbed her shirt from where it had ended up stuffed between the slats in her bed's headboard and flung it on.

Eyes narrowed, Dylan watched her cover herself up. "I guess this is your way of telling me you don't want to continue the conversation," he said, standing up and snagging his boxer briefs from off the floor.

"I think maybe you've been angry at your mother for taking the blame for your brother's actions for too long. And I think you're projecting that onto me. And that's not fair."

"My mother accepted blame when it should have been put on my brother's shoulders. Because of that, my brother never learned from his mistakes. She always made excuses for him, always made his actions her responsibility. He never grew up learning how to be a man. So yeah," he said, anger tingeing his voice, "I guess I am projecting that onto you. Because I see you doing the very thing my mother did. The therapists called it enabling, and—"

She laughed harshly, without humor. "Now you're giving me a lecture and therapy? All this, while my brother is out there under a death threat and the very monster capable of killing him is holding my son God knows where? And you're lecturing me on parenting?"

Bile rose in her throat. She fought the building nausea, swallowing hard to keep the acid down. Not long ago, she'd accepted that she was in love with this man. Now she wanted him out of her sight.

Yet the truth was, she *wanted* him in her life. *Needed* him. But they were too different. She couldn't open herself up to being with someone who thought the way Dylan did. In his eyes, Jax would always be a criminal. Peter would always be a recalcitrant kid. She'd always be a poor parent. And she'd never believe the way he did. She refused.

"Rachel, I don't want to fight," Dylan said, his expression fading from anger to compassion. "I'm sorry I said all that. Whether it's true or not doesn't matter at this moment. What matters is that you remain steady and stable and we get your son back. And your brother back into custody, safe and sound."

"I think you need to leave," she said, her voice hollow. She dropped her gaze from his and stared out the window, noting the gentle sway of the willow tree down at the creek. God, what she'd do to see Peter climbing that tree right now. Pain scratched the back of her throat. Yes, she needed to be steady and stable. And to get there, she needed nothing to do with the U.S. Marshal who stood before her, holding her bleeding heart in his hands.

"Are you sure?" he asked quietly.

As an answer, she bent and scooped his pants and shirt up off her floor, then handed the articles of clothing to him. He took the offered clothing with stiff arms, then put them on as she wrapped herself up in a sheet and sat back down on the bed.

"This 'complication' of ours has had its moments, Dylan. I appreciate you helping me get through this by distracting me. But it's time we both admitted it's nothing more than a physical need. I'm done. It's over."

Dylan's chest tightened, a vise squeezing the air out. He shoved his legs into his jeans, then zipped the fly, keeping his gaze fixed on Rachel. She wouldn't look at him, but by the way she held her jaw clenched and her eyes glittered with unshed tears, he knew what she'd said hadn't been easy.

And it hadn't been what was in her heart.

But the complication had increased to the point of being unmanageable. She was a woman determined to control her environment in a misguided attempt at protection. He was a U.S. Marshal—a man assigned to bring in escaped criminals. And one of those criminals was her brother. Rachel was right. Their complication had been fantastic while it lasted, but it was over.

He'd get over it. He'd get over her.

He had to.

Buttoning his shirt, he cleared his throat, catching her attention, although she still wouldn't look at him. "Fine. No more complication. Now it's time to get back to work."

"That's what you call this? You consider this work?" Rachel asked, gesturing to the phone.

The phone that still remained silent. Why hadn't Evans or one of his crew called Rachel yet to demand the money in exchange for her son? He plowed a hand through his hair and said, "It is for me. This is my job."

"It may be your 'job,' but it's my life," she said.

He couldn't argue. "It's about five-thirty. You said your brother will show up around midnight, in about six hours. We have to figure George Evans has people scattered around, looking for your brother. I doubt Evans or his crew know for sure when Jax will turn up, so in that we have an advantage. But I do believe they want your brother—even if they get the money."

"Oh, God," she murmured. "So even if we get Peter back, Jax will still be at risk?"

Her brother was as good as dead, he thought, but kept the words inside his head. Instead, he said, "Eat the cheese and crackers. You need to keep up your energy. I'm going to go downstairs and do some digging online. I have your phone calls doubled to my cell phone, so if you get a call, I'll immediately be on it, even if we aren't in the same room." He knew she needed space—needed to be alone for a while.

"Thank you," she said quietly. The tears that had made her eyes glitter suddenly spilled over, and she made no movement to stop their flow, but instead let them trail down her cheeks.

He fought the urge to kiss the tears away. To cradle Rachel in his arms. To croon that everything would be okay.

He couldn't. He just had to do his job, and hope that he did it well enough to bring her boy back to her. There were no other options.

Chapter 20

With Dylan downstairs in her kitchen, tapping away at his laptop, Rachel had the freedom to act on a plan she'd formed. Stacy had said that the money wouldn't be an issue, but Rachel wasn't counting on that. Money always mattered. And she'd make sure she had as much as she possibly could when the call came.

She'd take control. She'd get her son back.

Within twenty minutes, she'd texted Julia and had set up a quick liquidation plan, thanks to her neighbor Aaron Jacobson. Julia hadn't told Aaron why Rachel needed money, just that she might need quick cash, and soon. Aaron had agreed, and if needed, he'd purchase her entire ranch and all the stock.

With each alpaca worth up to ten thousand dollars and a herd of fifty, that meant a quick five hundred thousand available. Her land—about a thousand acres—was worth an easy million. All it would take was a few quick pushes of the button and Aaron would put one million and a half into her account. She had to hope it wouldn't come to that—hoped that Stacy was right and the money would never come into play—but she felt better about taking control and arranging the contingency plan.

Downstairs, Dylan's deep and smooth voice sounded. Rachel picked up the nearly empty platter—she'd managed to choke down the cheese and grapes but hadn't been able to swallow the dry crackers—and headed to join Dylan. No need for him to know of her plan to sell off her land—which was why she'd texted instead of talking on the phone. She supposed he'd be angry with her for not informing him of her plans, but at this point, she couldn't see how the action would compromise her son's safety. A contingency plan was just that, right?

She caught Dylan's attention when she entered the kitchen. He was sitting at the kitchen table, his computer tablet in front of him and a half-eaten sandwich on a plate off to the side. He quickly clicked off the tablet, then stood and took the platter from her hands. Turning to the sink, he asked, "How are you holding up?"

"Wobbly," she answered honestly. She placed her cell phone down on the table and stared at it, willing the damn thing to ring.

It was several minutes later that the phone rang, and a wave of pain made its way up her spine. She looked quickly at Dylan. "Do I answer it now?" she asked, almost breathless.

He nodded, then quickly pulled out his own phone from his front pocket and placed it to his ear. "Give it two more rings. I'm already connected—he'll never know I'm on the line. Remember, pretend you don't know your son has been kidnapped, pretend law enforcement isn't involved and, above all, keep the person on the line as long as you can."

And ask for proof of life, she mentally added, sitting down on the kitchen chair as her knees threatened to buckle under her. Goose bumps raised the hairs on her arms—as if the kitchen had suddenly gone cold. But that wasn't it—fear for her son was sending her into shock. *Keep it under control,* she reminded herself. She focused on the cracked tile Jax had promised to repair so long ago. How convoluted she'd thought life was back then, back before her brother had made his huge mistake. She never could have imagined this scenario, though. Never could have anticipated how horribly worse things could have become.

The phone rang again and she brought her attention back to Dylan, who nodded. Time to act. She pressed the button to connect the call, then as cheerfully as she could muster, answered the phone with a breezy hello.

"Rachel Kincaid?" a man's hoarse voice sounded across the line. When she acknowledged her name, he continued. "We have your kid."

Delay, Dylan mouthed to her from across the table.

"Oh!" she exclaimed, forcing brightness into her tone. "You must be one of the volunteers! Thank you so much!" Across the table, Dylan was making a drawn-out signal with his hands. She continued jabbering, working to fill the time with inane words.

Anything to keep the call going and help Dylan's team track the call. "He's not really a bad kid, you know, just a bit rambunctious, and impetuous. Doesn't really think before taking action. I suppose it's the ADHD—or maybe it's just being a boy. Where is he? Can I meet you somewhere?"

"Shut up," the man said harshly.

"Excuse me?" she said loudly, pretending affront. "Listen, you might want to get on your high horse and think I'm a bad mother for raising a kid who would run away and get an entire community upset, but that doesn't mean you get to tell me to shut up. Just put my son on the line and I'll figure out a way to get him back home." She glanced at Dylan, who smiled with lips pressed firmly together and held up two fingers. She'd done fine, but he needed two more minutes to get a trace on the phone.

"Your brat didn't run away," the man said. "He's been kidnapped."

A gasp tore its way out of her throat, and her heart-beat thundered in her head, blocking out sound. She struggled to remain upright. She no longer had to pretend—now she could be the panicked mother she truly was. "What do you mean? Is this some kind of joke? Why would you kidnap Peter, of all kids?"

"You have something we want, Ms. Kincaid. We'll give you your kid in exchange."

The money Jax had stolen. One million dollars.

"How much do you want?" she asked dully.

"Oh, we don't want money," the man said, with a sneer in his voice.

She frowned. They didn't want money? Wasn't this what everything had been about—chasing her off her land, trying to run her off the road, kidnapping Peter? Hadn't all this been put into place so George Evans could get his money back? "I don't understand," she said quietly.

"Your brother stole from me, Ms. Kincaid."

The man had used the word *me*. That meant she was speaking directly to George Evans—not even one of his flunkeys. "What did Jax steal from you? And how can I get something my brother stole back to you? Why don't you want money?"

"Stop asking questions. I don't just want the money your brother stole from me. I want the money and your brother. And you have twenty-four hours to get him and the money to me, or something very bad will happen to your kid."

"Peter!" she cried out. Sobs formed in the back of her throat. "Please don't hurt my son," she managed to choke out.

"Call the cops and the kid's dead."

An empty threat? Or the truth? Those members of this man's gang had already been tortured to death— an order made by the very man who held her son. Dylan made a violent gesture, catching her attention.

Oh, yes, proof of life. She needed to get herself under control and keep George Evans on the line— she needed proof that Peter was safe. She shoved the painful sobs down, deep, and willed her voice to work. "I won't go to the cops. But put Peter on the line. I'm not talking to you any more until I hear my son's voice."

But all she heard was empty space. George Evans had ended the call.

Without allowing her to hear her son's voice.

* * *

After the call from George Evans, Dylan managed
to convince a shaky Rachel that they needed to act
normal—whatever that might be. Evans might have
members of his crew spying on Rachel's ranch, so
he continued to play the part of Rachel's ranch hand
and went outside to dig a grave for the two alpacas.

Rachel went with him.

"You don't have to be here, you know," he said to
a quiet Rachel, who sat on a boulder next to where
he was digging a large hole in the earth. They were
about two hundred yards from the barn—in view of
almost any angle of the surrounding area. He'd made
sure both their cell phones had the full number of
bars, and he'd tucked his computer tablet into a cloth
bag Rachel had brought along.

"I know," she said, quietly. "But I want to be here
when you bury them. They were my responsibility,
and I failed them somehow. Just like I failed Josiah."

"Don't go there, Rachel. Their deaths were not
your fault."

She closed her eyes and shook her head. "With everything going on, Josiah's funeral has been put off
too long. It isn't right. I need to make sure the services are held in the next few days. I just hope…" Her
face crumpled as she no doubt imagined other funer-
als she might have to attend if their plan to get Peter
back safely didn't work.

"Rachel," he said, about to throw down the shovel
and go to her, but she shook her head and blinked
her tears away."

"No. No! You have to finish what you're doing.

And I have to be strong. We're going to get through this okay. We all are."

As they stared at each other, Rachel gave him a trembling smile. He nodded. "Believe it, Rachel." Then he got back to digging.

Soon the day had faded and evening was almost upon them. The sound of crickets surrounded them, and in the distance, frogs croaked out a sonorous song.

Under any other circumstances, the setting would be considered bucolic…beautiful. Romantic, even.

But not now. Not when the woman he loved was faced with the fact that she might never see her son again. His heart twisted up inside his chest, the ache he felt for Rachel making it almost impossible for him to breathe all of a sudden. Angrily, he shoved his foot down hard on the shovel, then lifted and flung the load of dirt up out of the pit and onto the pile nearby. He continued to work and had just finished burying the alpacas when Rachel's cell phone rang.

"Jax?" Rachel fought to keep her voice from trembling.

"I saw you on television, Rachel. Oh, God, is it true? Did they find him?" Her brother's voice sounded ravaged by fear and grief.

Nausea tore at her gut. Knowing George Evans had her son was one thing, telling her brother his nephew—her son—had been kidnapped was another. She wasn't sure she could make her throat work. Next to her, Dylan gave her a reassuring look. "Peter's been kidnapped."

"Oh, God! No!"

"Those people you got involved with?" she continued, "They know he's your nephew. They grabbed him at his grandparents' place and called me just a little while ago."

"They want the money," Jax said dully.

She hesitated before plowing forward. "They want you and the money, Jax. They want to trade Peter for you."

Silence met her statement. Worry added its unwanted presence to the nerves that were twisting her innards in knots. Why wasn't Jax saying anything? "Jax?" Her voice came out shaky. Uncertain.

"I'm so sorry," he finally said in a whisper. "I'd never have knowingly done anything to put you and Peter in danger. These people are bad, Rachel. Really bad. Once I get them the hidden cash, this will be all over. I'll trade myself for Peter, don't worry."

"But how?" George Evans hadn't told her how to exchange her brother for her son. And even though Dylan's team had a fix on the general location of the call Evans had made, no one knew for certain yet if the man was still at that location or if he'd moved on already. No one knew where Peter was.

She couldn't let Jax know about Dylan or the other marshals currently spying on the property. As much as she hated admitting it to herself, there was a part of her that didn't quite trust her brother fully.

"They'll find me. I promise, Rachel, that I won't tell them where I hid the money until Peter is safely back with you."

Wait—what did Jax mean, "tell them"? Didn't he have to go out to the property line and figure out where he'd buried the cash?

Realization hit. Her brother had known the location of the money all along.

"Oh, God," she breathed out, then clapped a hand over her own mouth. Her brother had lied to her. Had he actually run from Evans's men because he was afraid for his life, or had he run because he wanted to get to the money before George Evans could pry the location out of him? Anger spread through her, setting her limbs on fire. Jax wasn't the innocent victim she'd made him out to be. Dylan, with his caustic comments and jaded opinion of criminals, had pegged her brother more accurately than she.

What a fool she'd been.

All that money and time wasted on Julia's attempts to get Jax out on appeal. All that anguish Rachel had spent on thinking she'd not protected her brother enough. All the heartbreak thinking her brother was an innocent dupe—it had all been based on a lie.

Because her brother sure as hell knew what he'd been getting himself into when he took those drugs across state lines. And he sure as hell knew what he wanted when he ran from George Evans's men.

Jax wanted the money—for himself.

"Rachel?" her brother's voice sounded over the line, the same fear and worry apparent now as had been in his voice the day he called her at college to tell her their mom and dad were dead in their bed.

The sound of childlike fear in Jax's voice, reminding her of his innocent youth, just about broke her. Yes, Dylan was right—her brother was a criminal, and needed to pay his debt to society. But she was also right—Jax, as flawed as he was, was still her brother. Still a good person inside.

The fact that he was willing to sacrifice himself for her son proved the point. If he spoke the truth.

"Rachel, can you hear me?" Jax asked again.

"I'm here," she managed to get out.

"There's something else I need to ask you. I was hiding out behind the feed store just before you called and overheard Aaron Jacobson talking to someone on the phone. He was joking about loaning out Ginger to a city slicker—a guy pretending to be a bird-watcher. Aaron said that the man was really a U.S. Marshal. He figured the dude was out looking for me."

Rachel held her breath and looked frantically at Dylan, whose expression had gone grim. If her brother knew he'd go back to prison after the exchange, would he come back to the property? Would he risk his freedom for the life of her son?

"You aren't saying anything," Jax continued, his voice small. "I'm guessing that's the case, then, and the marshals are there, scoping out the place, waiting for me to come home."

"Jax," she whispered, anguish tearing at her chest. If her brother knew the feds were there, he'd run, and then her son— No! She couldn't think that. Couldn't bear to think of what could happen to Peter if her brother didn't cooperate.

"Sis, I'll do it," Jax said quickly. "I'll trade myself for Peter. But if the marshals are there, let me talk to them. I need to make sure they won't put me in custody until after you get Peter back, okay? I promise—I won't let anything happen to your boy. I—I—I—" He sputtered to a stop, then with a ragged breath, said, "I love him, too."

Dylan shifted, coming closer. He reached out a hand in a silent gesture for her to give him the phone.

Her stomach knotted and she began breathing in and out rapidly. Dare she trust him?

"Rachel," Dylan said, his voice a low murmur. "Trust me. I can help. This is what your brother wants, after all."

She looked up and held his gaze with hers. His eyes were soft, glistening, warm. Inside her mind, a sense of calm began to overtake the panic. Her heartbeat slowed and her breath came out in even puffs. She'd trusted this man with her son's life. Had trusted Dylan with her body, even. Had been prepared to trust him to bring her brother back into custody safely. What was different about now?

Nothing, really, she realized. Dylan was still the honorable man she'd fallen for. A man who did his duty, no matter what. He wasn't out to do her brother wrong—he was out to save the boys she loved. Peter. Jackson. A sob caught in the back of her throat. She trusted Dylan with Peter's life—she could trust him with the life of her brother. Silently she handed him the phone.

"Jackson, this is U.S. Marshal Dylan Rooney," he said, his voice even but a flashing pulse of tension shooting rhythmically through his jaw. "First, I want to commend you for doing right by your nephew. Second, I want you to know that your sister loves you very much. She's done everything she can to protect you from going back to prison, and she recognizes what a huge sacrifice you're making."

Rachel couldn't hear what her brother was saying

to Dylan, but she could see Dylan's gaze flicker, his focus shifting from one point of the room to the other.

"We need to work together to come up with a plan, Jax," Dylan continued, his calm voice soothing. He cast his gaze at Rachel. "Hold on a second, Jax. I want to keep your sister out of this. This is between you and me."

"No!" Rachel exclaimed. "This is about my son. I have to be involved. Don't kick me out!" Her pulse pounded in her ears. How dare Dylan tell her he didn't want her involved? Didn't he understand what this meant to her?

"Rachel, you need to trust me. This is my job— getting Jax in custody, yes, but doing so in a way that there's no harm done to anyone is my priority. And I need to feel free to make whatever decisions need to be made without you here. God," he swore, wiping a hand across his face, "I can't think when you're around, Rachel. And I will not, I repeat, I will not compromise your son or your brother. You need to let me work with Jax alone."

Emotions made the inside of her chest swell. He couldn't concentrate with her around? The way he'd said it, with the mouthpiece covered so Jax couldn't hear, told her it was because of how he felt in his heart, and not because she was an irritation. He loved her— he'd told her so.

If only she could allow herself to love him back.

If only there wasn't a chasm the size of the Texas Panhandle between them.

But if giving him room to breathe, to think, was what it took to get her son back, she'd give him all of Texas if that was what he needed. Yes, she trusted him. Trusted the lawman. And it wasn't because she had to—because he was her only hope in finding her boy again. It was because she believed in him. Believed he'd get her boy home safe…even as he slapped cuffs on her brother.

She leaned in close so her brother could hear her voice over Dylan's phone. "I trust Marshal Rooney, Jax," she said. "You need to, too. Do what he says." She pulled back and looked full-on at Dylan. "He's in your hands now," she whispered, then fled.

Chapter 21

Dylan found Rachel down at the creek, sitting cross-legged on the wooden footbridge that went over the shallow depths. She was skipping stones across the lightly burbling surface. Nearby, a bullfrog sounded a mating call—a sound impossibly deep for something that small. Dylan found himself suddenly experiencing a tug inside himself, from a place in his heart he didn't even know existed.

God, he'd miss this place when he returned to California.

He'd miss the hill country in Texas, with its impossibly brilliantly painted bluebonnets, with its chirruping crickets and frogs. He'd miss the scent of the creek and the sound the rushes made as the breeze tickled down the creek bed. Miss the dappled patterns the willow branches made in the new green grass as they swayed in time. He'd miss the fluff ball alpacas, with their big dark eyes so full of innocence and wisdom. He'd miss Peter and his smart-ass ways.

Most of all, he'd miss Rachel.

How was it the widow had slid under his skin when he wasn't watching? How was it she practically lived inside him? How could he bear to cuff her brother, put him in the transport vehicle and drive off into the sunset...without Rachel?

They'd been at odds throughout all this. He realized, though, that when it got down to it, he'd been obstinate in how he viewed her. In controlling the lives of her brother and son, in not allowing them to make their own decisions and ultimately their own mistakes, she hadn't been acting as his mother had all those years ago with his brother. No, that had been his own interpretation of Rachel's actions. Yes, she probably could have used a less tight leash with both Jax and Peter. Could have let them make their way into the world. And maybe, just maybe, if she had, none of them would be in this position.

But he couldn't fault her. It had been Jackson's choice to get involved in drug dealing—that wasn't Rachel's fault. In trying to protect her boys, she'd been acting as a mama bear—furious and protective and full of courage.

In no way had she acted like his mother—passive and fearful.

Hell, he'd pegged her wrong since the beginning. Had set up a barbed-wire fence between the two of them from the start. And now it was too late for them to make anything of the passion that existed between them. He could apologize, sure, but that wouldn't be enough. Would never be enough. Rachel would always see him as the big bad U.S. Marshal who sent her brother back to prison.

And even if she didn't see him that way, that was how he'd see himself. He'd let his past interfere with his present. There was no way out now.

He stepped closer and Rachel tipped her head up, glancing at him. She paused midchuck, then turned her head away and resumed skipping stones.

"Can I ask if you and Jax came up with a plan?" she said.

Dylan sat down beside her, letting his feet dangle from the footbridge. He leaned forward until he could see their reflections in the water—him, tight and corded, and Rachel grim-faced and with a determined set to her jaw. He fought the temptation to reach out and stroke her hair and instead tucked his hands under his thighs, sitting on them. "You can ask…"

"But you can't tell me," she said, continuing his unspoken statement.

"It's better that way, Rachel. The team has a plan in place, and we don't want you in on it. We may need to do things that…" He couldn't finish the sentence. Couldn't so much as hint as to the plan he, Jax and his team had come up with. Had to trust that Jax would do the right thing.

And he did.

Trust Jax, that is. Strange, how he'd come to this remote ranch out in Texas seeing him only as a criminal, and now? Now he knew Jax to be a loving brother. A self-sacrificing uncle. A man of compassion and intelligence. Yes, Jackson had done wrong, and no, he wasn't the paragon of virtue the way Rachel thought, but he wasn't a bad seed, either.

"I understand," she said quietly, then dropped a stone down into the water instead of skipping it across the surface. They both watched as ripples radiated outward, each one strong and forceful at the apex, then softening and finally fading away the farther away they moved from the point of contact.

With evening fast approaching, Dylan could barely make out the ripples, could barely see his and Rachel's reflections in the water. In the distance, an owl hooted, the sound startling Rachel, who jumped.

"Time to go inside," he said, standing.

When he reached down to offer his hand to her, she looked at it for a moment, as if contemplating the meaning of placing her hand in his. Of touching him. Of allowing him to get close. Then, deliberately, she placed her hand in his.

The moment their hands made contact, electricity bolted from his hand through his arm, straight through to his heart. He pulled her up suddenly, before she could back away, and then held her there, pressed up close against his body, her heat blending with his, her breath on his face.

Oh, God. He knew better. Knew he shouldn't be getting this close. Shouldn't be about to kiss Rachel Kincaid. But he did, anyway. He kissed her. Long and slow and sweet, the sound of her mewling in the back of her throat carrying him along a river of desire. Sweeping him along in a current of heat and want and need and—

Rachel's phone rang. She pulled back, dazed, then fumbled with the pocket of her jeans, working her phone out of the tight constraints. By the time she held her phone in the palm of her hand, he already had his out and was ready to hit the button to connect his phone to hers.

"I don't recognize the number," she said, her voice shaky. "What do I do?"

"Answer it. Could be George Evans on a burner. Pick up the call on the next ring. I'll be on the line with you, okay?"

She swallowed, the long column of her neck going tight with worry, but clicked on the call on the next ring. He did so as well, and placed the phone to his ear. Stacy would be listening in, too, and that reassured him.

"Mom?" a small voice came over the line.

"Oh, God! Peter!" Rachel cried out. Her body shook violently. Dylan put an arm around her and held her steady. "Where are you? Are you safe? Does the bad man still have you?"

"Mom, I'm fine. I mean, yeah, I've been kidnapped and the guy's a jerk. He gave me a peanut butter and jelly sandwich on whole wheat bread, the kind with those stupid nuts. And he doesn't even have any video games. Um…hey, is Dylan there?"

Odd. The boy's voice had gone from tight but a bit laconic to high pitched when he asked for Dylan. What was that about?

"I'm here," Dylan said. "Peter, are you alone? Can you tell us where you are?"

"The jerk is right here with me. He wants me to tell you something really, really important, but I told him I only would if I— Ow!"

"Peter!" Rachel screamed into the phone, her face going white at the sound of her son in pain.

"I'm fine," Peter said, his voice tight. "I promised I'd tell you his message but only if I got to thank Dylan for teaching me to shoot the BB gun the other day."

Rachel frowned. "Peter, when did you—"

Instantly Dylan reached out and pulled her phone away. She gasped, staring at his violent actions.

"What are you doing?" she ground out. "That's my son!"

He shook his head, narrowing his eyes at her and trying to convey the intensity of the moment through his eyes. She hadn't understood her kid's message. Peter had just given them two clues and Rachel was about to blow it. He brought his own phone back up to his mouth and said as calmly as he could, "Happy to teach you anytime, kid."

"Yeah, maybe next time we can do it in the dark."

Another clue.

"You got it. I appreciate you being a man. And for thinking the way you do." He could only hope Peter understood his cryptic way of conveying that he'd understood the boy's message. "Now, what was it the man wanted you to tell me?" He could hear murmuring in the background, and hoped to all that was holy that Stacy was getting a trace on the call.

"He says you know what he wants. Uncle Jax. You have until midnight tonight, or—"

The call cut off.

And Rachel fell apart.

"Oh, God, no!" Rachel heard herself screaming and realized she was pounding Dylan's hard chest with her fists as the tears streaming down her face blinded her. "What kind of sick bastard would do this? Kidnap a child and threaten to…to…" The rest of the words wouldn't come out of her mouth. But Dylan had to know what she was saying—he had to. How he could stand there, calm, rubbing his hands in circles on her back, seemed almost illogical when her own hands were shaking no matter how tightly she clenched them and her knees threatened to give way under her like the banks of a flooded creek.

And yet even as she didn't understand Dylan's emotionless state, she craved his strength. Craved his comfort. Slowly the sobs racking her body subsided, until she was left emotionally drained, sniffling against Dylan's warm chest. She fought to gain her senses, to make her mind work. She had to figure out what to do now—but no plan came forward no matter how hard she scrabbled her mind.

"Why didn't you let me talk to him?" she asked, her voice hitching.

"Rachel, there are parts of my job I can't share with you. And I know this is tough. Awful. Horrible, even. But I need your strength now. I know you have it— I've watched you over the last few days. You're strong."

"It's here," she said, knowing she needed to stand on her own two feet but not yet backing away from his warm embrace. "I'm here. I can function. Just tell me what you need to save my son." She paused, then added, "But I'm not sure my legs are working right."

Suddenly he swept her up in his arms, apparently uncaring of the fact that they'd essentially ended any possibility of happiness together hours earlier. There might be no future there, but she needed him, and he'd responded.

Within minutes he'd followed the path from the creek back up to the house, and settled her down on the ancient leather couch in the living room. There, she curled her feet under her as he wrapped her up in a faded and frayed quilt, made by one of her pioneer ancestors. He squatted and sat on his heels in front of her. She noted he seemed careful not to touch her. She'd gone stiff when he scooped her up but hadn't resisted him carrying her. He'd gotten the message she was trying to send him, though—it was okay for him to touch her if she needed the help, but not in any romantic way. That was over and done, and she needed to put it behind her in order to get her son.

But there seemed to be nothing she could do to get Peter. Nothing. She felt helpless—without any control.

"You okay?" he asked.

She nodded but kept her gaze fixed to the floor in front of her, unable to look at him. No, of course she wasn't okay. She was powerless—the sensation ate at her. Clawed around inside her, twisting up her insides. She'd already set up the sale of her land and assets, but money wasn't what George Evans wanted. There was nothing else for her to do.

But wait.

"Stacy was patched into that call, too, and she's probably already doing her thing, trying to trace the call, but I should go into the tack room and connect with the team, anyway."

"I understand."

"You okay here on your own? Want me to get

someone to take you to stay with your friend Julia while we...wait?"

"No." The fewer people involved the better. "You should go," she said abruptly. "I'm counting on you. We all are. Fix this, Dylan." The harshness of her voice surprised her, but when she cast a glance at Dylan, he seemed unfazed. How many times had he experienced something like this? she had to wonder. As a marshal, he was tasked to apprehend fugitives, not placate panicking mothers of kidnap victims. But he seemed to take everything in stride—even this.

A muscle on the side of his face flickered, and he stood. "I'll be in the barn. And, Rachel? You can do this. I know waiting must be incredibly hard for you right now, but that's the best thing you can do for your son. Wait, and let us handle this."

She watched him leave, a sense of calm settling down the urgency that had been churning inside her. Dylan was right. It wasn't that she had nothing to do—it was that what she must do was nothing. The sensation was foreign. Alien. After years of being the sole provider, the decision maker, the one holding the reins of her brother and son's lives, she now had to let go and trust others.

Her breath caught in her throat, and her heart fluttered in her chest—not from panic over the situation, but over knowing she trusted Dylan Rooney completely.

"Listen up," Dylan said to the several screens in the makeshift office in the tack room. All of his team members were on one of the screens, anxious faces gazing back at him. "We can't blow this. This comes down to trusting two people who haven't proven to be very trustworthy in the past, who have issues with law enforcement. Plus one of those people is a ten-year-old kid. The other person is the escaped fugitive we've been tasked to bring back into custody. And he knows we're after him. But this is all we've got, and that kid's life hangs in the balance."

"You sure we can trust these two?" Eric asked, worry etching his forehead. "Especially Jackson Kincaid—he's probably aware Evans is out to kill him. We already know George Evans is fully capable of killing a kid—after all, he'd had his own crew members tortured and killed when they couldn't deliver."

Dylan grimaced. Hell. He'd been in tough situations before, but this? Trying to rescue Peter—a boy he'd grown to admire in just a few days, a boy whose mother he loved? This bordered on impossible. He shoved the panic churning about in his stomach down low, forcing it away. No time for panic. No room for error.

"Uh, Dylan?" Stacy said.

He refocused, cleared his throat and said, "Thankfully Evans had the kid call with the ransom demand. From what I understood the kid was saying, he can escape once it gets dark, and he wants us to find him. I already know where—at the spring where we found the ranch hand's murdered body."

"You got that from the kid while Evans was right next to him?" Stacy asked, her skepticism clear by how she cocked one eyebrow.

"Kid's smart," he responded. "Really smart. Even his own mother didn't hear what he was really saying. He said I taught him how to shoot a BB gun—a clear indication that what he was saying was a message to me. I never taught him how to shoot. But I did see him shooting it by the spring. Now we just have to wait until dark."

"He's got to be close by," Stacy said, "if he's going to make it to the spring."

"That's what's so great about the kid's message— we can implement the plan we set up with Jax more securely once we know Peter is safe. I figure Evans probably has him stashed on the neighboring property, but we have no clue where. This is Texas—properties are thousands of acres. We have to wait for the kid to come to us before we get Jax involved. There's no way I trust Evans to turn over Peter after he gets Jax." Dylan turned to look at the computer screen with Eric's face on it. "You got men in the trees out at the spring yet?" At Eric's nod, he added, "And what about the bulletproof vest—you put that in the cache site where Jax can pick it up?"

"Vest is at the site, along with a burner phone with our numbers plugged in, and vice versa. The intel Jax passed on to you was right—there's an underground tunnel from during the Mexican-American war days that leads from the cliffs down under the field and comes out just near the house. He'll pick up the vest and phone and gun at the start of the tunnel, then will come out at the base and wait for our call. He assures us the tunnel is traversable—guess we'll have to take his word for it."

There was a lot of trust going on for a man who'd spent time behind bars. Dylan shoved his hand in his hair and blew out a breath. "No other options. We need Jax as close to the house as we can get, and we need him in cell range."

"Sir, are you sure you don't want to let Rachel Kincaid know what's going on? After all, it's her son we're in the middle of rescuing. And we're not, you know, the FBI. This isn't what we're trained for." Stacy's voice held respect but came out tight and worried.

Damn FBI. The team they'd sent had been waylaid when their private jet blew a tire partway down the runway. Because of the strewn rubber and steel mesh scattered about the tarmac, the runway had been closed. Although the FBI had been in constant contact with Stacy once they'd all learned of the kidnapping, their "help" hadn't been all that helpful.

"We can't involve Rachel," he said. "Not in this, at least. She has a habit of controlling the situation out of an attempt to help. We can't have that— We need to trust our training, our judgment and our instincts. Also, it's possible that she could react the wrong way, and if Evans is watching when we 'give' him Jackson, she might give the game away. She needs to stay in the dark."

"I just hope you're right about what you say the kid was trying to tell you," Stacy said. "And I hope you're right about Jackson Kincaid."

So did he. Everything that mattered in the world now rested on the shoulders of a criminal.

Chapter 22

Rachel busied herself in the house, doing nothing, besides tidying up a few dishes, answering emails about her alpacas and tallying receipts for her recent wool sales. Three hours had passed slowly, punctuated by the solemn ticktock of the hall clock. Night had fallen hours ago, and yet Dylan remained in the barn, presumably making arrangements to get her son back. And to save her brother.

Now, all the puttering she could force herself to do thoroughly completed, she sat on the bench at the kitchen table and sipped a cup of Earl Grey tea. The warm drink wasn't enough to keep her from shuddering, even though the house was warm. Two nights ago the temperatures had been nippy. That was springtime in Texas's hill country, though. Once the sun warmed the land, the land retained the heat at night. The cattle and alpacas would be comfortable from now on until autumn dropped the temperatures back down. No need for a barn for Aaron Jacobson's pregnant cattle. She wondered what he'd done with those who'd been close to calving since he'd lost the use of the pasture with the larger barn because of the vandalism.

Oh, God. She sat upright, worried excitement shooting adrenaline through her body. She knew where Peter was being kept. No wonder Dylan had pulled her off the call when Peter appeared to be lying. Her son wasn't fabricating some story. No, he'd been giving them clues. Clues where he was, what he'd be doing. Dylan had recognized her son's attempts, even when she hadn't.

She ran through Peter's words in her mind. If she had the clues Peter had given pieced together correctly, he was being held in a location close enough to get to the spring where they'd found Josiah's body. Somehow he had information that made her believe he could get away sometime in the dark. He'd surreptitiously informed Dylan where the marshals could find him after he escaped.

And she knew where that location was. Where he was being held.

But the question was, did Dylan know, too?

Dylan entered the house and was almost bowled over by a wide-eyed Rachel. "Steady," he said, holding her by the shoulders when she stumbled after charging into him. "Don't go outside now. We have everything in place."

"I know where they're keeping Peter!" she exclaimed.

He propelled her backward and kicked the door shut with his foot. His team assumed Evans and his crew were now on the property, watching their every move. The last thing they needed was a panicked Rachel trying to take control and blowing the whole operation.

"What do you mean you know where they're keeping him?" he asked.

"You thought Jax caused that stampede, to get me off the property so he could get the money without being seen by even me."

He didn't deny it.

"But it was George Evans, I'm sure of it. You marshals all knew where Jax was headed and set up your own sting operation. Why wouldn't Evans have done the same? And I know where he would have hid out— or where he would have stationed people. Aaron Jacobson's barn, the one in the pasture that had the fence line cut."

He froze. "Are you sure?"

"It's where Peter used to hide out, before I figured out it was his go-to place. Peter knows the place inside and out— If Evans and his crew are holding him there, he knows how to escape. He told you he was going to escape, right? That's what he was saying when you tore the phone from my hand. Don't deny it—I know it's true."

Instead of responding to Rachel, he pulled out his phone from his pocket. Instantly Stacy's face appeared on his screen. "You get that?" he asked.

"Got it and on it already," she said, her gaze focused on her own computer screen and the sound of her fingers hitting the keyboard coming through clearly. "Eric's routing a few marshals out there—don't worry, they'll be in silent mode. These guys are good. You and the farm girl make a great team, by the way."

He cast a quick glance back at Rachel. Yes, they did make a great team.

He clicked off the call with Stacy.

"You wired my place?" Rachel asked.

He nodded. "The day before. The whole house, actually. Stacy and the rest of the team have full access."

"You didn't need a warrant?"

Probably. Maybe. He'd been invited onto the property, though, and Rachel knew he was out to apprehend her brother. When bad things kept happening, he'd added the extra safety features.

"Rachel, things are going to happen suddenly now. I need you to trust that I'm doing the right thing, okay?"

"You're not going to tell me the plan?"

"No. After, I'll explain why."

"Just get my son back safe and make sure that bastard doesn't torture and kill my brother. That's all I ask."

"You know I can't promise anything. I won't lie to you and give you false hope. All I can do is tell you my team is good. Solid. We know what we're doing. Trust me with this plan."

A sudden rustling outside told him the plan already started.

Rachel turned and gaped at the figure outside on the porch. "Jax!" The word came out hollow, almost silent.

Dylan reached out and grabbed her arms again,

holding her in place. "You can't go to him, Rachel. Do you understand?"

"No!" she cried, twisting to get out of his grip. "I don't understand. Where's my son? Jax can't trade himself without Peter being present. Are your people out at the barn yet? Are they?" The last sentence had been ripped from her lungs and thrown in his face.

He hated himself for doing what he was about to do but forced the word from his mouth. "No."

"Jax! Jax!" she screamed again.

Her brother turned to look at her but remained where he was on the porch, at the very tip where it jutted out and was visible from the north, west and east. Jax, his face so very young, his stance so vulnerable that Dylan could see why his sister had fought to protect him for so long, gave Rachel a soft, sweet smile and tipped his head to the side.

As if he were saying he was sorry.

As if he were saying goodbye.

Rachel sobbed, her mouth going wide but no sound coming out. Dylan's phone rang, and he let go of her, whispering, "Stay still" even as he clicked the call on.

On the other end of the line, Stacy confirmed what he'd hoped to hear. Had needed to hear. It was time.

"Go!" he shouted, and hoped that in time, Rachel would forgive him for what he'd just done.

Chapter 23

Rachel couldn't seem to move, and instead watched helplessly, her gaze firmly fixed to that of her brother, as marshals swarmed the porch. Men and women in tactical gear had materialized from the shadows around the house and were now training their weapons on her brother.

Who stood stock-still, still smiling at her. She knew that smile. It was the sweet one, the smile he used only when looking at her or Peter. It was the same smile he used to have when their mother gave him a snuggly hug, or their father patted him on the back and told him job well done. It was Jax's smile. And she loved him for it.

"Get behind me!" Dylan shouted, grabbing her by the arm and propelling her backward to block her with his body.

She lost visual contact with Jax as she stumbled

and almost came to her knees. Gaining her balance, she peered from behind Dylan's wide shoulders, visually searching for her brother again. There. He still stood on the edge of the porch the way he had just a moment before, but now there was something in his hands. Something small and shiny and black.

Oh, God, no.

Jax had a gun.

And was raising it. Pointing it. Squeezing the trigger.

A percussive boom rent the air and suddenly her brother was jerking in time and space and her world was falling apart.

She collapsed, hitting the tile hard, a sharp edge gouging into her knee. The tile Jax had promised to fix the day before he'd taken off for California to transport heroin. On hands and knees, she shook, sobbing, aware of the blood trickling from her knee and blooming, coating the broken tile red.

No. Her brother had so much to live for. Why would he have chosen to die—to shoot at law enforcement? He had to have known he'd be shot dead if he so much as raised a gun at one of the marshals. Didn't he know what pain he'd be leaving behind by making that choice? Had he felt so trapped he thought death was his only escape?

And what about Peter?

Jax could not possibly have given up on his nephew. She couldn't believe that.

She reached up and grabbed the kitchen table, the worn wood warm under her cold fingers. With effort, she pulled herself to standing, then tried to push past a silent Dylan.

"I can't let you go out there," he said quietly.

Outside, marshals buzzed around, placing Jax's limp form in a black body bag. Rachel gagged. What kind of sick bastards brought a body bag to a kidnap exchange?

"Why did you have to shoot him?" she railed at him. "That was suicide by cop. He felt cornered. Trapped. As if he had no way out. Why didn't you convince him he'd be safe?"

"You'll understand soon," he said. "My task was to apprehend your brother. But my first priority was making sure your son came home safe."

"Right," she spat out. "And how'd that turn out? Peter is still in the clutches of a torturer, and my brother's dead!"

"Rooney!" a male voice called from outside on the porch. Eric. "You're needed—now!"

Rachel couldn't believe Dylan was walking away from her. He pulled open the door and shouldered his way past a couple of marshals in field jackets to join a marshal on the corner of the porch. She recognized the man as Eric, one of Dylan's team. His stupid team. His incompetent team. Why had she trusted them? They'd killed her brother. Their actions might even kill her son, if Peter wasn't dead already.

Somehow she made her feet move. Made her legs work. And followed Dylan out to the porch. Why? She didn't know. She simply couldn't believe this was over. Couldn't fathom her brother was dead and her son was God knows where. Didn't know if Peter was alive or dead.

"We found him," Eric said to Dylan in a hushed voice. "He was right where you said he'd be."

Rachel crept closer, her heartbeat so hard and pounding it echoed in her ears, but she knew what she'd heard—they'd found Peter. But alive?

"In the barn on the neighboring property?" Dylan asked.

"Yep. The team's bringing him here now." Eric nodded at the SUV that had just arrived.

Oh, God, he had to be alive. Rachel hugged the side of the house, trying to stay out of sight, but headlights swept the area, illuminating her. Dylan noticed she had come outside and was standing next to him.

"Rachel, go back inside," he demanded.

"No," she managed to get out. "I want to see Peter."

"You don't understand, that's not—"

But Rachel had torn from his grasp and was running down the length of the porch, toward the SUV. Alive? Would she find him alive, or…God, she couldn't even think the word. Couldn't bear it.

"Rachel!" Dylan yelled.

The car door opened, and a figure exited the vehicle. A man. Rachel halted. He was tall, well dressed and in handcuffs. A marshal followed him out, then slammed the door shut. Not Peter, then. Where was her son?

Rachel turned back to face Dylan. "Who is that, and where is my son?"

"The little punk-assed kid?" the man behind her said.

She whipped back around. Realization hit her hard. Made her stagger. She knew who this had to be. "Oh,

God. You're George Evans. You took my son. Where is he?" she asked, her voice low and throaty.

"You'll never find the kid." He sneered. "And I'll never tell where he is. He'll die, only unlike his uncle—" George Eliot nodded to the inert body wrapped in black vinyl at the edge of the porch "—he'll die slowly. Know how horrible it is to die from lack of water?"

Bile rose in her throat and for a moment her stomach heaved, but she managed to remain upright. "You bastard."

"You and your idiot brother screwed with the wrong man."

Dylan stepped between her and the man, Eric beside him. "Rachel, go with Eric and get back in the house. I'll explain everything in a minute, but not here."

"Yes, widow Rachel, go back inside," George Evans mimicked. "There's nothing for you here, anyway. No brother, no son…"

No! Rage filled her. Consumed her. Set her on fire and stopped her from thinking. The world in front of her blurred…all but one object. A black, shiny object on Eric's hip. As if the world had stopped spinning and time had frozen in place, Rachel saw her hand reach out. Felt the cold metal under her fingers. Hefted the weight and raised the gun.

Aimed at George Evans and placed her finger on the trigger.

Dimly, she could hear the ringing of a phone over the roar of anger in her head. In the back pocket of her jeans, her phone vibrated. And over the sound of the ring was Dylan's voice, shouting at her to put down the gun. To answer her phone.

Why should she take a damn call when all she wanted to do was shoot the man who'd caused the death of her brother and maybe the death of her son?

"Rachel! Listen to me. You are a good mother. You were right to believe in your brother. Believe in him and your son."

The world still whirled around her, but she could make out Dylan's words. Why, though, was he talking about her parenting?

"You're not a killer, Rachel. No more than your brother is. Answer the phone, Rachel. Grab hold of that control that keeps you so strong and put the gun down. Take the call."

Dylan thought she was a good mother? That she'd done right by her brother and son? That her brother wasn't all bad, the way he'd originally thought?

Still holding the gun pointed at George Evans, she reached behind her and slid her phone out of her pocket. The man wasn't going anywhere. But the call was important to Dylan. And Dylan was important to Rachel.

She was better with him.

She trusted him.

She believed him.

She let him take control.

Pressing the accept key, she held the phone up to her ear.

"Mom?"

The gun tumbled to the ground and Rachel followed it, going to her knees for the second time in the day. She couldn't speak. Could only rock back and forth, silently crying as she cradled the phone to her ear and heard the excited, happy voice of her son.

Vaguely, she was aware that Evans was stuffed back into his car and driven off. Then Dylan was there.

"Rachel, look." Dylan had bent to his knees and had wrapped his arms around her. His strong, warm arms. He pointed back to the house, to the porch.

She twisted, still holding the phone firmly to her ear, and watched as the second miracle of the night occurred.

Jax stepped out of the body bag.

Alive.

Chapter 24

Back inside the house, seated on the couch in the living room, Rachel sat between Dylan and her brother as they talked through the wild events that had just occurred.

"So you were shot with blanks?" she asked, seeking clarification.

Jax nodded. "I had what are called squabs inside my shirt. Someone else pressed a remote control button when the guns were fired, and the squabs went off, squirting out red gel." He grinned. "Pretty cool, huh?"

She shuddered. "Why pretend to die, though? I mean, Jax, they put you in a body bag!"

"So I can enter Witness Protection. The marshal here—" he nodded to Dylan "—said they'd capture George Evans alive. But the dude's one sick jerk, and he has connections everywhere. I wouldn't be safe unless he thought I was dead."

Rachel turned to Dylan. "So you had a plan to capture Evans but made sure it would keep Jax safe, not just in the present but in the future."

Dylan cleared his throat. "Of course, Rachel. I told you I'd do whatever it took to keep you safe. That included keeping your son and brother safe, too. Because they mean everything to you. You'd never be safe unless they were. And none of you would be safe if Evans thought he could still get to Jax through you or Peter. I'm just grateful Jax was willing to take the risks he did and help us. Thank you."

The last words he spoke directly to Jax, and Rachel was pleased to see her brother duck his chin and give the shy smile she used to see on his face when their father paid him a compliment. Yes, her brother was flawed. Wasn't perfect. But in the end, her parents—and she—had raised him right.

"And no one thought of informing me about this dramatic plan?" she asked.

Dylan shifted, settling her more firmly against his chest. "We needed Evans to be convinced your brother was dead. Your reactions needed to be sincere. Believable. And they were. Even though Evans wasn't on the property, he had someone videotaping it and transmitting it live. He was convinced enough to walk outside the barn to make his escape—and walked right into the arms of the marshals who were thronging the place."

"Had you figured out where he was hiding before

I told you?" she asked, tipping her head up so she could see Dylan's face.

"Nope. You gave us the key information we needed. And we were able to surround the barn and take out a few of his crew before he walked outside. Easy capture." He smiled, his eyes crinkling at the edges.

"But I thought you weren't going to exchange Jax until Peter was safe," she said, worrying the corner of her lip with her teeth.

"We held off on having Jax show himself until after we had Peter safe. That's the call I got—my team had found him at the spring. Once we knew your son was safe, I gave the order for the fake suicide by cop."

"You did great," she murmured to her brother. "I'll forever be thankful for what you did to save Peter."

"Speaking of," Jax said, looking around, "where is the little squirt?"

"About five minutes away," Dylan said. "A few of the marshals are bringing him here. Apparently he's a bit wet and muddy. Thanks to Peter's cunning, he escaped the storage cabinet in the barn where Evans had stashed him. And thanks to his quick thinking, we knew where to go to find him."

"At the spring," Rachel said quietly.

"Yes. At the spring. Which, by the way…" Dylan cleared his throat and looked hard at Jax.

"You find the money there?" Jax asked, his eyes wide and innocent.

"The briefcase was there, all right," Dylan said. "Money's a bit soggy from being stashed in a spring, of all places, but we have it in custody now. Thanks for turning it over to the authorities."

"It's all there. I didn't take any of it. Not even a C-note. When the guns went blasting during the raid, I ducked and hid. I saw the briefcase. Knew it had the money, so I grabbed it and slid out of the building through a ground-level vent."

"And came home to hide the money on our property." Rachel couldn't help the stern tone in her voice. Yes, she'd thought her brother had been killed and was relieved beyond measure to see him alive, but he never should have subjected her or Peter to drug money.

Jax dropped his gaze and lowered his head. "Yeah, I know. You taught me better, sis. But I was still being stupid. I—I wanted that money. Wanted us all to have a better life. I've had a year to contemplate my stupidity in prison. Believe me, I've learned my lesson."

"I want to believe you," Rachel said, "but one thing I don't understand. Why didn't you ever just tell me all of this, Jax? About the money? Why didn't you ever tell the cops? I mean, if you'd truly learned your lesson and the money didn't matter anymore…why did you lie and tell me you couldn't remember where you'd buried it?"

Rachel hated the confusion and mistrust she heard in her voice, hated the shadow of guilt that crept over her brother's face, but Dylan had been right. She couldn't take responsibility for everything. If she and her brother were ever going to have any type of relationship again, she had to confront him about his mistakes and make sure he was willing to do right by her.

"Rachel," he began, but then they heard the thumping of footsteps on the porch just as the door flew open.

"Mom! Uncle Jax!"

Peter flew at them like a missile, throwing his arms around her and Jax. Rachel wrapped her arms around her son and sobbed with relief. She sprinkled kisses on his face, telling him over and over again how happy she was that he was safe. It was only when she pulled back and swiped at the tears running down her face that she realized that her son was crying, too. That Dylan and Jax were crying. And that Peter was even including Dylan in his embrace.

Rachel's tears started flowing again when she saw that Dylan was hugging her son back just as fiercely.

"You did great, kid. I'm glad you're safe," he said.

"Thanks," Peter said. With a grin, but without letting go of Dylan or Rachel, he turned to Jax. "So, how many songs have you written since you've been gone?"

They all laughed.

Dylan rose and whispered to Rachel that he was going to give her and Jax some alone time with Peter but that he'd be close by. After squeezing her hand, he let go and walked to the other side of the room, where he began to talk to his teammate Eric.

They gave them almost an hour, enough time for Rachel and Jax to put Peter to bed before returning downstairs. Then, his eyes shadowed with regret, Dylan explained it was time for Jax to go. Eric would be taking Jax back into federal custody. Jax hugged Rachel and told her he loved her.

Before he left, however, he gave them one more bit of shocking news.

He explained that he had lied to Rachel about not knowing where the money was buried. The only reason he'd done so, however, was that he hadn't been sure whether her phone had been wired. Or who'd be listening.

As it turned out, Jax had had good reason to think not just Rachel's phone, but her computer and her entire house might have been wired, which was why he'd refused to speak to her at all after he was sent to prison. After Evans's men broke Jax out of prison, Jax had been running from Evans and his men, but they weren't the only people he feared might try to hurt Rachel and Peter. While it was Evans's money that Jax had stolen and Evans who'd broken Jax out of prison, there was another threat that had been lurking near Rachel all along—Sheriff Ryan, the man who'd hired Jax to deliver the drugs to Evans in the first place. Right before he took Jax into custody and handed him over to the DEA, he'd warned Jax not to say anything to anyone about his involvement, saying he had eyes and ears on Rachel and Peter and would make sure they died if Jax didn't listen to him.

To be safe, Jax hadn't uttered a single word about the sheriff's involvement. And in the likely event the man knew Jax had escaped and was headed to the ranch to retrieve Evans's money, Jax had sent Rachel that first email, worded so strangely because he'd wanted to deliver a message in case the sheriff was tracking her messages.

As Jax had explained himself, Rachel had retrieved the email and shown it to Dylan.

I ran. I swear I didn't shoot those men. As long as you and Peter are safe on the ranch, I'm coming. We can work out a deal. I'm coming home, but promise on the memory of Mom and Dad you won't tell anyone. Love, Jax.

As she reread the email, Rachel saw the message Jax had intended to send the sheriff—that someone else had shot the marshals, that he was coming home but wasn't planning on ratting the sheriff out, and that they could make a deal—so long as Peter and Rachel remained safe. In Jax's mind, his best bet for making any kind of deal, whether it was with Evans, Ryan or the cops, was by staying free and getting hold of Evans's money. But at the same time, he couldn't let Rachel know any of that in case Sheriff Ryan was listening.

"It turns out the sheriff was lying," Dylan explained after Jax left and just minutes after he made a call to have Sheriff Ryan brought in for questioning. "We found no evidence that your house had been wired before we got here. But the fact that Jax took such care with you, and that email message he sent you, shows how much he loves and cares for you. Yes, he made mistakes, but you're right, Rachel, there's nothing that you can't all work through so you can be a family again."

When he said the words, there was both happiness for her and sadness for himself in his eyes. She knew what that meant. That he didn't think the same thing applied to himself. What his brother had done wasn't something that Dylan was ready to forgive and move beyond…yet.

"You and your brother haven't seen each other in a long time, Dylan. I'm not saying you can forgive him, but maybe someday, you'll be able to see him. Talk to him."

He smiled and smoothed his thumb across her cheek. "Maybe. I could see you being strong enough to do that. To hope it might make a difference. But I'm not sure I'll be able to."

She reached out and took his free hand. "What are you talking about? You're a U.S. Marshal. You're braver than any man I know. *Better* than any man I've ever met. Plus…"

She hesitated and he squeezed her hand tighter. "What?"

"Well, if you think it would help, I could always go with you. To see him, I mean. If you ever wanted that."

"You'd do that for me?"

"Of course. I love you, remember?"

When he didn't reply right away, fear began to creep in. Had she misread him? Much had happened between them from the time when he'd first voiced his feelings. Had he changed his mind about her? Or was he worrying about other things? Struggling to imagine their lives intertwining? He lived in California, and as willing as she'd been to exchange all her livestock for her son's safety, she couldn't imag-

ine not tending to the land that had been in her family for six generations.

"Rachel," he said, his voice serious.

Scared, she interrupted him. "My life is a mess. I
have issues. My brother and Peter have issues. We're
flawed and we're going to continue to make mistakes.
But we can make things work, Dylan. I know we can."

Dylan frowned. "Of course we can."

"But...why are you frowning? Why haven't you
said..." She bit her lip.

He pulled her in for a hug. "God, I'm sorry. I was
just thinking about my brother. What you said about
visiting him. I can't promise that will ever happen,
Rachel, even knowing how important family is to you.
But you have to know how much I love you. That will
never change."

Relief flooded through her.

So there it was. That easily, he'd reassured her. Her
doubts floated away. Because Dylan Rooney was a
good man. A good man who kept his word and had
promised to keep Rachel and her family safe.

Her love wasn't dependent on him reuniting with
his brother. That was his decision and always would
be. He'd kept her safe, and she'd spend her whole life
proving to him that she intended to do the same for
him. She'd be a safe harbor for his heart.

Always.

"So are you saying I might not need to hire a handsome stud to muck out my stalls anytime soon?"

He gave a mock growl as he swept her up in his
arms. "I'm saying that as a marshal, I can work out
of Texas just as easily as California. I'll travel, and

be gone for a few days at a time, but I'll always come back to you. And it will make our reunions all the more exciting. I'm also saying you can hire anyone you want to muck out your stalls so long as you only have eyes for me."

She laughed. "Well, that's no problem. But be warned. I'm not just going to have my eyes all over you."

"Is that right?"

"That's right. Because I love you, too, Dylan Rooney. I might not have known it when you came riding up on your horse, but you're better than any knight in shining armor. You're a U.S. Marshal and I'm just so happy that not only did you get your man this time, you got your woman, too."

* * * * *

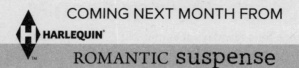
Available December 2, 2014

#1827 THE MANSFIELD RESCUE
The Mansfield Brothers • by Beth Cornelison

Falling for smoke jumper Amy Robinson is the last thing grieving widower Grant Mansfield has in mind. But when his daughter is kidnapped, Grant and Amy must work together to save his little girl. Now, if only he'd let Amy rescue his lonely heart...

#1828 COLTON HOLIDAY LOCKDOWN
The Coltons: Return to Wyoming • by C.J. Miller

To save Christmas in Dead River, Dr. Rafe Granger is working overtime to cure the deadly virus quarantining his hometown—while fighting his attraction to nurse Gemma Colton. But when someone sabotages their research, can this reformed bad boy win the day and get the good girl?

#1829 LONE STAR SURVIVOR
by Colleen Thompson

"Soldier" Ian Rayford returns from the dead, but can't remember anything but his former fiancée—PTSD psychologist Andrea. As an element of his past targets her, spy secrets become deadly secrets!

#1830 LETHAL LIES
by Lara Lacombe

With his cover blown, agent Alexander goes on the run with the alluring Dr. Jillian Mahoney. Yet with the FBI and a dangerous gang after them, separating the lies from the truth becomes a matter of the heart.

YOU CAN FIND MORE INFORMATION ON UPCOMING HARLEQUIN® TITLES, FREE EXCERPTS AND MORE AT WWW.HARLEQUIN.COM.

HRSCNM1114

REQUEST YOUR FREE BOOKS!
2 FREE NOVELS PLUS 2 FREE GIFTS!

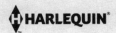

ROMANTIC suspense

Sparked by danger, fueled by passion

YES! Please send me 2 FREE Harlequin® Romantic Suspense novels and my 2 FREE gifts (gifts are worth about $10). After receiving them, if I don't wish to receive any more books, I can return the shipping statement marked "cancel." If I don't cancel, I will receive 4 brand-new novels every month and be billed just $4.74 per book in the U.S. or $5.24 per book in Canada. That's a savings of at least 14% off the cover price! It's quite a bargain! Shipping and handling is just 50¢ per book in the U.S. and 75¢ per book in Canada.* I understand that accepting the 2 free books and gifts places me under no obligation to buy anything. I can always return a shipment and cancel at any time. Even if I never buy another book, the two free books and gifts are mine to keep forever.

240/340 HDN F45N

Name	(PLEASE PRINT)

Address		Apt. #

City	State/Prov.	Zip/Postal Code

Signature (if under 18, a parent or guardian must sign)

Mail to the **Harlequin®** Reader Service:
IN U.S.A.: P.O. Box 1867, Buffalo, NY 14240-1867
IN CANADA: P.O. Box 609, Fort Erie, Ontario L2A 5X3

Want to try two free books from another line?
Call 1-800-873-8635 or visit www.ReaderService.com.

* Terms and prices subject to change without notice. Prices do not include applicable taxes. Sales tax applicable in N.Y. Canadian residents will be charged applicable taxes. Offer not valid in Quebec. This offer is limited to one order per household. Not valid for current subscribers to Harlequin Romantic Suspense books. All orders subject to credit approval. Credit or debit balances in a customer's account(s) may be offset by any other outstanding balance owed by or to the customer. Please allow 4 to 6 weeks for delivery. Offer available while quantities last.

Your Privacy—The Harlequin® Reader Service is committed to protecting your privacy. Our Privacy Policy is available online at www.ReaderService.com or upon request from the Harlequin Reader Service.

We make a portion of our mailing list available to reputable third parties that offer products we believe may interest you. If you prefer that we not exchange your name with third parties, or if you wish to clarify or modify your communication preferences, please visit us at www.ReaderService.com/consumerschoice or write to us at Harlequin Reader Service Preference Service, P.O. Box 9062, Buffalo, NY 14269. Include your complete name and address.

HRS13R

SPECIAL EXCERPT FROM

H HARLEQUIN®

ROMANTIC suspense

Returning to Dead River is anything but welcoming
for Dr. Rafe Granger, who lands himself in the middle
of an epidemic…and discovers a connection to the
powerful Colton family he never anticipates.

Read on for a sneak peek of

COLTON HOLIDAY LOCKDOWN

by C.J. Miller

Dr. Rafe Granger would never escape this rotting purgatory.
His return had brought with it a terrible series of events:
an unidentified virus was claiming victims by the dozens,
the virus research lab had been trashed and a murderer had
escaped the local prison and was adding to the terror and
paranoia of every person in town.

Rafe entered the clinic through the single metal entry
door. The smell of smoke hung in the air. Behind the recep-
tion area, the clinic's patient files had been pulled from the
shelves and littered the floor. The culprit had done much
worse to Rafe's office and the lab.

Dread pooled low in his stomach. What had been taken?
The most critical work had been stored in the lab.

Rafe checked over his protective gear, pulled it on and
entered the lab, noting the lock was broken on the door.
Anger and frustration shook Rafe to his core. The inside
of the lab was a disaster—tables overturned, equipment

thrown to the floor and petri dishes and beakers smashed on the ground. But the most alarming thing was what had been done to the samples. The small refrigerator they'd been using to store the carefully labeled Vacutainer tubes was open and emptied.

Rafe let loose a curse he almost never used. This situation was beyond all repair.

He felt a hand on his back and whirled around, coming face-to-face with Gemma Colton, one of the clinic's registered nurses.

"Where are our samples?" Gemma asked, sounding shocked and panicked. Her green eyes were filled with concern. As many times as he had looked into those green eyes, the vibrancy and beauty of them struck him every time. "Who would do this?"

"Not sure. But that virus is deadly on the street," Rafe said.

"We already have an epidemic and now we have to worry about someone running around with vials containing the virus," Gemma said, her voice shaking.

Rafe heard shouts and banging from the clinic. He and Gemma exchanged looks. What else could go wrong?

Don't miss COLTON HOLIDAY LOCKDOWN by C.J. Miller, available December 2014 wherever Harlequin® Romantic Suspense books and ebooks are sold.

Copyright © 2014 by Cynthia Miller

HRSEXP1114R

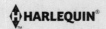
HARLEQUIN®

ROMANTIC suspense

Heart-racing romance, high-stakes suspense!

BETH CORNELISON
brings you the next installment of
THE MANSFIELD BROTHERS miniseries
THE MANSFIELD RESCUE

Available December 2014

*A single father discovers the price of
revenge and the power of love...*

After his wife's murder, Grant Mansfield vowed to stay true to her
memory and to protect their children. But fate has other plans.
His temporary houseguest, injured smokejumper Amy Robinson,
has him burning with a white-hot attraction. And the single dad's
nightmare comes true when his older daughter is kidnapped.

Grant is just the man the adventurous Amy never knew she
needed, his children the family she never knew she wanted.
Before she can rescue his lonely heart, the handsome widower
must become a hero. Only Grant can rescue his little girl.
But time is running out...

Don't miss other exciting titles from BETH CORNELISON's
THE MANSFIELD BROTHERS:
PROTECTING HER ROYAL BABY
THE RETURN OF CONNOR MANSFIELD

Available wherever books and ebooks are sold.

HRS78978

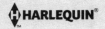

ROMANTIC suspense

Heart-racing romance, high-stakes suspense!

LONE STAR SURVIVOR
by Colleen Thompson

Available December 2014

A soldier's memories are more dangerous than anything he's encountered in the line of duty

"Killed in action" a year ago, US Army captain Ian Rayford shocks everyone when he stumbles half-dead onto his family's Texas ranch. Suffering from post-traumatic stress disorder, his former fiancée, a psychologist specializing in PTSD, arrives to help Ian recover. But not everyone wants her to unearth the dangerous secrets he's carrying.

Now engaged to another man, Dr. Andrea Warrington fights her feelings for Ian even as she helps him remember how much they once loved each other. Yet the closer Ian gets to his past, the more someone else has to ensure the treacherous truth stays buried.

Don't miss other exciting Harlequin® Romantic Suspense titles from Colleen Thompson:
LONE STAR REDEMPTION
THE COLTON HEIR
PASSION TO PROTECT

Available wherever books and ebooks are sold.

www.Harlequin.com

HRS78992

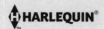

ROMANTIC suspense

Heart-racing romance, high-stakes suspense!

LETHAL LIES
by Lara Lacombe

Available December 2014

Trusting the man she loves could cost her her life

Putting her faith in someone who lies for a living isn't the safest thing Dr. Jillian Mahoney has ever done. But to stay alive, she has to believe the undercover agent—who's kidnapped her to prove his innocence—isn't a traitor to the FBI. And to help him, she must deny their intense attraction as they run from two vengeful killers.

Her captor, Alex Malcom, *has* lived a life of lies—some worse than others. Still, there's one truth he's reluctant to disclose to Jillian, the woman of his dreams. One that could stop their relationship cold.

Don't miss other exciting Harlequin® Romantic Suspense titles from Lara Lacombe:
FATAL FALLOUT
DEADLY CONTACT

Available wherever books and ebooks are sold.